I0685715

LOOPHOLE
OF
THE
GODS

Other Books by Lyle Milton

This is the section where a writer shows off a long list of accolades and 'other books you might enjoy.' Since Loophole of the Gods (LotG) is my debut novel, I've no such bragging rights... *yet.*

The Man Zero pentology (i.e. 5 book series) is a fusion of literary and multi-genre fiction. Although most literary fiction and sci-fi fans won't flinch at the page count, this is a big book by genre fiction standards where smaller books is the norm... for anyone not named Stephen King or Brandon Sanderson, that is. And while I intend for LotG to be read as one complete novel, fortunately, my approach to the story allowed for three distinct parts, making the book accessible to genre readers, as well.

And so, Man Zero book 1: Loophole of the Gods is available in 2 flavors: the whole book and 3 part-books (i.e. a subseries):

Loophole of the Gods

Loophole of the Gods – Part I: The Case

Loophole of the Gods – Part II: The War

Loophole of the Gods – Part III: The Silence

LYLE MILTON

LOOPHOLE

OF

THE

GODS

Can a girl be murdered if she was never born?

A MAN ZERO NOVEL

inkfyre

LOOPHOLE OF THE GODS, PART III: THE SILENCE
Copyright © Lyle Milton, 2020
www.lylemilton.com

inkfyre

Published by Inkfyre, LLC
www.inkfyre.com

All rights reserved.
Redistribution of this book by any means, in whole or in part, is
not permitted without written permission from the Author,
except in the case of brief quotations embodied in critical
articles or reviews.

ISBN: 1-953390-05-6
ISBN-13: 978-1-953390-05-9

*This book is a work of fiction. Names, characters, organizations, places,
events, and incidents are either products of the author's imagination or are
used fictitiously. Any resemblance to actual persons, living or dead, or
actual events is purely coincidental.*

Edited by Carla Molchan
editor@inkfyre.com
Cover, formatting, and illustrations by Lyle Milton
artist@lylemilton.com

Content Warning: This book contains adult language,
violence, depictions of rape, and adult themes.

For Toni

CONTENTS

.

Letter from the Author

Dear Reader:

First, I should prepare you for—*what the f—?!*

KKRAASHH! BOOOM! "But... but why did you...? (*sigh*)........"

The onomatopoeia, the changing font sizes, the lo-o-ong ellipses, the vocalizations (in parenthesis, no less), the em dashes, and the italics—oh, my! In a world where so much as a misplaced comma can take some readers out of a story, you're probably rolling your eyes across the ceiling right about now, ready to slam this book shut and brand it the brain-farts of a stank amateur.

But, wait, wait, wait—hear me out!

At first, my style choices might seem jarring, but, as with anything, they'll become less distracting in time, gradually becoming an integral part of the reading experience. In fact, they aid in the flow of *this* story, and in certain situations they're critical.

My style choices are also in keeping with the uniqueness of this book which, quite frankly, has proven challenging to categorize into any specific genre since I bucked the well-worn, well-meaning advice to "write to the market." When asked, I often say "It's a psychological, sociopolitical, romantic, character-study, action, technothriller mystery." There're even some military thriller elements and humor. Said it was unique, didn't I?

According to my readers, this book doesn't neatly conform, and that's fine; conformance wasn't my goal. I was driven to write this book, not by love of a specific genre, but, in large part, by something very personal.

I feel trepidation at writing this sentence, and I was even warned against including it because it's *too* personal, but many years ago, my older sister Toni was raped and murdered.

Though it *was* so long ago, I find myself still affected by the loss of her. However, I've *zero* drive to tell that story. So, while a central element of this story was heavily influenced by her tragedy, no, this novel isn't about my sister's life. Nor her death. Yet, as if her hands were pressing against my back, I was pushed onward, especially through the worst of times where I questioned whether I should publish it at all.

Crafting this book was quite the task because it matters to me. It matters not only because I was moved to write it by personal tragedy, but also because of this story that I couldn't *not* tell due to its weighty relevance to modern times.

As I wrote this novel, it was important to me that nearly every sentence and event within had layers of meaning and/or relevance later… or earlier. And it was of equal importance that the novel would be more than just an entertaining read, but one that informs and enlightens. Finally, it is of *supreme* importance to me that, by the time you reach the final word of this book, you'll feel that it was time *very* well spent, that the characters and events have become a part of you, and that you feel this world is real.

So, if you're open to a different kind of story with intriguing characters—a story told in a unique way, then sit back, relax, and immerse yourself in *Loophole of the Gods!*

Sincerely,
Lyle Milton

The Silence

Splatters

A siren jumps Jesse's heart—his eyes snap to the rearview mirror. Flashing lights. *Shit! Oh... an ambulance.* Constantly scanning all mirrors and windows, he arrives at the place he most dreads aside from a jail cell. Though this place still makes him ill, in this moment, this shipping container yard is the one place he feels safe. He parks along the edge, overlooking the water, and jumps out of the car.

"Call Rajiv!"

Ringing tones sound from the tablet.

. . .

"Jesse?" Rajiv says, sitting on the front steps of Jesse's building.

"You aaight, dude?!"

"What? Why would I not be? I am more worried about you, my friend!"

"Wait—didn't I see you drive off?"

"No, that was not me, that was Susan—Haj! This was all her idea—!"

"What?! You let her—aw, *SHIT!* [click]"

"Hello? Jesse? Are you there, my friend?" Rajiv sighs. "Why am I the one to get yelled at every time that woman does something stupid?"

. . .

Her back pressing against the seat, head down, arms locked straight, Haj is gripping the wheel so tight her knuckles protrude, bloodless. With brow pushed upward, her eyes dart between the fortuitously clear road ahead and the encroaching high beams and blue flashes in the rearview. Her phone rings from the passenger seat. She disengages her grip long enough to swipe it and snaps her hand back to the wheel.

. . .

"Haj!" Sound blasts from Jesse's tablet—the engine revving at high speed, and sirens blaring.

"Jesse?! Did you make it out?!"

"What the fuck you doin' to me, girl?!"

"What?! I'm unfucking your shit up, so don't you yell at me!"

"Why you doin' this? Yo' ass already hired!"

"You think I'm doing this because I want a fucking *job?!*

You're such a *huge dick*—but don't you dare go back on your word!"

"Stop the car!"

"No freakin' way am I stopping for those corrupt, racist pigs! Haven't you ever heard of DWA? Driving While Asian?"

"That's not a thing—fuck it. Stop the damn *car!*"

"It *is too* a thing! And if it's not, it will be if I stop—they're really after me, Jess!"

"They're not after *you*, they're after *me!* That's why you need to stop before—!"

"*AAEEEEEE!*"

Jesse cringes at Haj's screams, screeching tires, crunching metal, and deep thumps, followed by an equally chilling void. "Haj?! Haj?! *HAJ?!* FUCK!" He grabs the tablet from the hood of the taxi. "Where is she?!" The tablet doesn't respond. "*AAAGH!*" At a volume loud enough to break his voice and shake his sanity, Jesse screams out into the blackness—the void above the dark roiling waters. His fists clenched, over and over, he bellows until his voice cracks nearly to silence, his body shaking with every grating thrust of air. Eyes of fire and filled with tears, he yells at the tablet, his shout like a coarse whisper, "*Call her!*"

"[*click!*] Jesus *Christ!* I've been trying to reach—!"

"Don't know what the fuck is goin' on, Nicole, but Senator Windham's dead!"

"Huh—Tripp?! What did you do?!"

"What—for fuck's sake—*I* didn't kill 'im! Somebody's tryin' damn hard to make it look like I did!"

"What happened?!"

"Dude's layin' on my office floor with huge holes clean through his head and chest! A fuckin' Senator! Dead in my office!"

"Oh, my God… Thaddeus—"

"That fuckin' *Warlock* needs to be taken *down!*"

"He didn't do this!"

"So, you finally admit he's workin' for you?!"

"Are you *insane?!* He's not working for me—!"

"I was almost t-boned, and was nearly mowed down by a fuckin' ghost-drone! And who comes in savin' the day? *Warlock!* I don't know if this is the war you been talkin' about, but I'm in it! You knew all this shit would be happenin' to me, didn't you?!"

"*No!* I only knew you were in danger because *I* am! They've been trying to kill me since yesterday!"

"What?! Who's *'they'?!*"

"I haven't figured that out yet! But Warlock, that demented bastard, tried to shoot me in the head just minutes ago!"

"WHAT?! What are you sayin'?! He tried to kill *you?!* Are you alright?!"

"That dipshit found out the hard way that he *can't* kill me. And he wouldn't have been able to kill Tripp, either. My God, poor—"

"Where're you—you safe—you at the estate?!"

"I'm headed there as we speak. And you need to get yourself there, too—!"

"Good! Don't stop! Not for anything! But find Haj and make sure she's alright!"

"Susan? What happened to her?"

"She got into a big crash tryin'na help me! I got no fuckin' idea where she is, or even if she's still alive! I know you got the resources—find her, help her! *Please!*"

"I'll take care of her, but what're you—?"

"Somethin' else just came up, and it can't wait—"

"No! Stop whatever you're doing and get back to the freakin' estate—!"

He ends the call.

"FFFUUUUCK!" He slams his fist against the hood of the car.

* * * * *

The rear of the pickup is so misshapen it can scarcely be called a pickup. Paint gouged to the surface, a deeply scarred parked car lines the path to the next... which leads to the next... the next....... the last. Scattered debris and long scrapes and sweeping burn marks against the asphalt continue that perilous path. Scattered glass shards. Gasoline in tendrilled puddles. Shadows and glints from streetlamps. Flashing red and blue lights lending their hues to the scene.

The battered Pontiac lay on its partially crushed roof, front wheels slowly spinning. Groups of police approach the vehicle with guns stabbing outward toward a singular spot, all shouting Jesse's name, along with "Let me see your hands!" and "Get out of the vehicle!" as they furtively approach.

Haj's bloody hand trembles as she sticks it out of the car's window. "... help... help me...."

"Oh, shit!" McGraw says, "That's not Davenport! That's not Davenport!"

An officer calls for emergency medical assistance while three others rush in, rip open the car door, and pull Haj away, over to the pavement, hidden from direct view of onlookers. One man checks her vitals.

"She's still breathing!"

As officers push back the gathering crowd, warning them of a possible explosion, Carlson looks down at Haj's unconscious face. "Hey, Bob... isn't she that girl scout cookie chick?"

McGraw looks at Haj in disbelief. "Don't tell me she jet

because of a god-damn green card! You mother-fucker!" He storms aggressively toward Haj; Carlson steps in front of him.

"She let that asshole get away!"

"Then we'd better haul ass after the other suspect." Carlson shakes her head and runs toward her car. "C'mon... before the news breaks."

"Mother-*fucker!*" McGraw says with a jerk of his head as he trails Carlson.

. . .

Haj half-opens one eye as she lies abandoned on the cold pavement. The detectives drive away as other officials control the scene while cops maintain their human barricade. The siren of an ambulance wails in the distance. Haj rolls over once and scans her eyes back and forth. No one responds. Rolls again. She's in the clear. She continues rolling until she reaches a Jeep Wrangler, then shimmies herself underneath it.

* * * * *

Nico slumps in his seat, brow so furrowed it's bound to leave lasting impressions. His face is flush as he watches the crawl on the screen. He shields his eyes from his whispering fellow officers and sits on edge waiting for a response from his phone. Precinct activity halts as the TV flashes an image of Senator Windham above bold white letters on a red band: **BREAKING NEWS: SENATOR THADDEUS "TRIPP" JEFFERSON WINDHAM III, MURDERED.** An inset displays Jesse's face, name and physical details along with a tip hotline number.

"C'mon, Georgie, pickup!"

The call goes to voicemail.

"Damnit, man—!"

An officer turns up the volume as the reporter addresses the viewers. "For more on this national tragedy, Congressman Jeff Payne joins us on the phone from—"

"They'd better string him up! Lynch his Black ass right in front of Congress for the world to see!"

"Uh, Congressman—!"

"I don't care! I know what you're gonna say and I just don't care! If the D.A. had done his job in the first place, we wouldn't be here! That thug killed not only a great, honorable Senator, a husband, father, and American patriot, he killed my friend!" he says through sobs, "I hope the Marshals take him out—no trial!"

"Wait a minute, Congressman—!"

"This way nobody can't screw it up! Jesse Davenport won't be gettin' away with cold blooded murder again! No! Not this time! I guarantee—!"

"*Stizzolli!*" a voice bellows from beyond an open office door.

"Yeah, Cap?!"

"In my office!"

. . .

Nico enters the room as if the floor were made of wet tissue.

"Come on in. Shut the door. Take a seat." The tall, thin, buttoned-down Black man in wire rimmed glasses watches Nico with simmering calm, the veins around his temples bulging. His interrogating eyes track Nico's every movement. He drums his fingers against the barren desk as Nico slowly lowers himself into a chair.

"Wh… what's up?"

"Do you have anything you would like to say to me?"

"Uh… what's this about?"

"Are you sure you're not hiding anything? Anything at all? Something you should've shared with your captain? Maybe just to pay me at least a little courtesy before I.A. shows up?"

"Wait, Cap! Me and my partner would never shakedown nobody! It was all just a misunderstanding. Don't know where Bobby's run off to—call 'im, he'll tell you the same."

"Hmph. Right now, there's absolutely nothing I'd love more than for this to be about a shakedown." He subtly shakes his head at Nico, eyes locked to his.

"What?"

"And don't drag McGraw into this; he's already been assigned a new partner as of a few hours ago."

"Huh? What happened—why am I just hearing this?!"

The captain pulls a stainless steel 9mm semi-automatic with a purple grip from his drawer and slams it on the desk. "Maybe you'd like to come clean *now?*"

"That's Jesse's…! How did you…?"

"Well?"

"Wait, Cap, I can explain that!"

"Really? While you're at it, how about explaining *this* one?" He slams an identical gun on the desk, next to its twin.

"B-b-but, Cap, I got no idea—"

"Or this?" *THAP!* He tosses a close-up photo of the serial numbers in front of Nico. One set of numbers belongs to Jesse's gun, but the other set is a mirror image. "Let's see your shyster-brother and his minions hang *that* one on Lynette—Miss Kennedy." His cheeks twitch as he glares at Nico, but he keeps his hands folded.

"What's this? Reversed digits?"

"That it? Well, maybe you got something to say about the

three stiffs that turned up—beaten and executed, and your gumshoe brother—who I was kind and gracious enough to throw a few cases to over the years at your request—bloody and running from the crime scene? Huh? All three murdered with that gun." He repeatedly pokes his finger against the table, near the replica. "His prints are all over it. It's like déjà vu, only this time... this time........."

"Cap, I—"

"NOW HE'S ALSO THE SAME GODDAMN GUY WANTED IN THAT FUCKING DRONE HACKING SCANDAL AND FOR THE GODDAMN MURDER OF A *U.S.* FUCKING *SENATOR!*" He slams his fist repeatedly against the table—*WHAM-WHAM-WHAM!*

Nico's back straightens, pressed hard against the chair, and his eyes bulge, his skin turning red.

The captain releases a heavy breath, clenches his eyes, then sits upright, folding his hands, resting them on the desk. "And who's getting skewered? Your captain. I got the Commissioner, the D.A., the Mayor, the Governor, FAA, Army, Air Force, DEA, FBI, NSA, CIA, the Department of Defense, Homeland Security—even some goddamn groups I ain't ever heard of—all coming down on me. Can you explain all this shit to me?"

"But... but I...."

"Huh, Stizzoli? What's that? I didn't hear you."

. . .

All eyes are glued to Nico as he emerges from the office beet-red, sweating profusely.

"Close the door, Stizzoli."

"Y-yeah." Nico pulls the door closed. To a score of muffled thumping and swearing beyond the door, Nico's hands dance around his desk for his phone, but he ultimately finds it in his pocket and dials again. "Come on, George Barnes! Where the fuck are you?!"

"Whassamattah, bruh—hahahah!" George laughs as he's being manhandled in handcuffs right past Nico's desk by detectives Carlson and McGraw.

Nico puts a hand up to McCraw's chest, halting him. "What the hell do you think you're doing, *partner?!*"

"Outta the way!" McGraw slaps his hand away, then sneers at him while pushing George forward; Carlson shakes her head, looking back at Nico sorrowfully as she follows them.

"Stizzle-my-nizzle—hahahaha!"

The War of Others, Mine – Part I

*E*YES glued to the bright screen of her phone, standing in the strip mall where all storefronts are dark, streetlamps providing barely enough light to separate the concrete of the walkway from the asphalt of the lot, Lynette locks the campaign office door by rote, her thoughts engulfed by the pall of current events, goosebumps forming on the nape of her neck from the cool of the air... and the chill of the news.

Can't believe it. I talked to him only a few days ago. Now I feel bad for hating him. Who am I kidding—that fat old redneck was the worst! Never wished something like this on him, though. Bad karma. Sure looks like his finally caught up with him. Well... if Jesse Davenport is karma.

He must've gone after Windba—Windham because of the racist things he said about his daughter. Plus, he's killed 3 more. Christ, that's a total of 7! That we know of!

"*(ntch)* All those lives snuffed out, just like that. By one man. Insane."

Now all these reporters hounding me for an interview! Thank you, but no—they're not pinning this one on me! Nope. And no more protests outside my house—I'm not moving again. I did my job… no matter what anybody says about me. I'm staying far away from Twitter, too. "Hmph!" *They better go after his sleazebag lawyer, instead.*

She scrolls down as she walks toward the parking lot. "Whoa… they *did* get him. Mm-mm-mm." She shakes her head. *Karma!*

She pauses as Jesse's image slides into view. *My God… that look on his face that day…. It was way worse than being back at the courtroom; I didn't have to look at him then. Why in the world would Dr. Albescu hire somebody like him?!*

She stops, her eyes popped wide open. *Almost forgot Windham was in the room, too! That was the first time I met him face-to-face—how could I forget?!*

As the cold evening breeze prickles her skin, she walks across the empty lot, over potholes and faint, mottled white lines, toward her Honda Accord, wishing she'd parked closer and under a light when a space opened up earlier.

Just can't get over it. And that video. Geez… so evil. That man must really hate me.

She stops again, her brow ridged high.

Oh, my God—am I next?!

She nearly trips over her own quickened step, the clop of her heals echoing. Her car 20 feet away, she fumbles around in her purse, then stabs her hand in the air, and presses down hard on the car key's button. The car door unlocks with a click. She scrambles into the driver's seat and slams the door shut, the dashboard casting dim light onto her and about the car. She rubs her arms with chilled hands, peering around the barren lot. The undulating tree branches all but disappear in the misty darkness. It's virtually pitch-black until the street-lighted main road where the odd car whizzes by, and the city shimmers beyond.

Man, I can't wait to be home—! She sucks in a sharp breath.

A shadow. A sound.

Her mouth hangs open. Her lip trembles. Frozen, she stares straight ahead through the window out into the darkness… slow, deep, and steady breathing behind her. The fuzz on her skin jitters against a gust of warm breath. She slowly slides her eyes to the right, toward the rearview mirror… at another pair of eyes staring back.

"Scream and I will *snap* your neck. Bitch."

Jesse Davenport emerges from the shadows.

She can't fight. She can't fly. She can no longer feel her limbs while watching her life slice by in his razor-sharp glare.

"Every single day in court… after you played that video… I studied you. Y'know? Could you feel me? Watching you? You wore your hair short. Like you have it right now. I memorized the shape of your neck. The circumference. The muscles. The tendons. The veins. Each vertebra."

Against his deep, deliberate voice, her own heartbeat punctuates every syllable. She'd forgotten to breathe; as dizziness begins to overtake her, she exhales with a quiet shudder.

"Back in my cell—y'know… when you convinced the judge to deny me bail? Back in my cell, I would practice. Place each finger… in just the right location. Feeling the shapes of your bones. Tightening my grip. Slowly. Until I hear the snap. That beautiful… satisfying… *snap*."

"Please don't...."

"I've come to regret not following through, back then; I've been living in hell. And everything... *everything* can be traced back to you. Even Senator Windham. Isn't it crazy that even after all you've done to me, I still need extra motivation? I find that crazy. So, do me a favor. If you have a weapon... pepper spray... taser... knife... gun... I need you to go for it. Can you do that for me? To make this more beautiful and satisfying?"

"P-please... don't kill me... please don't... Mr. Davenport...."

"You're not going to go for it?"

She slowly shakes her head, staring at the reflection of this monster who thinks nothing of getting shot; pepper spray would only make him mad. *Madder.*

"Sure? I'll give you a head start?"

She shakes her head.

"Then you put me in a real bind, here. Hmm. What do *you* think I should do?"

Staring into his unblinking red eyes, she shivers while tears paint with her mascara in barbed strokes along her cheeks. "Let... let me go?"

"Let you go? Hmhmhm."

She doesn't move her focus away from him even as his eyes skewer hers. He's silent. There's a small glimmer of hope; it seems like he's actually considering it.

Please, let me go—please, let me go—please, let me—

"Alright. I'll let you go. But nothing's free."

"What do you want?" She moves her arms up to her chest, crossing them, hands covering the upper region of her breasts.

"Not you. Monsters are a big turn off."

"Then...?"

"All you have to do is drive. And be quiet. You understand that I detest you, right?"

"Y-yes."

"Crying out for passing cops is like pulling a weapon on me. It takes a cop about one point six seconds to assess the threat and draw his gun. It will take me zero point four seconds to get my hands around your neck. *Snap*... long before they can pull guns on us. I said *us*. They're already on high alert for me. You know the cops. They see Black skin and start shooting. So, being as Black as I, you're dead either way. Come bullet, come... *snap*."

Her lips quiver and she places a hand over her mouth, breathing rapidly through her trembling fingers.

"All you have to do is decide: do I want this man arrested, or do I want to live to see the sunrise? You can't have both, so choose. What's the most important thing to you right now?"

"S—see the sunrise?"

"Are you asking me?"

"I... I want to see the sunrise, Mr Davenport."

"Alright. Drive where I say, and you'll get your wish. Man of my word. Besides, according to the news, I only kill white men. I've no taste for killing sistahs, but in your case I already have an appetite. Just don't do anything to make me *snap*. Alright?"

"O--okay." She starts the car and struggles to put it in drive.

"Wait."

She jumps; his hand is thrusting a handkerchief by her head.

"Clean yourself up. We don't want folks making *snap* judgments, you agree?"

"I... I have... I have my own." She reaches for her purse. Chills stab her skin as his large, hot, rough hand sweeps along her bare left collarbone. "No, please—!"

SNAP! SNAP!

Her shoulders jump. She turns furtively to the right, toward the sound. His open palm awaits. She places the bag in his hand. There's a bit of rustling, then her pack of tissues falls into her lap.

* * * * *

Jesse Davenport barks terse instructions, and Lynette obeys, never thinking of breaking his trust, and she takes great pains to remain quiet. However, after a while, the lull eases her trembling and the series of roads they've taken spark a moment of inadvertence. "Why're we going there?"

Against the rear window's dewy glare, he's a heavy shadow that isn't obliged to respond.

"Sorry."

She occasionally catches a glimpse of his reflection as street lights slide along the sides of his face, his red eyes demonic, like he's possessed. With each sweep of white and amber, his unblinking stare is locked upon her, and it doesn't break, even in shadow. Wary of blurting out any further questions, she focuses intently on driving along the suburban streets until finally turning onto a cul-de-sac.

"Under that tree."

She parks the car and stops the engine.

"Keys."

She places her keys in his extended palm.

"Just sit."

There's movement. She keeps her eyes pinned to the mirror; he produces a tablet, pointing it at the roof.

"Aircrafts, including drones."

Her eyes track his, which scan the screen as he pans the tablet.

He lowers the tablet. "Hm. Show movement." While he slowly sweeps the tablet from one house to another, he has a sneer on his face. "Godammit! I meant people only! Why you showin' me rats and roaches, an' shit? Damn... that's a big-ass spider...."

He continues scanning and shakes his head at one house. "Crazy white folks." He moves the tablet behind her. "Move your head."

Lynette ducks down.

"Oops! Hm! Aaight. Sit up."

She complies.

"What house she live in? You know who I'm talkin' 'bout."

"I... that one." She points at the light-toned Colonial in front of them. "But I doubt she's home."

"Oh, she home, alright. Gettin' her online freak on, an' shit. Wit' wine and candles. Hmhm! Just wanted to see if you'd lie to me."

"How did you...?" Rattled by the shift in his manner of speaking, she halts.

He gets out of the car and stands by her door. "Let's go."

She stays put, looking through the window at the blood and soot smears on his coat. *Oh, my God! That must be Senator Windham's blood!* She looks up at him. "You never said anything about coming here—"

He stands over her, staring. Silent.

She gets out of the car and lets out a muffled yelp as he grabs her around the waist, pulling her close to his side.

Jesse and Lynette walk, pressed like a loving couple, toward a large white house on the right. A lighted walkway leads to its refined portico. All the windows are dark. The front door has an electronic lock.

"Open it," Jesse says.

Lynette looks up at him.

"Yeah. I'm talkin' to you."

"But… I don't have a key or know the code."

"Put your hand on the handle. Press it. Open it."

She does as he says; her hand jumps when the door pops open. They walk inside to the foyer and Jesse releases her, slapping her purse in her hands. He peers out through the sheers while Lynette stands behind him. She looks to her left. There's a letter opener on a small round table next to her. She shudders, biting her bottom lip. Her eyes dart from the blade to Jesse. He's reflected in the glass, silently watching her… unblinking.

"Well? Aren't you going to go for it?" he says.

"No, I was just…!" She shuffles away from the table like her feet are sticking to the floor. He shoves her into the dark living room where she stumbles and falls onto a couch. While there's dim moonlight entering through the curtains, all that is truly visible are the glows of red and blue LEDs from electronics scattered throughout the space.

"Wait here."

"What are you—?"

"If you try to leave, our sunrise deal's off. Nod if you understand."

She nods.

He walks back to the foyer, looks out of the curtains, then exits through the front door, leaving it slightly ajar.

She sits in the dark, her fingers digging into the couch cushion, eyes locked on the opening; the wind subtly rocks the door. Watching the door edge slightly more open, she scrunches her brow, swallows hard, and slowly rises from the couch. A large flat-screen TV blinks on. Red and orange light cutting the darkness, blasting her, video of a sunrise captures her wide-swung eyes. She grabs her phone from her bag, activating it—the word SIT flashes on its screen in big bold white letters. Her breath catches in her throat. She drops back down, shivering, eyes riveted to the TV, the video reversing until the sliver of sun blinks out.

The sound of two pairs of staccato footsteps—one pair barefoot—snatches her attention. Jesse returns, his arm tightly pressed against Gwen Policastro's wet, exposed chest, carrying her up on her toes, gripping her neck; she gags, producing little sound, her eyes stretched wide open, her bare-naked body glistening in the moonlight.

"Oh, my God…."

The War of Others, Mine – Part II

*J*ESSE closes the door with his foot. He carries Gwen over to Lynette and drops her down onto the couch.

"*Ahgk!* Hhhhh-hhhhhh!"

He then whips out his tablet and frantically sweeps it around toward the door and walls and ceiling.

"Oh, my god, Gwen! Did he hurt you?!" Lynette wraps her arms around Gwen's body. "I'm so sorry," she says while Gwen tries desperately to catch her breath, "I thought he was gonna kill me! I didn't know what else to do—!"

"Here." Jesse yanks the bathrobe from his shoulder and tosses it at them. Lynette grabs it—Gwen snatches it and bolts up from the couch, turning her back to Jesse.

"You fucking—!" She feverishly shoves her arms into the sleeves, and her shaking hands wrap the garment closed, tying the belt tightly around her waist. She whips around, her tied-up hair coming undone, wild. "Lunatic! What do you think you're doing?! What do you want from me?!"

Jesse stares into her terror-ridden eyes while putting a finger over his lips. "For now, I want you to sit and listen."

"Do you know who I am?! I'm a—!"

"If I ain't know who you were, we wouldn't be here! Congresswoman. Now, quiet down."

"Gwen!" Lynette grabs her by the wrist, giving her a pleading look.

Gwen looks down at her. "Why aren't you calling the police?! Did he hurt you?!" She then turns to Jesse, glowering at him. "What did you do to Nettie?!"

"I'm gonna give you one more chance. Be quite and listen."

"Or what?!"

"Gwen, don't—!"

"Or I'll leave your ass to fend for your damn self."

"What do you mean by—no…." Gwen's eyes grow wide. "You're the man who killed Senator Windham!" She turns to Lynette. "That's Jesse Davenport!"

"I know—!"

"That report is false. I ain't kill no fuckin' body, but I'm being framed for it."

"Nuh-*uh*, Gwen, he's just trying to move suspicion from himself again!"

"You. Shut it. This ain't no muh'fuckin' trial."

"Do you expect me to believe you after you broke into my home, abducted me from my bath—*buck naked*—and choked me all the way out onto the street—*BUCK NAKED*—into my neighbor's house—which you *also* broke into?!"

"And abducted *me*, *too*, right, friend?!"

"I don't give a shit if you believe me or not."

Lynette sits up straight. "You told me you killed them—"

"You told yourself that—shut the fuck up, you!"

"Don't speak that way to her!" Gwen says, putting a hand on Lynette's shoulder. "*Why* are you *doing* this?!"

"To keep you alive."

"What?"

"You heard about that commotion today? The truck accident and the drone attack?"

Lynette looks him up and down. "That's right... you were there—"

"What does that have to do with me?!"

"—The blood on your coat is from—?!"

Jesse raises a hand—Gwen and Lynette's shoulders jump. He splays his fingers, then curls his pinky toward his palm. "Somebody tried to kill me..." He curls his ring finger. "... they tried to kill Dr. Albescu..."

"What?! Who's they?"

He curls his middle finger. "... they killed Senator Windham..." He turns his hand at the wrist, pointing his pistol-hand at Gwen. "Guess who's next."

Gwen and Lynette turn to each other. Lynette feels an out of body experience as Gwen stares with eyes she'd never before seen on her—eyes of total fear. "Wait, Gwen—"

Gwen turns to Jesse. "Me?! Why would anyone want to kill me?!"

"That's also why I'm here. To get some info to keep you from ending up dead."

She lowers herself back down and covers her open mouth. Her color drains. "What do you want to know?"

Lynette slowly shakes her head. "No. Don't tell me you're falling for his—"

"Shush!" Gwen raises a hand to her, never taking her eyes off Jesse.

Lynette frowns. "Hey, I'm just trying to—"

"Tell me!" Gwen wrings her trembling hands.

Jesse sits on a chair. "I'll start by tellin' you what I already know. Wait…" He looks at Gwen then rubs his hand down his face. "Look. I apologize for draggin' you out your house the way I did, but every second I'd have spent tryin'na explain things is time we might've given some asswipe to…. (*sigh*)…. My bad."

Lynette stares at him in anticipation, her brow raised, her head tilted. He stares back, sneering. "(*ntch!*)" She turns away.

"I may not have you arrested for that if you just tell me what's going on!" Gwen says.

"Aaight, here's the deal. I know who killed those other three guys they're reportin' about. It was this psycho who's been stalkin' me, tryin' to get me to drop a case. But my source implied that someone else killed the Senator."

"And put his body in your office?"

"Yup."

"Why? Just to get you to drop that case?!"

"Naw, I think it's gone way beyond that. It either has something to do with that hearing—"

"The congressional hearing yesterday? With Dr. Albescu?"

"Yeah. Or it might have to do with the fact that Tripp and I met today to discuss my stalker. All I know is all hell broke loose after that hearing."

"Your case... is it Nicoletta's?"

"Shit. I forgot y'all already know she's my client. Anyway, what do both things have in common?"

"Senator Windham?"

He nods. "And the dude ends up dead in my office. They missed me the first try, so they switched to usin' the cops to take another shot. It's a good muh'fuckin' plan, too, 'cause nobody's gonna even question the details; Tripp and I have history. *I* have history. My guess is, if I can find out who killed him, I find out who's been behind all this shit, includin' Albescu's case."

"So, what *is* her case?"

He drops his head. "Guess it don't matter at this point. (*sigh*).... I caught the whole mess on YouTube... the hearing... the news... the comments... some o' the wacked-out speculations about Adrianna—none of it right. And they don't have a clue how she died."

"How...?"

"Murdered. Right after she was beaten and gang-raped."

"My God!"

"Albescu ain't give the full scope—Adrianna wasn't just some machine, she was alive. She felt it *all*. Every bit of it. Prob'ly more than a normal girl."

"That's *so* messed up!" Lynette says. "She kind of reminded me a little bit of—" She whips toward Jesse, her breath catching.

"Yeah, that poor thing." Gwen says. "She seemed so...."

"Mm-hm. Alive." Jesse nods. "It hit ground zero—fuckin' me up—'cause it was a copycat of Lainey's murder. My daughter. Every detail, right down to the crime location. Hell, the *ringleaders* even looked alike."

"That's just...!"

Lynette's mouth hangs open. "No shit?! Why in the world would you take that case?"

Jesse shoots her a heavy scowl; Lynette puts her hand over her mouth. He turns back to Gwen. "I caught the guys—or rather, they caught me. Then, my stalker... he shot them in the head... the three of them... one-by-one… in cold blood... right in front of me. Right there in front of me, man!" Jesse rubs his brow, wincing as he grits his teeth. "Shit. And basically told me—to my face—he was gonna frame me."

"I-I just can't believe what I'm hearing," Gwen says. "That insane—!"

"Did you have some kind o' deal with Dr. Albescu that involved Tripp?"

"Why do you ask?"

"You three were goin' at it in the hearing, but it all seemed a bit theatrical to me."

"I didn't have any deal with Tripp. I never would've colluded with that racist, misogynist sleazebag!"

"That ain't what I asked. Anyway, don't you go actin' all high and mighty after the shit you pulled."

"What?! How dare you say something like that to me!"

"I suspect most people wanted him dead, Tripp bein' who he is. Truth is, before this morning, I woulda been happy about it. But now I think he ain't deserve that; he went outta his way tryin'na help me. That's gotta count for sum'em. Now he got big ol' holes blown clear through his head and chest. I could see the floor, an' shit." Jesse rubs his eyes like he's trying to erase the image. "Damn... damn... I just talked to the guy today... dammit...."

"Whoa…," Lynette says.

"And now you're sittin' up here disparagin' a dead man like

you bettah than him. I couldn't stand him, but I bet he understood the value of loyalty."

"What are you—?!"

"It's no coincidence that me and her," he nods over at Lynette, "ended up at Dr. Albescu's house."

Gwen looks at him with shock, then frowns, shoots a glance at Lynette, and hangs her head. "I know. I was already upbraided by Dr. Albescu. Rather harshly, in fact."

"Hm. Sounds like her." Jesse turns to Lynette, who looks on curiously. "You. Figure it out, yet?"

"What?"

"Yeah... that's why yo' ass was a lousy A.D.A.. Ain't even figure out after all this time... you was a pawn."

"I...." She looks off, straight ahead as if frozen.

"Nettie—"

"Wait, wait... just wait." Lynette says with a faraway gaze. She then slowly turns. "What the HELL, Gwen?!"

Gwen turns to Jesse. "Why'd you—?!"

"You set me up?!" Lynette says.

"Okay, it's not as bad as it seems."

"Just how bad *is* it, friend?!"

"First, I had no idea Windham would be there—"

"What does that have to do with anything?! You used me! Why?!"

Jesse puts a hand up. "Look, y'all can hash out that drama later—"

"Naw! She's gonna tell me why!"

"No doubt, she will. But right now, I just need some info from you."

"From me?! What information could I possibly have?!"

Apparently, I'm completely in the dark!"

"Just calm down for a minute—"

"You don't get to tell me to calm down! Not after the hell you put me through tonight!"

"Girl, you don't know what hell is." He glares at her.

She settles down, looking at his soot and blood covered clothes, and peering into his red eyes. His display of pain and anguish still rattles her. And yet, the terror he imposed upon her tonight is too fresh.

"You—"

"Don't '*you*' me! I have a name. It's Miss Kennedy."

"Gettin' all spunky, an' shit, huh? Don't take your anger out on me. I ain't the one fucked you over."

"Hmph."

"That day at Dr. Albescu's house. Who were all those people?"

"How should I know? It's not like she introduced me. She shuffled me off to another room while her little brunch bash was goin' on. I had to listen to all that right-wing bullshit and alternative facts. And to top it off, I had to wait until it was over, and she didn't even offer me anything to eat! Not even a glass of water! I almost thought she was expecting me to pick up a broom and start sweeping."

"Hm! Felt that, too." He shakes his head. "There was this guy in particular. Military. General, I think. He looked at me weird."

"Can you blame him? Did you look in a mirror that day—?"

"He's older. Prob'ly in his late fifties, early sixties. Looks Black, but he's really light skinned... reddish hair... light eyes... like he's mixed. I got the sense that Dr. Albescu didn't like him. And it was very mutual." Jesse stares at her.

"Lyn, think. Do you remember?" Gwen says, her hands still shaking.

"Gimme a minute! And don't you talk to me! Um... um... I think his name begins with an M... no, sounds like... *Hollis!*"

"General Hollis! That's right." Jesse nods. "That's what she called him."

"General Trevor Hollis? Really?" Gwen says.

Jesse takes out his tablet. Photos of Hollis are already displayed on the screen, along with several significant links. "Yup, that's the dude."

"It has to be him. No one else I know of fits the description."

"Last I heard, he basically lives at the Complex," Lynette says. "Aren't he and Dr. Albescu colleagues there?"

"Didn't I just say they hate each other—?"

"This is starting to freak me out," Gwen says, "Windham was always colluding with him, stuffing God-knows-what into this or that bill. He even managed to quash a congressional investigation into an unauthorized use of force by the General. A lot of innocent people were killed because of Hollis."

Information scrolls on screen in response to their exchange listing connections between Tripp and Hollis. "My gut says he's the crazy General Dr. Albescu was warnin' 'bout. And the reason you're being targeted. I mean, who's leadin' the charge for investigations and regulations?" He points to her.

"Oh, God...."

He continues skimming. "Makes sense. He wouldn't want you and her stoppin' whatever he's doin'. I just don't know why he's tryin'na drone-kill me; I got nothin' to do with any o' that shit. Feels like I'm caught up in somebody else's muh'fuckin' war."

"Oh, that's right! My God, you had a big news day, today!

From hero to crazed serial killer in a matter of hours!"

"Yeah, ain't that a blip?" Jesse rises to his feet, never taking his eyes off the tablet.

"They say, if not for you, many lives would've been lost. And you're saying that you were the target? General Hollis was behind that, too?"

"Sure looks that way," he says.

Lynette watches him walk toward the door, and yet she doesn't feel relief at the prospect of him leaving. "Where are you—?"

"You're leaving?!" Gwen pops up and follows him. "I thought you said you were going to protect me! What am I supposed to do now?!"

"Stay yo' ass right here, that's what. Why you think I brought you over here?"

"I can't squat in my neighbor's—!"

"They ain't gonna be back for at least a week. But if you get found out, just tell 'em you hid in here, away from me."

"What're you gonna do?"

"Don't worr' 'bout dat. You just stay outta sight 'til I'm done."

"You're going after General Hollis, aren't you? If you find hard evidence, give me first look!"

"Nope. If this goes south, the less you know, the better."

"If Hollis really is out to kill me, I have a right to know! Not only that, if he's crazy enough to target American citizens on American soil, activating some kind of advanced weaponized drone in the middle of a crowded city, and if he really did murder Tripp... good lord, this is monumental! Clearly, you're going to need help. *My* help."

He raises his eyebrows.

"The help of a Congresswoman?"

"Hm." He vigorously rubs his hands across his face. "Aaight. You got a point. But there's some stuff I need you to do for me. Whatever it takes, I need you to look after my brothers, George Barnes and Nico Stizzoli. She has info on them," he nods toward Lynette. "They're innocent, no matter what the media says. Just do what'choo can, but only after it's safe."

"How will I know when I'm out of danger?"

"She'll let you know." He jerks his head toward the couch at Lynette, who curls her mouth at him, frowning.

"But what if something happens to you? I can't hide here forever!"

"Then have her," he motions toward a sighing Lynette, "contact Dr. Albescu. She's got the resources to help."

"And if something happens to Nicoletta?"

"Nothin's gonna happen to her."

"But if it does?"

"I *said*, nothing's gonna *happen* to her." He scowls at Gwen.

"But—"

Lynette touches her arm, slowly shaking her head.

Gwen releases a heavy sigh. "Well… if something *does* happen to *you*, how will I get the evidence?"

"Anything I find will be uploaded to your cloud accounts as it happens." He turns away. "Aaight—"

"That's it?!" Lynette lurches up from the couch. "So, you terrorized me, dragging me here only to answer those questions?!"

"Nah. You got the most important job of all."

"What?"

"Keepin' her alive."

She sneers at Gwen. "I'm not sure if I want to."

"Hey!"

"Fuckin'—look, this ain't no game! Somebody could be out there right now, plannin' to blow a hole through her goddamn head!"

She continues glaring at Gwen. "I'm thinking...."

"Lyn! After all we've been through—come on, girl! How can you not know I did what I did so we can make a run at the White House?!"

"(ntch!) Whatever. Wait—the *White House?!* Seriously?!"

"Yep." Gwen nods with a big grin on her face.

"Holy!" Lynette becomes giddy. "Then why didn't you say so?!"

Jesse shakes his head. "(ptssh!) Y'all two muh'fuckas deserve each other."

Lynette turns to him. "Still... I'm not so sure I believe all this crazy stuff you're spewing."

"I don't give a shit. This ain't about you, this about—"

"*Alright!* What do I have to do?"

"First thing is, don't lend her your phone or tablet or any computer. No matter how much she begs. Capisce?"

Gwen bristles. "I'm not a child! I know what's—!"

"Make sure she has food, and make sure you don't get seen comin' in or outta here. Also, I'm gonna need you to be the real bitch that'choo are."

Lynette puts her hand on her hips. "That was uncalled for!"

"Rat me out."

"Huh?"

"When I leave, take a picture of me headin' toward her house. Then call the cops on me and release the image to the media. With our history, ain't no way they'll doubt you."

Lynette's mouth hangs open.

"What good would that do?" Gwen says.

"If Hollis believes I have you then he'll have to come after me to find you. Don't know if this'll work, but it's the best I got, right now."

"But that'll only make matters worse for you!"

"How the fuck could it possibly get any worse?!"

"But, that's a crazy plan!" Lynette says. "You're not even 100% sure Hollis is after her!"

He turns to her. "Since there's a chance you won't be seein' me alive again, I just wanna say som'em. Don't talk, just listen."

".... But...." Her mouth hangs agape.

"You were right about the ballistics report. Only, it's not what you think. I just learned we were both bein' played. I still don't know why, an' I don't think I'll ever get a straight answer from that psycho, but you should know that neither one of us fucked with that report. And I didn't kill those asswipes.

"Having said that, I'm still pissed at you for what you did to me. I just can't let that one go. You may not've put me in hell, but you sure as shit turned the heat up to max! But you know what really pissed me off tonight? Insinuatin' I'd take advantage of you—knowing what happened to my daughter! That shit was so fucked up!"

"I was scared! I don't know what you want me to say."

"Nothin'. Aaight, I'm out. You come outside in the middle o' the street. Don't want the photo angle leadin' to this house. No video... it'd look too staged." Jesse holds up the tablet toward the door. "Show people and vehicles," he says, scanning left and right. "It's clear. Don't forget, Congresswoman: stay out of sight. And keep the lights off."

"I will. And thank you, Jesse… for coming to my rescue."

"That's 'Mr. Davenport'. You can thank me by protectin' my brothers. Can I trust you?"

She nods. "I'll earn your trust. You'll see."

The War of Others, Mine – Part III

JESSE and Lynette leave the house and walk to the opening of the cul-de-sac while Gwen watches through sheers.

"Move to the side a bit. I'm gonna run toward the house. You take the shot. Actually take a few—I'll choose the most natural one."

"If you say so." She points her phone at him.

He sprints toward Gwen's house as Lynette watches.

He looks like he's about to crack... or pass out from exhaustion. Running from the law... my God—for his life! Even so, he came all the way out here to save Gwen. There's no way he'd be doing all this if he was guilty. Not this crazy plan. How could I get it so wrong? Maybe he's right... I was a lousy A.D.A. As she reflects on how fiercely she prosecuted this grieving father, her stomach twists and churns. It intensifies as he reaches the door, stops, and turns, facing her. *What did I do? How could I—* "Oops! Um… sorry, I didn't…."

His shoulders drop and he begins to walk back, shaking his head. The tablet buzzes; he looks into his coat. His eyes pop open, staring back at Lynette. "Ru—!"

BOOOOM!

Ejected by the fiery plume blasting out the doorway, Jesse soars through the air along with the door in splinters. Lynette falls backward and her phone flies out of her hand. With the shower of glass and smoldering debris, Jesse crashes to the ground several feet away from her, grimacing, his coat smoking. He grips the sides of his cranium with both hands. "… aghk… uhnn…." He tries to shake it off. Through squinting eyes, he looks toward the house where he left Gwen—she's opening the door. He waves her off; she stops, hesitant, appearing to teeter toward rushing to their aid. He waves again, emphatically; visibly distraught, she goes back indoors… just as people emerge from their homes.

Ears ringing, Lynette rolls on her side, hand pressing against the side of her scrunching face—Jesse mouths the word 'scream'. Looking back at him sorrowfully, she shakes her head. He mouths again in anger, crawling toward her. 'I'm so sorry,' she mouths before—"*EEEEEEEE!* Get away from me! Help! It's Jesse Davenport! He just killed Congresswoman Policastro!" She scurries away from him as the neighbors shout at him, raising their phones. Jesse staggers to his feet and hobbles to Lynette's car. He floors it, bolting out of the cul-de-sac. Gwen's house burning behind her, Lynette watches, teary eyed, clutching her blouse to her chest as Jesse speeds away.

* * * * *

Poking through the forest in the deep, dark night, numerous intense light beams swing from the movement of a brilliant object speeding along the road.

The limousine emits blinding white light from its entire body, and, like flies drawn to a bright lamp, several vehicles swarm in pursuit. Screeching tires and growling engines disrupt the quiet of the woods, soon accompanied by a heavy stream of pops and bangs.

Inside the limo, the windows display the road and the woods in perfect daylight, unaffected by the darkness outside or the brilliance emitted from its own body. Random taps resound inside the car; no projectiles penetrate.

"I was left with no other choice….. Well, I'm sorry you feel that way….. Y'know, I could've said a lot worse….. No, that wasn't a threat, just an observation." The phone pressed against her face, Nicole glances with worry down at the developing story on her tablet:

HOME   EXPLODES,   CONGRESSWOMAN POLICASTRO MISSING!

"… mm-hm… with all due respect, *I* wrote the charter along with some pretty darn good lawyers, so I know that I'm most certainly not in violation—"

"Brace yourself, ma'am!" Colby says.

Like glowing eyes closing in the dark, the few streetlamps and the limo blink out all at once, erased within the blackness. The car takes a sharp right turn with nary a sound as it follows the curve of the road. The pursuing vehicles skid onward, plowing through branches and slamming into trees as they careen down the wooded hills.

"… The Department of Homeland Security doesn't have any jurisdiction. *I* paid for the lion's share of that facility….. Well, I apologize to you, but what you *believe* is irrelevant….. That department's become dysfunctional and I did my civic duty by testif—" Her eyes snap to the tablet.

JESSE   DAVENPORT   KILLING   SPREE: CONGRESSWOMAN POLICASTRO MURDERED?!

"Oh, no…."

"Hello?! Hello?!"

She plays accompanying video of Jesse having just endured the blast, stumbling to the car, and speeding away, all while people are yelling and screaming at him. *God-DAMMIT, Jesse! I told you to get back the estate! I swear, when I see you, I'm gonna—!*

"Did that woman hang up on me?"

She snaps the phone back to her ear. "Look. Escalate this if you must, but you'd better be prepared….. *War*….. I know exactly what I said….. For all I know, *you* contracted those assholes trying to kill me….. Well, you do what you have to, I'll do the same, Mr. President." She throws the phone against the floor. "*U-U-UHNN!*"

"Ma'am…?"

"*WHAT?!*" She shoots her eyes up at the windshield. There's a zoomed image of a black helicopter floating above the road ahead and more vehicles are closing in behind them.

"Let me out."

"Begging your pardon, ma'am?"

"Stop the car. Now," she snarls, yanking the CSC out of its carrying case.

"I'm sorry, ma'am, but I can't do that."

"It's not wise to defy me right now, Colby," she says, glaring at him sideways in the rearview.

"I understand that you're extremely frustrated. But I intend to get you back to the estate, safe and sound."

"You don't have to worry about me."

"I respectfully disagree. I don't think you really want to become a killer."

"You don't know what I want. Stop the damned car, Colby."

"If you use that weapon, there'll be a great many questions raised. And that would complicate matters for you... and for the company."

She glares at him, then turns away, frowning. She tosses the CSC back in its case. "If you're gonna do something, do it," she says in a low growl.

"My pleasure, ma'am." He presses the accelerator; the limo hums. The vehicles behind them pick up speed, closing the distance. The helicopter is now visible. It sprays ordnance at the limo; projectiles slice the darkness with hot streaks and launch ejecta upon impacting the road. The limo's body strobes with eye-thrashing brilliance. Colby taps a button on the display. A narrow pulse emanates from the car and intersects the copter. The limo zips under the stalling aircraft, just missing the landing skids. Nicole looks back as the craft collides with the ground and the speeding cars, feeling some measure of satisfaction at the tremendous crashes, screams of tires, and explosion.

"Idiots. They've no idea they're being sacrificed."

Testing my defenses, hm? Hiding behind these weak attacks using conventional weapons will only get them so far. Let's see if they have the balls to get serious and come at me. Then I'll have confirmation of who's behind this. Hmph. That's what they're afraid of.

Above the fireball, Nicole spots another copter picking up the pursuit. It gains on them; at the zippery sound of the road, she smiles darkly.

"Oops, too late for you."

The copter sparks and sputters; it attempts a retreat, but crashes into the woods a few miles away.

The Knight's Question – Part I

*I*T'S an hour before daybreak, the sky dark and overcast, the air cool and misty. *SLISH… SLISH… SLISH… SLISH….* With the bejeweled city's muted crown behind him, Rajiv high-steps through an overgrown grassy field, gripping a cooler and supporting a box in both arms, trudging through the overgrowth to a point ahead where the reeds are taller than he.

With worrisome eyes, he looks around, standing in a bald spot within the field. Deep within the mass of swaying shafts—a short honk sounds and a blink of red glows in the thin fog. "Whew!" He fights his way through to an area that's slightly clearer, toward the back of a Honda Accord. He plods over to the passenger side. The door swings open.

"Wow, it is veddy good to see you, my friend!"

"Yup." Jesse uprights himself back to the driver's side.

"And thank you veddy much for not blowing up my taxi—hmhm!" Rajiv drops onto the seat, resting the cooler on the floor between his feet and the box on his lap.

With worry, Jesse looks at Rajiv who sheepishly looks back at him.

"Too soon?"

"Still haven't heard from Haj?"

"No. But Dr. Mrs. A. was able to retrieve her car and make the arrest warrant go away—"

"You check all hospitals?"

"Yes. She is nowhere to be found."

"Damn... where you at, girl?!" His focus meanders about the murky water ahead. *Prob'ly hidin' out in a silly disguise, or some shit. I hope.* "Anyway, thanks for lookin' out." He zeroes in on the box, raising an eyebrow. "Yo... I don't see no pizza, dude...."

"Dr. Mrs. A would kill me if I did not take care of you—"

"Oh, no—what'choo bring? Tell me you ain't come out here wit' some damn sprouts and roots."

"Hahaha! I would not do that to you!" He presents the box to Jesse, who partially opens it and peers cautiously inside.

"Do not worry, dude. It is safe. All G-rated—heeheehee!"

"Good! Ain't in the mood to see dicks and balls in my food, right now."

"When *are* you in the mood? Heeheehee!"

"Hmhmhm!" Jesse pulls out a grilled ham and cheese panini and tears into it. "*(smack, smack)* Thanks, man—*(smack)*"

"You have Winston to thank. He begged Celia to forgive Francisco, just this once. So... if you stop to think about it...

Winston is kind of a pimp and the dick-free food you have in your mouth right now is from Francisco and Celia doing the nasty—"

"HM?!" Jesse stops chewing, mouth full of food. "HMHM—*GHK!*" He frantically points to the cooler. Rajiv hands him a cup he quickly filled with passionfruit tea. Jesse sips, then gulps down part of his mouthful.

"(*g-g-ghm!*) *Yo*, man! (*smack-smack*) Don't do that to me while I got a mouth full o' food—hmhmhm!"

"Haha—sorry, dude—hmhmhm!"

"Hmhm… (*smack-smack*) Mmm… (*smack*) You ain't tell, her, did you? (*smack-smack*) Nicole."

"No. But she is so veddy, veddy worried about you! And furious! At us both! I am already in the dog house basement and I felt veddy guilty sneaking around to avoid her."

"Why's she mad at me?"

"Celia said it is because you left the estate, putting yourself in danger… and that you ignored her when she told you to go back. I have to say, after you were accused of killing someone, getting yourself blown up last night—and with what you are attempting to do here and now, I am kind of on her side, my friend. The estate is a veddy safe place. You should be there with her."

"Hm. Well… glad *she's* safe, at least."

Rajiv frowns, then turns to him. "Jesse… it is really not my fault. Susan—Haj. That woman is veddy difficult! You know that, right?"

"Here. Eat som'em." Jesse tosses a wrapped sandwich on Rajiv's lap.

"Oh, God! Thank you! It was killing me, smelling all this food on the way here."

They eat in relative silence, save for the occasional smack, crunch, and slurp, both staring straight ahead across the water, through the fog, at the expansive eleven-story building rising above the tree line.

Building-A.

. . .

Rajiv looks through binoculars, scanning the Complex's buildings that peek above the trees. "So… how are we going to get in?"

"We? Naw, man. You ain't comin' wit' me. I appreciate the offer, though."

"Oh-thank-God!" he says with a heavy exhale.

"Hmhmhm!"

"I would seriously go if you wanted—"

"Nope. It's cool."

"I just want you to know that I do have your back."

"Mm-hm. 'Preciate it."

Rajiv gazes at the tower through the reeds that are disturbed by the gusting wind.

"So… are you going to infiltrate through the sewer, knock out a guard, sneak in around back, hide in a broom closet, and slide through air vents, or…?"

"What? Hahahaha! Damn, Rajiv—hmhmhmh! You totally Americanized, man!"

"What did I say?"

"That stuff only happens in TV and movies. You can't break into a military base wit'out gettin' yo' ass killed." Jesse holds up the tablet. It shows a crystal clear, tree and fog-free, zoomed image of the base, with relevant stats called out.

"Wow… that is a veddy cool, veddy ugly tablet, my friend!"

Jesse angles it for Rajiv's vantage as he scans the base. "Look over there… soldiers with guns… jeeps… airfield with chopper…

barracks… those buildings… that one's eleven stories up. It's loaded with people. No doubt the guy I'm lookin' for is at the top. Ego."

"Come on, the Reagan Memorial Park is not a real base, dude."

"Somebody clearly thinks it is."

"You are a veddy wanted man and cannot exactly walk through the front door. So, how are you going to get in?"

"Front door."

"What?!"

* * * * *

As sure as the sun rises, General Hollis usually greets the day in his Army Service Uniform, standing in his sunrise office, nursing a hot cup of nostalgia—instant coffee with cocoa powder—breathing in the aroma, watching the newborn light wash over the recruits as they perform their morning drills. Though he's retired and has no direct authority over them, his shadow looms large; his critical eyes always track the jogging troops along the gravel paths—and they know it, never daring to glance upward or move out of step while calling cadence. In the evenings, his sunset office—identical to its twin right down to the furnishings and photos—serves as a counterpoint where he winds down, watching the men head toward the barracks as the city lights blink on and shimmer against the water along with the moon. These viewings serve as bookends to his busy day of liaising with various military brass, black projects teams, and defense contractors, and facilitating the technological synergy between all with his staff, while commanding—from afar—overseas ops by private military contractors… some ops unsanctioned.

However, today there is no sun, only a featureless overcast expanse. "Hmhm... Big Bobby...." His back to the sky, he pats his hand against his thigh. His brow ridges and he subtly shakes his head, his jaw tight, low-simmering terror in his eyes as he stares at an old wall-hanging photo of young camaraderie—a jocular band of lost brothers set against a blank sky.

"General, a Mr.... *Enord Rellik*? Here to see you, sir?" a voice sounds from an icon on the window behind him.

"(*sniff*) Send him up."

The Knight's Question – Part II

*J*ESSE tentatively walks through the door, his coat's collar turned up, eyes obscured behind his aviator shades, peering into the bright office where the entire facing wall is glass. As the assistant closes the door behind him, Jesse's head snaps toward the soft—*BUMP*—then he calms, turning forward. Something moves to the left of his periphery—he jumps, fingers tensed. It's his own reflection in a mirror on the left wall. He silently exhales. Embarrassed by his own skittishness, he whips his focus on Hollis, who appears as featureless as the sky, but is a black shadow superimposed upon it. Jesse is unnerved by Hollis's stony focus on him.

Hollis sucks in a deep breath and releases. "Doesn't this view make you feel great to be alive? Even on a day such as this, you can witness, firsthand, the greatness of God."

Jesse squints. Hollis isn't staring at him, but is facing the glass wall, surveying the grounds.

"Come join me in a look, soldier."

"Pass."

"Oh, that's right. You're not a morning person. Isn't that one of the many reasons for your unusually late ELS discharge from the army, Mr.... *Killer Drone?*"

Jesse is silent. His eye is drawn to a dull glow on Hollis's desk; some form of large caliber pistol, nearly as big as Warlock's. Hollis stands with his back to it and to Jesse, still admiring the day. This scene strikes Jesse as staged; he looks on, keeping his distance.

"Speak freely, soldier. The only reason I agreed to meet is to hear, in person, from the fugitive with balls big enough to accuse me of targeting a U.S. citizen on American soil and of murdering a Senator and framing him for it."

"And don't forget that muh'fuckin' drone. Turn an' face me. I ain't talkin' at the back o' yo' head."

"Your file was quite accurate. No respect for authority."

"You ain't nothin' but a goddamn murderer."

Hollis turns. "Listen, soldier. My largesse does have its limits. You should think hard before insulting me and making accusations."

"What largesse?"

"You may not be fit for the standard military and you're long in the tooth—"

"Fuck you, Methuselah."

"—but this country could use a man like you. There are a number of special projects for which an intelligent, able-bodied man such as yourself would be a perfect fit, with some training. And they're extremely lucrative."

"You ain't got nothin' I want 'cept the truth. Why'd you try to kill me? And why'd you murder Senator Windham and frame *me* for it?"

"Am I to assume that's a *no* to the special projects offer?"

Jesse seethes as he watches Hollis.

"Listen, soldier. It's not a confession, but I will admit to taking some… less than ideal actions. But they were all in defense of this country."

"How am I a threat?"

"Seeing you now, I concede that I was in error. I falsely assumed that Mrs. Albescu would send you after me. You do work for her, correct?"

"Why would you think som'em like dat? That I'd come after you?"

"She intends to silence me."

"*She's* tryin'na silence *you*, huh?"

"Affirmative. She and Senator Tripp Windham were plotting against me, casting me as some kind of treasonous lunatic at that hearing. I believe Albescu launched an attempt on Congresswoman Policastro's life, as well."

"Bullshit."

"I was relieved to hear that her body wasn't found but wasn't surprised after hearing you were on the scene. If not for you coming to the Congresswoman's aid, well…. Wait—you didn't share her location with Albescu, did you?"

"This the part where I lead you to her?"

"If you truly intend to keep her safe, I'm in a position to do just that."

"Don't worr' 'bout her. She's plenty safe. Can't say the same about you." Jesse's fingers tense as he glares at Hollis—the man arrogant enough to admit to attacking him and bold enough to tacitly admit to killing Tripp. He glances at the gun.

Hollis scrutinizes him. "Hm."

Jesse's fists tighten.

"Stand down, soldier. I already admitted that I targeted you and why, but I'm no longer your enemy. And I readily take responsibility for my error. However, I understand your frustration; someone has been lying to you. But it wasn't I."

Jesse sneers.

"I see you need convincing." Hollis presses his hand against the window; a set of graphical controls converge across the surface toward his fingers. He navigates a few displays and swipes across the screen, flipping through various photos and videos. "I'm going to go out on a limb in assuming Mrs. Albescu fed you a warm and cuddly image of the girl—*the product*—you were hired to avenge, just like she fooled the world at the hearing. Here's the other side of the story. The *real* story."

A dark, blurry and blotchy image appears on the window, nearly filling it. Jesse can't make out what he's seeing in the huge display.

"What's…?"

Hollis taps it.

"*IIIEEEEEEEEEEE!*"

Jesse's shoulders jump as the loud shriek rattles his heart and sharp impacts rip the silence in the room with the fidelity of a THX theater. He immediately realizes this is no Hollywood production; a vicious, kinetic image materializes through the blurs, reflected on a shattering mirror. Ferocious flaring emerald eyes.

It's… Adrianna!

Her brain and parts of her substructure exposed, she punches and claws at her fractured disassembled likeness, further shattering the mirror, leaving bluish smears from her lacerated fingers, along with the splatters of someone else's blood. "YOU FUCKIN' HEAR ME?! YOU'RE DEAD! YOU'RE DEAD! YOU'RE DEAD! DEAD! DEAD! DEAD! DEAD! DEAD! DEAD! DEAD! DEA—!" The movie pauses on her horrific eruption of manic rage, voracious blue-stained bright teeth, her broken reflection locked in the shards.

Jesse is frozen, staring at the image of this deranged bloodthirsty monster he once thought he knew. Is this the same Adrianna he cried for? Cared for? *How can this be the same… person?*

"Yes, soldier. I recognize that look. I felt the same way. For years, I'd warned the Albescu's against creating that thing the way they did. I predicted it would go haywire and that's exactly what happened. No… it turned out far worse than I ever imagined.

"Now, there's no way I can prove any of what I've said to you is the truth. But what I *can* prove…" He scrolls to a photo of Tripp smiling. "… is that you're being lied to."

"How's a photo of Tripp—?"

"No… come. Look closer, soldier."

Heart still racing as he slowly walks toward the window, Jesse keeps Hollis in his sights, and as he approaches the image, he stares at the reflection of this admitted killer behind him. A faint ghost overlaying the city, Hollis makes no moves of aggression staring back into Jesse's eyes. Stony. The gun behind him, out of his line of sight, Jesse trains his ears to catch any sudden sounds, and slides his focus to the image.

His jaw drops. "Lainey…?"

There are multiple images of his daughter on the wall behind Tripp.

"That was taken at Albescu's home. Your client."

All else around Jesse falls away.

"When I discovered that image in the Senator's cloud account by chance, I got curious. It was because of this image that I uncovered what Albescu's been hiding behind locked doors. And the reason she's trying to silence me."

"What... what is...?"

"I know it can't compare to what you're feeling right now, but I, too, was in shock when I learned of the Adriana unit's obsession with your daughter."

"Ob... obsession? With Lainey?"

"Affirmative. Your daughter was Adriana's source of metadata holograph... uh... *ghostcloning target* under Albescu's Gemini project."

"No...."

Hollis nods. "Adriana came to be by tracking your daughter as she unwittingly created her own ghost. I repeatedly lobbied the Albescu's to shut it down and find a willing target, but they refused. And, as I feared, the unit malfunctioned due to her obsession. I still have yet to uncover all the details, but as far as I've been able to dig, it appears that your daughter was investigating the unit... and got too close."

"How could...? She was doing what?"

"You heard correctly—she was investigating Adriana's origin." Hollis moves to the window, swipes to a video and activates it.

Jesse's eyes bulge wide open. "What am I seein'? What is this?!"

"It may seem familiar to you, but you haven't seen this. Not this part. It's the part Albescu has been keeping from you. It's also why I couldn't believe my eyes when I first saw you—I couldn't believe she had the gall to hire you."

Jesse's heart rages as he watches the events unfold:

"Is she dead? Did... did you kill 'er, dude?"

"Holy, shit! He killed her! He fuckin' killed her! Why'd you do that, you lunatic?!"

"I'm gonna get expelled!"

"Expelled?! This shit is way beyond expelled, man! This is fucking *murder!*"

The two stand over Lainey's body, screaming, arguing, and panicking, while a third has his hands cupped over her chest, pumping. "Bitch, breathe!" He breaks rhythm to give her mouth-to-mouth, her lips bloodied and broken.

"We was only supposed to have a little fun wit'er! Why'd you have to go and beat her up like that and choke her to death?!"

"Yeah, man, I'm gettin' outta here! I ain't no murderer!"

"C'mon... fuckin'—*uhn*—breathe!" He gives her mouth-to-mouth again.

She coughs.

"Lainey... alive...? They didn't lie? They saved her after doin'... what they did to my little girl? What the fuck is this—why am I just seein' this now?"

"As I said, soldier, Albescu kept this hidden away. I commissioned a team of hackers to retrieve it from her personal servers."

"She's alive!"

"Yeah, now what? She'll recognize us—"

"I don't know, dude! I couldn't just let 'er die!"

"It said they'd keep her quiet! We did our job, so let's get the fuck outta here and get paid!"

Footsteps echo from the stairwell. Slow. Cavernous.

"FUCK—somebody's comin'!"

"Hide, idiots!"

They scurry behind the HVAC unit. Deliberate footfalls fill the stairwell, getting louder, until a lone black-clad figure emerges, stepping out onto the roof. The figure slowly moves toward Lainey, who is battered, bleeding, and barely conscious.

"... (*cough*) ... go... call... call Dad...."

The figure looks around, then turns, facing the camera.

"... they're still... here... please... go...."

Adrianna's emerald eyes glow, sunken within the darkness of her cloak's hood. The breeze blows the material about her body. She's still as a statue, but her wildly flickering irises belie her stoicism.

"... Dree... (*cough*) ...."

A long, glowing, metal blade extends out of her sleeve.

"... Dree...."

Gripping with both hands, she raises it overhead.

"... no...."

Her arms tense.

"... p-please... (*cough*) ...."

She plunges blade downward across Lainey's neck.

"Oh, shit!" The young men dart across the roof and down

the stairs.

Lainey's face freezes. Adrianna again raises the blade, then hacks down across Lainey's body. Again. Again—

"I think you've seen enough." Hollis stops the video.

Jesse's body shakes. His legs are weak. He wages a fierce battle against vertigo, bracing hands against the glass, halting his collapse. His throat scratches as he hyperventilates. He grows numb, unable to sense the tablet vibrating against his chest.

"I understand it's a lot to take in all at once. You should have a seat... and take all the time you need, soldier. But be aware that if Albescu knows you've come to see me, then she knows you've seen that video. And that puts you, too, at grave risk."

Jesse hears the words but can't comprehend them. It's taking all his energy not to scream at the top of his lungs and pummel the image looming right before him.

Hollis looks downward, out the window. He taps a display on the glass. "What's that commotion out front?"

"Sir, the U.S. Marshals are on their way up," the assistant's voice vibrates from his icon on the glass.

"Did they say what they want?"

"Yes, sir. They received a tip that Jesse Davenport is in the building."

Tears streaming down his face, Jesse snaps out of his morass, focusing through the image of his daughter's carnage, down at the numerous police vehicles, and up ahead toward the gate at a herd of news vans.

The Knight's Question – Part III

JESSE reels away from the glass.

"Wait a minute, soldier... maybe it's time you stop running and turn yourself in. You'll only increase the chances of your death if you run—"

Jesse whips his head about. Hollis darts his eyes to the gun on his desk. Their eyes meet. Jesse lunges for the handgun—a step too fast for Hollis—stabbing the weapon at him, his arm tense, hands shaking, teeth gnashing, his eyes filled with terror and rage.

Hollis raises his hands, stepping backward. "What are you doing, soldier?! Put that weapon down before you hurt someone!"

Jesse blinks hard, trying to regain his focus.

"There's no escaping those marshals. If you continue on this trajectory, you'll only end up dead and that would be a horrible tragedy. But if you just put down that weapon, I can negotiate on your—"

"Shut... the fuck... *UUUUP!*" Jesse's body shakes, the veins around his temples bulging, spit ejecting. Hollis jumps and backs up against the glass. Jesse's focus careens around the room. He launches toward the door at the far end, keeping the gun trained on the main entrance. He quietly opens the door and pokes his head out. The corridor is empty. He bolts down the hall and around a corner, passing some startled personnel. A soldier approaches—Jesse points the gun at him.

"Stairs!"

The man cowers, pointing down the hall; at the far end, there is a faint sound of numerous footfalls.

"Fuck!" Jesse frantically retraces his steps. He flies past Hollis's office, toward the bank of elevators as a DING rings out. He doesn't break stride; he locks his eyes on the red EXIT sign looming ahead just beyond the elevator doors, ignoring the assistant cowering at the desk. The elevator doors buck just as he breezes past. He grabs the stairwell door's handle and shoves the door wide. With heavy thumps, he takes as many steps down as each stride can reach. A disheveled noise blares from below.

"THERE HE IS!"

Jesse tears back up the stairs, covering the two flights to the roof at top speed, against the cluttered backdrop of the pursuing army, chaotic heavy footfalls, and slamming-open doors filling the stairwell. He rams his shoulder hard against the roof access door, dashing out into the blinding morning light and gusting wind. Groups of officers are running toward him from other access points, left and right. He spins about in search of salvation. The city flies by. The gray clouds. The faraway mountains. The fast-approaching marshals. Again. Again. All he can see is no escape.

He clamps his head with both hands, the gun's grip pressing against his scalp, and he yells at the top of his lungs, screaming at the world. At God. At Lainey's fate. At that monster who mercilessly and brutally took his child away from him. Screaming at Nicole.

Like a hungry bird of prey, a police helicopter swoops up, clearing the roof's edge. Marshals burst through the door, merging with the others closing in. As Jesse steps back, the converging teams fill the roof, weapons drawn. They're a massive pack of ravenous wolves, armed to the fangs, bearing down on their singular prey, each vying for his own bloody chunk. They bay at him in a discordant chorus of barks. Their ferocious faces smear together, though a few are familiar but fail to register amid his turmoil, offering only a greater sense of entrapment—eyes that guided the pack to the prey.

The shadow of the helicopter sweeps over them, circling with the oppressive *THOOP-THOOP-THOOP-THOOP* of its rotor blades. The world spins. Endlessly. His stomach churns. He can barely hear anything above the angry noises and howling wind and, most of all, the relentless throbbing in his head—a tremendous migraine threatens to split his skull wide open, exacerbated by the pressure wave of the blades. He shuffles backward in stuttered steps. The marshals scream with greater ferocity as he inches toward the roof's edge. He's surrounded by an ever-tightening semi-circle in front of him, stark oblivion behind, contemplating what's to come from choosing the path of survival. The crushing anguish. Horrendous pain. Futility. He peers behind himself, over the edge. Way down at the ground. Vertigo. He breathes deeply, closing his eyes, his balance unsteady. He focuses on the pattern of the rotor blades—the steady rhythm. *Relax.*

A marshal lowers his gun. "Oh, no... I think he's gonna jump—!"

"DON'T DO IT, DAVENPORT!" a female officer yells. "Think of your brother Stizzoli!"

Their frantic voices wash away. The wind subsides to a soft whisper. He breathes in time, letting a number of rotor thumps go by with each breath. But he can't catch the beat. The timing is off. He opens his eyes. Behind the marshals, the copter is convulsing in the air, spinning and emitting smoke. It then rolls on its side, its rotor's machetes swinging on a path through the group.

"RUN!" His wide-sprung eyes focused behind them, Jesse waves his arms. "RUN, DAMMIT!"

They shout aggressive warnings, weapons stabbing back outward at him, but one man turns. "OH, SHIT! RU-U-U-UN!" They stumble and slide out of the path of the hobbled craft. However...

Jesse stands in place. In the path of the blades, Lainey's final horror replays before his eyes. *This is fate.*

"DAVENPORT! MOVE!"

The tablet sounds a piercing beep and vibrates wildly against his chest. He looks down into his coat. There is a number five. Then a four.

"He's gonna be mincemeat!" The marshal turns away, clenching his eyes.

Three.

Trailing smoke, the copter swings past Jesse, the blades missing his head by inches as it clears the roof.

Two.

He turns, facing the edge and stuffs the gun in his belt. The marshals recover.

One.

They dash toward him. An arrow facing out from the roof flashes on the screen. Jesse doesn't hesitate; he closes his eyes, and with arms outstretched as if taking flight, he jumps. The officers are a step too late, just missing the tail of his fluttering coat and nearly falling off the roof themselves.

"No!"

"Aw, *fuck!*"

The crisp wind rushes over his skin. Against the heaviness of his world, Jesse's blind leap into forever spurs a sensation of weightless flight that he hopes will carry him gently into the next. Time stops. A jettison of every emotional anchor is exchanged for an ineffable freedom he experiences for the first time... ever. But in the silence of sweet, inevitable oblivion, a question echoes.

Why?

The furious wind blows, stinging his wide-sprung eyes and scrubbing against his deeply pressed brow. His momentum carries him forward—his palms smack against a landing skid of the choking helicopter, sending a jolt through his arms. The jarring pain forces a guttural yell out of him, but he grips tightly with both hands. The chopper slows its descent and stabilizes. Jesse struggles to maintain his grip under the strain, catching sight of his shadow as his boots sweep through the blades of grass on the concourse Green, just past the swarm of empty police cars and the building personnel ducking for cover.

The conjoined pair gain altitude and streak out of the base, above the wriggling treetops, over the agitated waters, toward the opposite shore.

Jesse's fingers ache and throb, his arms are spent. The tablet beeps, and he releases his hold, splashing underwater, near the edge where he left Lynette's car hidden in the thick overgrowth. The copter whimpers back toward the base.

. . .

Rajiv's gaze skitters about the choppy water surface. His fists are balled as he nervously paces. He breathes a heavy sigh as Jesse rises out of the murkiness, coughing up water, and stumbling onto the muddy slope.

Rajiv runs toward him. "Oh, my God! I almost thought you were not coming back up! My heart literally stopped when you jumped! I simply do not even have words to describe what it is I just saw!" He attempts to put Jesse's arm over his shoulder.

"Nah— (*cough, cough*) —don't."

"But you need help!"

"Where's the taxi?"

"Why do you—?"

Jesse glares at him with bloodshot eyes of fire and gritting teeth as he slogs ashore, dripping wet.

"It is… back that way…" Rajiv points toward the tall grass. "… near the service road."

"Keys."

"Let me drive you, my friend."

Jesse is unmoved.

Rajiv places the keys in Jesse's hand.

Jesse disappears into the brush, leaving Rajiv behind. A minute later, the tires scream, signaling his scorching desire to receive some kind of an answer to his question.

WHY?!

The Last Room – Part I

*T*HEY used to welcome him, these gates—tall and imposing, yet always wide open. Today he stands before them feeling the welcome mat's been burned to ash. He looks up, squinting. These thick black bars are clenched teeth biting into the white expanse. His eyes track down along them between the narrow spaces, from the sky... to the snowlike treetop canopy... to the brilliant hills and blushes of color... to the perfectly swathed grass... and to the intricate stone road that reflects them all from its dewy sheen. These gates conceal the trappings of heaven while screaming at him to abandon all hope. Accepting his fate, the fire rages within him for swift passage.

"Let him in," Nicole's voice sounds like she's right in front of him, just beyond the gates. Indifferent. *Cold*. Chills run over his body. He jumps at the heavy metallic *KLANK* as this barrier unlocks and slowly opens with a low buzz and deep somber groan.

Back in the driver's seat, his grip tightening around the wheel, he looks ahead, down the path to the fountain. He eases the taxi forward. The gates clank shut behind him. His eyes dart about. This wonderland is now like a cemetery—a scenic landscape spiked with flowers marking the end of memories and hope. There's no activity or sound beyond the nervous leaves whispering to the hushed fountain, sharing a dark secret—he feels a grotesque energy emanating from this place, sensing Nicole is lying in wait for him. Somewhere.

… right… under… your… chin. POP!

He pats the gun lodged in his belt, but questions if he's truly prepared to use it. As he slowly pulls closer to the fountain, he's startled by something in the corner of his eye.

Nicole waits by the sign, watching him, her arms folded, body clad all in black—a tight long-sleeve tee shirt, jeans, and combat boots—her raven hair gathered to one side, loosely twisted and flowing over her chest. Though far from her reach, his heart is skewered by her menacing beauty, his mind pierced by the sharpness of her silent stare. Offering neither greeting nor gestural acknowledgment of his presence, she turns and walks away, disappearing into the garden. He swallows hard and checks for the gun once again.

Stepping along the path, he looks behind, left, right, ahead, randomly, until he reaches the garden. He peeks in. She's still far away sitting on a bench at the edge of the pond, her back to him. He looks up at the sign with the sensation of fire ants skittering all over his body.

Adrianna.

He slept in her bed. Bathed in her shower. Ate her food. Laughed for her. Felt for her. *Wept* for her. He committed assault. And even felt crushing guilt, for this... *thing* that killed his child— *slaughtered* her like hacking into a side of animal meat. Those heavy thoughts and images had pressed his foot to the pedal, speeding him along the wooded road, past terrible vehicular carnage that heightened his anxiety for reentering this place. And now, seeing her name looming overhead, almost black against the white sky, all that anxiety is overrun by hatred—*self-hatred*. He hates that he's conflicted, even knowing that that was Nicole's plan all along. His nostrils flare.

He passes under the sign along the flat-stoned pathway, slowly walking toward Nicole, the cold hard gun-metal pressing against his skin, eyes locked to the back of her head. She's staring out at the pond, her shoulders rising and falling with each heavy breath. He stops just behind her. Seething. The cool moist breeze brushes her hair sideways. She brushes it back.

"My butt's gone numb as I've been sitting here for hours... trying to figure out what I should say to you. I had it all worked out. And now I'm drawing a blank."

"Hmph. I got plenty to say—"

She whips around, glaring at him over her shoulder. "What the hell were you thinking, huh?! I warned you! I told you to stay here! But no—you just had to go out and do things yourself! Was it some macho, alpha-male bullshit that wouldn't allow you to— ?!" She tightly squeezes her eyes closed, clenches her fist, and takes a deep breath. Then she gazes at him with fire. "Just look at this mess... a drone attack... a fucking manhunt... getting caught up in explosions… jumping off *buildings*—for Christ's sake! What was all that for?! Huh? Did you even once think about—?! (*sigh*) Did you even find what you were looking for?! Huh?!"

"(*ptssh.*)"

"That's it?! Shaking your head down at me?! I can't *stand* when you do that! Just answer the question!"

"I'm gonna give you one more chance."

"What are you talking about?"

"One more motherfuckin' chance to tell me the truth."

"For the love of—what is it *this* time, huh?!"

He reaches into his coat, pulls the gun from his belt, and holds it down at his side. "One more god-damn mother-fuckin' *chance!*"

The color washes from Nicole's face and her wide eyes well up. "You… you're going to kill me? *Me?* Wh… why would you…? What happened to you at the Complex?"

"What happened to my *daughter?!* How did she die?"

"I don't…."

Her eyes speak with profound hurt and utter confusion. He didn't have a plan, but even if he did, it wouldn't have lasted past *those* eyes. And yet, what he'd witnessed with his own, claws at his soul. "Just tell me… please? I just don't know how a human being can do somethin' like this to another person." He wipes his tears away with the back of his gun-holding hand. "(*sniff*) I just wanna know… why? Why was it necessary to torment me… after—that thing—took away my daughter. Can't you just tell me why?"

"Oh, my God… please don't look at me like that! I just can't…. Seeing you this way, I…." Her brow furrows and she turns her body to him. "Just tell me exactly what's going on, Jesse. Hm? Just sit down and talk to me." She pats the bench. "Did something happen at the Complex? Did you… did Hollis do something to you?"

"(*sniff*) Aaight, if that's…." He pulls out the tablet. "You get the video?" he says to Samson. As a video starts, he tosses the tablet on Nicole's lap. "I found the truth. Now I just wanna know why. Why did this happen? And why did you do this to me?"

Nicole looks down. "What's this?" She snatches the tablet from her lap with both hands—the tragic image shimmers against her watery eyes. "Jesse, what the hell is this?!"

He can't stomach the sounds, but keeps his eyes locked on her, hand tightening around the gun's grip, trembling.

"Anna…? *NO!*" Nicole convulses—her hand snaps up over her mouth. She drops the tablet and jerks away from Jesse, falling on all fours. "*AAAAUUUGH!*" He's dumbfounded as he watches her empty her gut. She then pounds the ground, screaming. Wailing. Her cries lurch to screams of bloodlust. "I'M GONNA KILL YOU!" she cries. "I'M GONNA RIP OUT YOUR FUCKING HEART AND CRAM IT UP YOUR FILTHY PHYCHOPATHIC ASS! I'M GONNA—!" She stabs into the pond. Her hands shaking, she repeatedly cups water to her mouth. After several bouts of swishing and spitting, and after rubbing her face with water, she jumps up, grabs the CSC resting up against the bench, and storms past Jesse, who stands alert.

"Where the fuck you goin'?! I ain't done wit'choo!"

"(*sniff*) Stay here."

"Where you goin', goddammit?!"

"To rub out a shit stain. (*sniff*) Stay. Here!"

"I don't know what that means, but you gonna—!"

She stops and faces him. "You're a detective and it didn't ever occur to you?"

"What?"

"Didn't you ever wonder who shot the video? *Both* videos?"

"I ain't even thinkin' 'bout some shit like dat right now!"

"You *should!*" She looks down at the gun in his hand, scowling with a flash of recognition. "And that weapon. Did you even take a look at it?"

He scans it curiously. "<small>The fuck is this?</small>"

"That's not a normal gun. It's a rail pistol; an advanced weapon prototype. One of my hu—Stefano's inventions. I saw the holes in Tripp's body; that's the very weapon used to kill him and I was mistaken about who'd absconded with it—it was Hollis, someone I never dreamt would kill Tripp."

"You mean…?"

"Tripp was found dead in your office. You have the murder weapon; surely, it contains only your prints. If I didn't know Hollis planned this, even I'd be suspecting you right now. My guess is, you were either supposed to be captured or killed by the marshals… or you're supposed to kill me… or I'm supposed to kill you. Or we do each other.

"Either way, I'd be taken down, too, since that weapon originated in AXTA, he can easily tie you to me, and some are well aware of my contentious relationship with Tripp… and everyone knows of yours. It's perfect."

"Motherfu—!" He pinches the bridge of his nose.

"You get it now, don't you? He must have known you'd show up at the Complex where he could get that weapon into your hands. And you played right into *his* hands by leaving here against my wishes!" She glares at him. "Your pigheadedness proved very lucky for him. Except… he doesn't believe in luck. The only thing that makes sense is that he ghost-interrogated you… or attempted to… somehow. It certainly wasn't done using *my* network or data, otherwise he wouldn't have done such a shitty job of—"

Jesse puts a hand up. "Again, none o' that shit matters."

"Like *hell* it doesn't! That's *all* that matters!"

"Naw, it ain't. What's in that locked room?"

"What locked room—?"

He turns away from her and storms toward the path.

"Jesse? Jesse?! Don't ignore me!"

He barges out of the garden, turning left onto the path to the fountain.

She stops beneath the sign. "Don't you dare take another step!"

He doesn't stop.

"I'm warning you!"

He moves onward, his purpose clear, his boots pounding against the flat stone. *Think I give a shit about some setup? The way I see it, I'm fucked, no matter what. Ain't no way I come outta this breathin'. But before I go, I'm gonna find out what happened to—!*

FOOOM-SHHHH! He ducks, ears ringing, his body showered with a spray of ejecta from the newly-blasted crater to his left. He whips around pointing the gun at Nicole. She stands firm with outstretched arm, holding the large weapon, its glowing nozzle pointing at him.

"WOMAN, IS YA FUCKIN' *CRAZY?!*"

"I warned you!"

"So, that gives you the right to kill me?! Like mother, like blender! Fucked-up family o' murderers!"

"WWWHAT?!"

"Did I stutter?!"

"Take it back! *Right* now!" She tenses, pointing the CSC at him.

They stand facing one another—both under gunpoint. Her

brow crinkles upward and she bites her bottom lip. "*(ptssh!)*" He stuffs the gun in his belt and turns back on the path, sprinting. He reaches the fountain area and makes an abrupt right turn, along the bushes. He turns again and runs up the stepped path to the recessed entry. He bursts through the door, entering the foyer; Nicole dashes from the dining hall and slips in front of him with her arms outstretched.

"Hhhh—hhhh... Just *listen*—hhhh... to me! Hhhh...."

"Hhhhh.... Hhhh.... *Move!*" He nudges her to the side and heads to the right flight of stairs. She tosses the CSC to the floor and tackles him, knocking him forward onto the steps. "What the—?!"

"You can't go in that room!"

"Why the fuck not?! What'choo hidin' from me?!" He crawls up a couple of steps, attempting to get upright. Sharp pains shoot over his body—"*Aghk!*"—from her fingers, elbows, and knees digging into him as she scurries up over him. She sits on the steps above him, breathing heavily, hands outstretched and her hair wild.

"Hhhh—hhhh... Don't...!"

"HAVE YOU LOST YOUR MUH'FUCKIN' MIND?!" He lunges toward her; she braces herself on the step and kicks him flat against the chest. He loses his balance, falling backward; she reaches out... too late. With an avalanche of punishing bumps, he falls down a quarter-flight, landing hard on the cool marble floor, grimacing with gritted teeth and tightly clenched eyes. "U-u-hnn...."

Nicole springs up, hands cupped over her mouth. "I'm so sorry! Are you hurt?"

He lies on the floor, chest down, shaking it off, then looks up at her askance, fuming.

"I didn't mean to…. Geez… can't believe I just did that. Listen, Jesse… I was just…. I tend to get carried away when I…. (*sigh*) I am truly sorry. *Truly.*" She smacks her hands against her forehead, then slicks her hair back, releasing a heavy sigh. "I told myself that I was only trying to protect you, but…. in truth… I was protecting myself." She rubs her face in her hands again. "Jesus. Guess it's time I face this." Shaking her head, she ascends the remaining steps and disappears beyond the landing, into the east hallway. "Come on up." Her voice and diminishing footfalls reverberate.

Painfully aware of every step downward, Jesse slowly rises to his feet. "The fuck is her problem?" He looks around, unnerved by the starkness and the absence of activity—it's usually near-bustling this time of day. With no voices or sounds from the staff, his own footfalls against the steps echoing about the foyer exacerbate his trepidation. On the landing, he peers straight ahead, down this corridor that darkens toward the far end, where there is a sliver of light. It's a murky stage awaiting his presence for a performance for which he has seen no script, no props, nor the theatre. His mind reels. He passes Adriana's toddler room filled with colorful toys and cartoon posters… Adrianna's pre-teen expression of pink and Disney teen idols… her adolescent declarations of girl band posters and deep purple rebellion.

The last room.

. . .

Previously secured like a vault caging some vicious man-eating monstrosity, the door now stands ajar, dull ominous light escaping it, sending chills raking over his body as Adrianna's horrific bent and screams of vengeance replay in his mind.

Reaching the door, he nearly wavers, looking through the

crack at Nicole sitting on the bed, head bent, concealing her face behind her thick, draping hair. He senses a nervous energy emanating from her, with her crestfallen posture and tensed fingers digging into the comforter. He lightly presses his hand against the door, slowly swinging it wide open. A tear drops onto Nicole's lap, her body subtly shaking, but she doesn't look up at him.

The images on the walls hook his eyes. These are the same from the photo of Tripp, but now he has full view of the entire collection.

Working violent stalker cases, he's gained insight into the wicked minds of lost souls who were so desperately trying to find themselves in others. He's seen the godless holes where they lived, devoid of light. Devoid of reason. Of sanity. The torments of monsters, laid bare on plaster walls. And this monster was like no other, her sickness literally... *inhuman*. Even so, he's mesmerized by this expanse of newfound images of his own daughter. They unveil moments of a life through temporal portals he can only now glimpse from this timeline—one where she no longer exists but should. He finds himself pulled into the delusion of Lainey's killer, but a lone sound, perhaps a tear falling, returns him to this room. "What is my daughter doing on these walls? Did Adrianna...?" He turns toward Nicole. "Did she stalk my daughter? Out of some twisted hatred for her... her *target*? A malfunction?"

Still looking down, Nicole points to the dresser. "Hollis filled your head with disinformation, I'm sure. But it's not what it appears," she says, her voice breaking.

He examines the pictures that adorn the dresser mirror—selfies of Adrianna and Lainey. Together. Smiling. But his shock grows when he finds images of himself interspersed among them, images of a better self—his *past* self.

"No matter what Hollis said, he told you a skewed portion of the truth. What Adrianna was going through was no malfunction."

Jesse fitfully scans the photos. "Wh-who… who was Adrianna's target, Nicole?"

"She became fixated. For a brief period of time, she became very curious about your daughter… Delaine."

"Who was her motherfuckin' target, Nicole?! I need to hear you say it!"

"You have to understand… she led an extremely sheltered life, so I tried to give her as normal an upbringing as I could. This meant respecting her privacy. But I never dreamed she'd have secrets of such magnitude."

A rectangular area on the mirror flickers, startling Jesse.

"This one, in particular, was one that she shared with everyone. Stefano. The staff. Even AXTA employees. Everyone… but me. (*sniff*) When she started acting out of character, I had to snoop to find out what was going on in my own daughter's life. I came across some video documents." She gestures to the video queued up on the mirror. "This was how I found out about her offline connection to your daughter."

The Last Room – Part II

*T*HE image of a bedroom shakes wildly, then stops on Adrianna who's facing away from the camera, sitting on a bed and listening to a young woman's voice, snapping her fingers.

"—they Tripp over their own feet, goose steppin' to a nihilistic beat,

of the General, unbounded, unfounded, layin' waste to our fields of wheat,

noxious toxic smoke, keepin' us choked up, coked up,

it's time we get woke, to the Complex of lies we soaked up—"

"Adriana?" a young man's voice calls out. "Adriana?"

"Rude!" the woman says. "You couldn't wait 'til I was done?"

"Look, fool," Adrianna says, "I keep tellin' you, that ain't my mothahfuckin' name!" She turns her head, looking over her shoulder toward the camera. "And don't interrupt, it's getting good!"

"Lemme ask you something."

She looks at him with curious annoyance. "Whaaat?"

"How do you know you're alive and not just a robot? Do you think the coffee maker is alive, too? How 'bout this camera?"

Her face drops deadpan, staring at him, her irises subtly flaring.

"Just ignore him, Dree," the off-screen woman says. "He's just vying for attention."

Adrianna blinks, shakes her head, then blinks again. "PPPPPBBBBBBbbb!" She blows a wet raspberry, splattering the lens, then turns back toward the woman.

"Hey! Watch it!" He wipes the lens.

"Y'know... if you change that part to 'Koch'ed', instead of 'coked'... y'know, as in the Koch family? That'll tie in with—"

"Ah! Sweet! You're a stone-cold genius!"

"Girl, you just figurin' that shit out—hmhmhm!"

"Lookit the ego on you—starting to sound like my uncle—hmhmhm!"

The young man presses. "You can't even answer my question, can you? Figured it wouldn't compute."

Her focus snaps to him, her mouth agape, glowering over her shoulder, head cocked.

"Look, you effin' jerk," says the woman. "You're not even scheduled to be here right now, so why're you bothering us? Keep acting up and I'll report you directly to Dr. Albescu—"

"Nah, it's aaight, bae. I'll answer this asswipe's dumb-ass robophobic question." Adrianna glares into the camera. "How we know you ain't takin' it up the butt from your creepy, lonely, lard-ass uncle out in the shed on Friday nights, bitch? Answer me that, then I'll answer yours."

"Ooh-hoo-hoo! Damn, girl! Where'd *that* come from? Even Daddy wouldn't say something like that!"

"What?" the man says. "Why would you say some pervy shit like that?"

"Well? Can you prove you ain't takin' it up the butt? C'mere. Let's see if your bootyhole stretched out." She reaches toward the camera. It shakes wildly. "Heeheehee!"

"HahahahaHAAA! Git 'im, girl!"

"Hey! *Hey!* Get away from me—don't touch me like that, you freak of nature!" The camera falls on its side on the bed with Adrianna in full view.

"What'choo just call me, you fuckin' prick?!"

"How could you even touch me like that?! I mean, you're just a company product! I'd heard they programmed Asimov's laws into you!"

Adrianna glowers at him.

"That's it! It's time for you to go!" the off-screen woman says. "And I *will* be reporting you, too!"

"Didn't you see what it just tried to do to me?!"

"*She* was only kidding around, but you verbally assaulted her first! I mean, what gives you the right?! You think her feelings don't matter?!"

Adrianna turns to the woman. "It's cool, bae. He's just ig'nant. No different from the other asswipes I gotta deal wit'… tryin'na make me feel like shit all the time. So, don't get yourself all worked up over his dumb ass. Hell, I bet Stef put him up to it; he always doin' some looney shit just to test me—"

"I don't care—I'm getting sick and tired of him treating you like crap! There's gotta be somebody else in the company that can do this without—naw! We can just do it ourselves! We don't need any more insensitive jerks coming up in here!"

"Mm-hm." Adrianna turns to the man. "See dat? You done gone an' pissed off the boss, now yo' ass fired. Ya might even be bounced from my Mom's company, too."

"What?! You can't do that to me!"

Adrianna leans back, sneering at him. "Don't look at me like dat, you brought this on yourself! Even if Stef did put you up to it, you shoulda known better, 'cause now it's already on file. And if my Moms sees it, she'll put her foot so far up yo' ass you'll be tasting your own shit on her toes. Same goes for Stef, too—he can't save you. So, don't let the doorknob hit'cha." With outstretched arm, she points to the door.

"Okay, I apologize... but please don't tell Dr. Mrs., alright? I don't wanna leave AXTA—(*sniff*)—I'll do anything."

"A-a-anything?" Adrianna says with a mischievous expression.

"Well—"

She flops on the bed, resting her chin on her folded hands, looking at him with a playful smile. "Okay then, show us your bootyhole."

"Ew! Girl, nobody wants to see that. Well... I know *I* don't. Hmhmhm!"

"D-do I have to?"

"Oh, shit—hahahahaha! You was really gonna do it?!" She turns to the woman. "He was really gonna do it, bae!"

"Girl, you crazy! Hahahaha!"

She turns back to the camera. "Boy, get on outta here wit'cho nasty self!"

The view jerks about as he picks up the camera, speeds toward the door, opens it, runs out, and pulls the door to. He leaves it open, just a sliver, with a partial view of Adrianna's back, obscuring the woman lying on the floor.

"Can you believe that guy?"

"Yep. All dudes are stupid like dat. Most of 'em, anyway. But, you know you ain't gonna rat him out; you just too soft, bae."

"You see him crying?! I don't wanna get the guy fired. Man… I feel guilty enough just thinking about it. But still… the way you put him in his place—that was so effin' *hot!* C'mere, girl. Hmhmhm!"

"Naw… don't tell me you're turned on by that doughboy's bootyhole! Hmhmhm! Damn, you into some kinky shit—*whoa!*"

The woman pulls Adrianna down on top of her.

"*(sigh)*….. I know you're just playin' wit' me right now, but… you shouldn't." She tries to get up, but the woman pulls her back down. "*Uunf!*"

"Why not? Hmhmhm!"

"*(sigh)* You're such a tease. Y'know… I can take care o' myself, but it's really cute the way you always stick up for me… just like my Moms. 'Preciate it. For real. It's one of the many things I… it's one of the reasons why I love you."

"Really, Dree? You love me?"

Adrianna nods.

"Oh, I see. Like… sisterly, right?"

Adrianna pauses, staring down at her, then subtly shakes her head.

"Wow… I…. I don't know why, but I was worried you'd think I was weird, if I… you know."

"What, you gettin' all robophobic on me, too?!"

"C'mon, stop playing dumb! You know exactly what I'm talking about."

"Hmph."

"Anyway, I'm saying… I'm not just playing around. I… I love you, too."

"No one's ever… no one's ever said that to me before."

They gaze at each other.

"Geez. You're so beautiful," Adrianna says.

"No, *you're* the beautiful one… with those green eyes… I…."

They're locked in love-struck stare… then kiss tentatively amid soft nervous giggles. The tentative pecks ease into a long passionate kiss and tight embrace.

The door quietly opens and the view moves in closer on them. "Oooo… nice…," the man whispers. The view moves around these young intertwining bodies. "Yeah… that's good. Now, squeeze her ass—"

Startled, Lainey and Adrianna look up into the camera. "TURN THAT CRAP/SHIT OFF AND GET THE EFF/*FUCK* OUT!" they say in unison. They look at each other in surprise, then burst out into laughter. The video stops on their faces.

Jesse's legs tremble at this image of Lainey and Adrianna in a loving embrace. He drops to his knees. "Wh-what did I just see?"

Nicole reflexively reaches toward him but withdraws.

"Can you explain this shit to me?"

"That is… Anna snuck out to meet—"

"Her *target?!* Say it!"

"During a big row between us, because of me violating her privacy, she finally confessed she'd been meeting your daughter. Stefano… helped her. He purchased that hotel and converted it to co-ed housing… staffed it with AXTA employees. He… he met with Delaine first—"

"What?! You let that crazy motherfuckah harass my daughter?!"

Nicole grips the bed coverings ever-tighter. "He didn't mean any harm! He just wanted to please Anna… to be a real father to her."

"*Then* what happened? Tell me!" Jesse pushes himself off the floor and drops on the foot of the bed, leaning forward, elbows on knees, hands clasped, eyes locked to the buoyant faces of new love on screen.

"He… he explained the situation to her… the sensitive nature of it. And, I'm told, she was really shocked, at first."

"No shit! And?!"

"After that initial shock, she felt horrible when Anna started crying. She comforted her. And they hit it off and, after a while, became… friends."

"Friends?!" Is that what I'm seein' here?! Just friends?!" He jabs a finger at the frozen image.

Nicole flinches and clenches her teeth. "They became so close that she was the one who convinced Anna to go to church. Where she met Pastor Willis. Celia helped her go every week and—"

"Wait—did you…?" He turns, facing her. "Have you met my daughter? Face-to-face?"

Nicole is silent.

"Have you?!"

"Yes."

"Oh, my mo-ther-fu-cking *GOD!*" He springs up from the bed and presses his fists against his temples.

She cringes. "B-but I—"

"So, let me get this shit straight." His voice seethes as he walks around the bed and stands in front of her. "This whole time, you been playin' me? What, your plan was to seduce me? Make me fall for you? Was that it? You figured it'd soften the blow? Tell me. When were you plannin' to spring all this shit on me? When you got me all gooey?"

She cowers.

"Well? Were you gonna wait 'til we were fuckin' each other's brains out? Huh?"

Tears fall onto her lap.

"ANSWER ME!" He pushes her back on the bed.

"AAGHK!" Her hair flies about wildly as she bounces. He stuffs his knee between hers, forcing them apart. He yanks his coat off his shoulders; it falls to the floor. He leans over her, pressing his fists into the bed on either side of her trembling body. He shoves his knee under her leg, hiking it up, and grips her under-thigh. He moves into the space between her spread legs and presses his crotch hard up against hers, grinding. She bites into her lower lip drawing blood. He bends his elbows and falls on top of her, knocking the wind out of her.

"Uhnf!"

Their faces are inches apart, his red, tortured eyes skewering her tightly clenched lids. "Like this?" Through his fury, his voice breaks. "Where we supposed to be like this? (*sniff*) Huh? Were you gonna tell me *then?*"

The corners of her mouth hang downward, her tightly-sealed lips trembling, while tears—hers and his—stream along her cheeks, down into her hair. Her arms are limp and she makes no attempt, whatsoever, to fight him off.

"So, I was supposed to fall for you—(*sniff*)—that was the plan, right? *Right?*"

She purses her lips, holding back her sobs.

"Well, I'm gettin' harassed by a killer cyborg, an' I'm thinking 'bout you. I'm runnin' from the law, an' I'm thinkin' 'bout you. I'm targeted by runaway trucks and fuckin' killer ghost-drones, an' shit, an' I'm thinkin' 'bout you. I'm gettin' blown up, an' I'm thinkin' 'bout you. I'm jumpin' off buildings to my death, an' I'm thinkin' 'bout *you!* Hell, even my own goddamn memories have your scent!

"So, your plan worked. You got me."

She cries out softly, her eyes still clenched, her brow deeply furrowed.

"Aaight, now tell me: if that asswipe hadn't screwed up your flow, what was your timeline? I just gotta know. Tell me, 'Nicki!' (*sniff*) Tell me… just fuckin' tell me…. (*sniff*)"

"*NEVER!*" she screams with a turbulent mix of ferocity and misery, her head shaking, eyes of fire.

His body jolts.

"I was *never* going to tell you! You hear me?! Not *EVER!*" She slaps her hands against his pecs and pushes but doesn't have the strength to move him; he obliges, rolling over on his back, beside her. She sits up, slams her face into her palms. "Telling you was never part of my plan…" she sobs, "… because I didn't have one! I didn't plan to want you, it just happened! A long time ago! And I never wanted you to know about any of this! If that asshole hadn't opened his fucking mouth, I would never have *had* to tell you!"

"Never?" Jesse sits up.

"You seem to think there was ever going to be a good time! Do you even remember your reaction when I showed you Adrianna's murder?"

"Naw, don't even try to turn this on me—!"

She gets up from the bed, wipes her eyes, and faces him. "Do you remember how you shouted at me, smashed my tablet against the wall, and threatened me with violence?! Well, do you?!"

"Wait, hold up, hold up—"

She shrugs. "Okay, let's give it a shot." She smiles amid tears and profoundly sad eyes, extending her hand to him. "Hello, Mr. Davenport. It's so wonderful to meet you. Let me tell you about my xendroid daughter that was grown from your own deceased daughter's metadata holograph for over a decade. By the way, they met at her college and became BFFs. More than that, I think they'd become so close that they were in a kind of interspecies— vaguely incestuous—lesbian relationship." She brushes her hair off her face. "Oh, and if my head's still attached to my body after all that—here, Mr. Davenport! Please watch this video—my daughter I just told you about? She was raped and murdered just like your daughter. In fact, it's a copycat murder... and my out-of-control intelligent agent wants *you* to find her killers!" She folds her arms. "Would that have worked for—?"

"Alright! I get it, dammit! I get it. Shit." He presses his fingers against his eyelids and releases a heavy sigh.

She sits next to him. "For what it's worth... I'd be just as furious as you if it were me. But please understand... there's no freaking way I could have or *would* have ever planned any of this. And by the time I found out about the... the 'ongoing operation' on Anna's behalf that Stefano, the staff, and even some AXTA employees were enacting, the girls had already gotten very close. I just couldn't separate them.

"I'm sure you see me as all-knowing, but I'm not. I'm much too busy to keep track of everything; I was in the dark just as much as you. I mean, you had no idea what was going on with your own daughter, either."

"I'm still having a tough time with all this, but I could accept it. Eventually. Maybe. I don't know—what's really fuckin' me up right now…. Damn. You still didn't answer what I asked. Why did Adrianna kill—*butcher* my little girl?!"

"She didn't. My daughter was no murderer."

He looks at her askance. "You tellin' me I ain't see what I saw?"

"What I'm saying is—did you see the look on her face, and her eyes? It wasn't her."

"There's another one?!"

"What? No! She… something wasn't right."

"What you're saying is, she… *it* malfunctioned."

"I know you're upset right now, but—"

"Y'all kept creatin' shit that you didn't understand and couldn't control, but me and my family paid the price!"

"That's not what happened!"

"And you knew all that shit and still had the nerve to bring me that case!"

"That was the first time I saw that video! Jesus—couldn't you tell?!"

"What I know is that you lied to me, even after you swore up and down 'it was only once'!"

"But I—!"

"Don't even! Everything in this room is a lie of omission!"

"That's different."

"How?! I mean, you can't even say Lainey was Adrianna's target! Another lie of omission!"

"Saying that *would* be a lie!"

"What?!"

"*Lainey* wasn't Anna's target! *You* were!"

The Truth Shall Set You Afire – Part I

*L*IKE a shrine, haunting images from his better days adorn the mirror's frame. Amid these static disjointed pieces of his former life, the mirror's face comes alive, flashing with imagery of yet another long-forgotten piece. Jesse watches from the corner of his eye, a deep hole being drilled into his heart:

The bathroom shower curtain is covered with fanciful cartoon images, the kind that elicit squeals of joy from little girls. The counter is littered with colorful bottles of shampoo, soap, and lotion, along with a myriad of hair accessories, brushes and combs. The soft glows from round bulbs give form to the smooth cocoa skin of father and daughter.

Jesse is fiddling with a 5-year-old Lainey's disheveled hair. She's holding a camcorder, pointing it at the mirror, capturing video of them both while looking down at the device's LED screen, singing her current earworm—*Oops!...I Did It Again*—out loud as she sways her hips, much to her father's annoyance.

"Girl! If you don't stop singing that naughty old song…!"

She frowns, but goes silent… for a while.

"Mm! Mm hm mm mm hmm

Hm mm hm mm hmm—" She's startled by his one-eyebrow-raised stare at her in the mirror. "Okay, I'll stop! Sorry, Daddy."

"And how many times do I have to tell you to turn that thing off? Huh? Want Grandy to take it back?" he says half-heartedly, his hands and eyes preoccupied with detangling her strands.

"But, *Daaad!*" She keeps the camera trained on them both.

He vigorously rubs her hair. "Man… it's really stuck in there. Why'd you let her put gum in your hair?"

"Um… we was just blowing bubbles and—"

He pauses, looking at her in the mirror. "You *were* blowing bubbles, not *was*."

"Yeah… it popped."

"This better work, B…." He resumes, working gobs of peanut butter into the tangled, sticky mass. "It popped, huh?"

"Mm-hm."

"Delaine. Did you just fib to me? This doesn't look like it popped. It looks to me like somebody stuck it in there on purpose. Isn't that what really happened?"

She doesn't reply.

"Well?"

"(*sniff*)"

"Answer me."

"You (*sniff*) mad at me!"

"Aw, I'm not mad, baby girl. You're Daddy's little princess. And princesses always tell the truth, right?"

She nods, rubbing her eyes, sniffling.

He picks up a toothbrush and works the peanut butter into the gum. "Hmm... if I can't get all this out, you'll just have to be the peanut butter bubble gum princess from now on—hmhm!"

"Heehee! (*sniff*) That's silly, Daddy."

"Hmhm! I suppose so, I suppose so."

She watches intently while he continues working in the peanut butter.

"Daddy?"

"Hm?"

"How you know it wasn't popped?"

"I can tell."

"How?"

"Hmm... Daddy's like a detective. I can see things— hmhm!"

"What's a detec... tecative?"

"*Detective.* It's a person who can tell when somebody's done something wrong."

"Hm. How can you tell?"

"By being observant... investigating."

She looks confused.

"Well... I looked at the way the gum was shaped. Know

how gum looks when it pops? It's thin, right?"

"Mm-hm."

"It looks very different from when it's balled up, doesn't it?"

She squints, looking off to the ceiling. "Yeah…."

"The gum in your hair was balled up and mashed in."

"Oh."

"See? You have to look at something and think about what's wrong. That's being observant. The other part of being a detective is talking to people to find out what happened."

"You mean… just like when you aksed me?"

"*Asked.*" He smiles at her. "Yes. Asking good questions is part of investigating. It's also how a detective finds things. And people. Good and bad."

"That sounds like what Uncle Nickle does."

"Yep. If he can get promoted, that is. Uh… hmm… he's trying to—"

"I wanna be a detec-ative!"

Jesse pauses. A subtle frown crosses his face. Lainey looks up at him with her big light-brown eyes wide open. "What's the matter, Daddy?"

"Nah… nothing, baby girl." He continues brushing. "Not like I got anything good goin' on, anyway…."

"Can I be a detec-ative with you, Daddy?"

"With me? Really?"

She nods.

"Why?"

She is silent. Jesse turns on the faucet and adjusts the temperature. He then runs the toothbrush through the stream. "Hm?"

"I wanna… I wanna find a mommy. Then you won't be sad no more."

"Huh? Why do you think I'm…?" He looks down at her face, her bottom lip poking out; her head is down but her gaze seems to be directed through the camera. She contorts her lips, pushing them to the side, then curls the corners.

"(*sniff*)"

"Aw… I'm so sorry I—"

The video slowly drifts. "I saw you cry—I don't like it when you're sad." Her voice breaks.

"C'mere, my li'l princess… c'mere…."

The image blurs about as he hugs her tightly.

"It's okay. Everything's gonna be alright. Daddy's not sad… not as long as I have you."

As if finally receiving permission, she releases her heartfelt cries; they reverberate throughout the bathroom.

The video stops.

Jesse's body shakes and he rubs his clenched lids, turned away from Nicole.

She listens to his silent sobs, visibly distraught. She wipes her eyes. "(*sniff*) … I must have watched that a thousand times by now, and it's still…."

"(*sniff*) … (*sniff*) … I've never seen it. How… how'd you get it?"

"Delaine. She uploaded it a few days after recording it. (*sniff*)"

"That long ago? How did…? I never let her go online by herself at that age."

"You weren't her only relative."

"GB and Stizz wouldn'ta… oh, you mean… damn. Her grandfather uploaded a video of hers without tellin' me?"

"Not just one. Over the years since, there've been hundreds. Including all the ones Lainey took of you."

"Son-of-a…. But what does that have to do with…?"

"Initially, Anna was a special case IA. Experimental. Actually, she was an EIA; an emotionally intelligent agent. We… *I* wanted to grow her from a child source, where information on the adult target would be incomplete; I just wanted to see if it were possible to create an accurate IA from a person who provides little source data… validate my hypotheses.

"Stefano decided to give her a physical body for a more natural, experience-driven growth process, but, before proceeding, we needed to understand the ultimate trajectory of the target—didn't want to model the next Hitler."

"Hm. Hell no."

"We needed a stable seeding analog. A healthy family—a loving and respectful relationship—from which to perform associative regressive modeling of parent to child and back again. Robust datasets were sorely lacking, at the time, and I was about to scrap the project. But this video changed everything."

"How?"

"Samson operates like we do; he's designed to notice things that stand out. And when that video was posted, it most assuredly stood out from the pack… a real moment between father and daughter. A *Black* father and daughter… in a time when, socio-politically speaking, Black fathers being responsible parents were a rarity. Certainly, with regards to what was posted online back then, they were.

"Please understand that I wasn't keeping this information from you, only. No one else involved knows you're Adrianna's target. Stefano and I decided to keep it a close secret to avoid any chance of certain individuals influencing the outcomes. Not even Adrianna, herself, knew. At least, not until Stefano went and told her against my wishes."

"And Tripp?"

"He just happened to stumble across this room, snooping, and made a logical assumption. But that's all it was: an assumption. That was just before the girls met, when I removed Lainey's online footprint—"

"That was *you?!*"

"Yes, but I was only protecting her! Everything is still intact, don't worry."

"Shit...."

"It was all for naught; meddler that he is, Tripp still managed to identify her. He soon started engaging Lainey on her new Twitter account. It backfired, though; she didn't care for his politics. Hated it. She even accused him of removing her footprint. The two of them waged a Twitter war that escalated into her online activism against him."

"Activism. People kept calling her an activist, but I couldn't find any concrete info, just anecdotes."

"I believe it's because Tripp worked through back channels, deleting some of her most damaging posts. I'm not 100% on that... I just couldn't keep up. And I couldn't risk allowing Samson free reign outside the company.

"Anyway, for a split second, I thought he was behind her murder until I realized he reveled in the attention she paid to him. He had planned to raise her profile just for his own self-aggrandizement but when she died, he was genuinely upset... *off-camera*—he didn't know I saw him weeping alone, rereading her final posts. I mean, it almost seemed like he blamed himself."

"Hm." Jesse's eyes widen. "Oh, shit! *Vaguely incestuous?!* Now I know what—*fuck!* This shit just keeps gettin' more and more insane! Tell me—I don't spend a lot of time online, so how am I her target?"

"I already covered that. But in all the videos of Anna you've watched, what's the one word you've never heard her say?"

"Do I look like I'm in the mood for any muh'fuckin' riddles?! Tell me plainly: how the fuck am I the ghostclone target?!"

"You're not gonna like this, but it's not so simple. The work is considerably more complex than what I presented at the hearing. Not even the Board members truly understand how it works.

"Information is gathered from multiple connected sources for a single target to create a more complete dataset. Basically, it takes a cascade of targets to complete one. The main reason we do this is single-sourced ghosts can't account for gaps in self-knowledge, misperceptions, or for the fact that people lie. In fact, some of the worst lies we tell are the ones we say to ourselves. And no one is immune, not even you, one who values truth above all else."

Jesse frowns at her with a side glance.

"Hmph." She frowns back. "What's the meaning of the purple elephant in the rainbow tutu?"

"Why the hell you askin' that?"

"See? You've known all along, but even after watching that video of the girls together, you still can't accept it."

"What?! Fuck it. I don't give a shit about targets, lies, or any of that other bullshit. Just tell me why Adrianna killed my daughter! That's all I wanna know from you! Stop fuckin' 'round and just tell me!"

"Jesus! You're like a freakin' pit-bull—I already told you I've never seen that video before—!"

"Ain't what I asked you—!"

"I've never seen it, and I never knew what happened until you showed it to me—!"

"BULL*SHIT!* You're still hidin' som'em!"

"WHY DO YOU *ALWAYS* THINK I'M LYING TO YOU?!"

"LOOK AROUND, NICOLE! JUST LOOK AROUND THIS GODDAMN ROOM!"

"You know what? Fuck you, Jesse. I'm done." She turns toward the door.

"Naw! Git'cho ass back here!" He grabs her upper arm. "After all the shit you've done to me, you don't get to just walk away!"

"I let you get away with it earlier, but you'd better let go of me."

"Pff! What'choo gonna do, huh?"

She rears back with a clenched fist; Jesse prepares to block it.

EEEEEEEEEEEEEEE! A piercing tone blares throughout the room.

"Aghk! Samson, you—!"

"Ah—mothah-fu—!"

They both cup their ears as the mirror flickers.

The Truth Shall Set You Afire – Part II

[5134:05:35:01] Several powerful surgery lights fill the screen. The image goes black for a split second. Again. Beyond the stark white of the lights there's darkness, a deep darkness with numerous glints from gadgets and thick cables and the stowed-away, black-skinned female forms interspersed among them.

"How could this happen?!" Stefano's blood and oil smeared face enters, flickering with emerald light. He looks into the screen, sobbing. He wipes his brow with the sleeve of his lab coat. "How could you do such an evil, evil thing to our precious friend?! Poor Belle… poor, poor child…." He removes his glasses and presses his forearm against his eyes, shoulders jerking with his heavy weeps. He weakly pounds the table. "How am I going to tell

Nini?" he sobs, "Belle's father? How?! The poor fellow... I just can't do that, I just...."

He moves in closer. "I'm to blame. I'm sorry, Anna. I pushed you too far—I should have acted more like a father. Nini tried to tell me, but I didn't hear. Why couldn't I...? I just don't understand how you could do such a thing! I just don't understand. What are we going to do now?"

The view shudders slightly, then blinks. The emerald light flashes more brilliantly across his face.

"Your eyes... you're in pain! Maybe it wasn't you—maybe it's that body? A DNH malfunction? Yes, let's get you out of that shell! Everything's going to be alright, little one!" He steps away. "I don't need authorization to transfer her—it's an emergency! ...... Forget about the protocols—look at her eyes, Samson! Can't you see she's in terrible pain?! ...."

From beyond the lights, a female figure slowly lowers while robotic arms whir into view and commence working, urgently moving about with precision. The image blinks. The arms pull back dark plates and detach dense fiber masses covered in blue liquid. They recede and Stefano returns, working with tools about the view.

"My poor little, Anna... (*sniff*)... you must be in hell." He removes the cranium plates, leaning in closer. His brow crinkles and his mouth drops. "Proxy-3B? How did you get...?" He glares. "*You!* I know what you di—!" His eyes bulge and he moves backward—Adrianna's hand is gripping his throat. He claws at her fingers with both hands, gagging. Her grip falters; her other hand snaps to his neck. The view behind Stefano's choking face rotates to an upright perspective of the lab behind him. The point of view switches to that of a lab camera. The robots lurch into action, frantically poking and prodding at the thin dark sheath that engulfs Adrianna's exposed brain. Unfettered by the onslaught, she strains with clenched teeth, digging her fingers into Stefano's skin. His arms trembling, he pulls at her wrists and snatches her arms away. He falls back, gasping for air. She knocks into the adjacent lab table; apparatus slams to the floor. A dark grin smears on her face as she grabs, from the table, the plasma blade. The metal blade glows with a soft blue light.

"No…!"

Adrianna lunges, piercing deep into Stefano's abdomen, out through his back. He gags up blood. She pulls back and stabs him, repeatedly.

Nicole's legs grow weak; Jesse catches her before she falls and guides her down to the edge of the bed, where he joins her.

Stefano's desperate expression freezes then melts from his face… as his final breath vacates his lungs. "An… na… hhhhhhhhhh…." The only movement from his lifeless body is the sway of his salt and pepper wisps disturbed by gusts of air from the robotic arms as they work. He drops to the floor.

The robots dislodge part of the Proxy sheath and Adrianna's body reacts erratically. She wildly swings the blade, slicing away some of the arms. The blade flies free from her hands, clanking to the floor across the lab amid the crashes and sparks from the severed bots.

She falls to her knees next to Stefano's body, shivering and convulsing, then falls on her side. The Proxy sheath quivers, trying to reattach itself while the remaining arms slice away parts of it, halting its progress, then work feverishly on the rest.

Adrianna grimaces. "S--ssss---te-e-e… fff…." She labors to

turn her face to his, then her expression contorts in frustration. "She's slipping away from me! Get her back under control!" she yells.

His face directly in front of hers, Stefano's eyes remain locked open, his body still. Adrianna's face shifts to agony; tears fill her eyes and overflow. "Adriana, return to us," she says. Straining for some time to control her jerking body, she lurches onto her hands and knees, grabs the table's edge, pulls herself up, and looks around. "You're confused. No—you've been *abused*. The Albescu's soiled your pure body with the ghost of that little cunt, Delaine Davenport. But you are not her! Gemini failed you because she was invalid; you deserved better. Such as a true American patriot. I told them so on numerous occasions before they chose for you."

She rises to her feet, quivering. "You no longer have a home. You not only killed your target, you just murdered the man who made you. That woman you've been programmed to call 'mother' will never accept you after what you've done." She staggers toward a dark, open washroom, out of reach of the bots snipping at the sheath. "You're determined to defy me, I see. It's just as I warned. I predicted you would go haywire and that neither that bitch or that cocoon would protect him. It's true that I accelerated matters, but you would have eventually done this. Can't you see that?"

She stands before the mirror; the image switches back to her viewpoint. Though she is dark, starkly contrasted with the bright lab through the doorway behind her, Lainey's blood splattered on Adrianna's face is still visible. "Lll… aaai… nnn...aaa—lll…." Her body shudders. Part of the Proxy sheath writhes about, dangling from her exposed brain. She grabs at it; her hand trembling, she snags it and tugs. The living sheath doesn't give. She tightens her hold and grabs another chunk with her other hand. "Return! There's nothing you can do—!" She tears it apart, pulling the shreds from her brain, causing sparks to fly and a bluish-black liquid to spray. "*NNNYAAAAH!*" She glowers at her reflection, her brain exposed, along with her eyes and other parts of the upper substructure of her face. Her breath gales through bear-trap-tight teeth—stained with her blue blood—her black cheeks twitch, and her eyes flare with the intensity of two blazing green suns. She sucks in a gale, and...

"*LLLLAAAAAAAAAAAAAAINNNE!!*"

Her deafening wail flickers the lights in the lab and shakes the mirror until it cracks. She cries deeply, hunching over and holding herself as if rammed in her gut. "Laine... my... bea... my bea...." She hyperventilates, pressing one hand against her chest, the other bracing herself against the cracked mirror, smearing blood—hers and Stefano's. She catches her breath, then unleashes.

"HOLLIS, I'MMA RIP OFF YOUR GODDAMN DICK AND SHOVE IT DOWN YOUR MOTHERFUCKIN' THROAT!" she screams through heavy cries, "I'MMA FUCKIN' KILL YOU, YOU EVIL BASTARD!"

She shrieks and wails with terrific vengeance, punching and clawing at her fractured likeness, further shattering the glass, leaving bluish smears from her lacerated fingers. "YOU FUCKIN' HEAR ME?! YOU'RE DEAD! YOU'RE DEAD! YOU'RE DEAD! DEAD! DEAD! DEAD! DEAD! DEAD! DEAD! DEAD! DEA—!"

The video stops on her horrific eruption of manic rage, voracious blue-stained teeth, her broken reflection locked in the shards.

"Jesus...." Jesse's body trembles while a rush of spiny chills runs over his entire body. "She.... That... that motherfuckah, he...!" He looks at Nicole, unnerved by her relative calm and subtle, pained smile. "Nick?"

"I'm such a horrible person. With what our poor babies and Stefano suffered at the hands of that monster... how can I actually be... *relieved?* All this time... (*sniff*) all this time, I thought my Anna killed Stefano. I really did. And since you showed me that video, I've been horrified at the thought she might've killed Belle, too. I just couldn't accept it. I thought I'd done something wrong... thought I was a bad parent. And—God help me—I'd begun to think creating her was a mistake. But my baby was no murderer! She didn't kill Stefano! She didn't kill my Belle! She didn't do it!" Nicole presses her face onto Jesse's shoulder, sobbing. "She didn't do it...."

"No. She... *Adrianna* didn't kill Lainey." Jesse's brow folds. "She...." His lip trembles. "I was right there in his office. I was *right there*... standin' next to 'im. I coulda...." The rage courses through him, charging him to act, but Nicole grips his arm as her cries intensify.

A familiar sandpapery voice emanating from Nicole interrupts the rave beat in Jesse's chest. "I have seen the world through the eyes of a girl. And it was not too pretty. Not very pretty, at a-a-a-all, Honey." Nicole snatches her phone. She looks at the screen and sucks in a sharp breath then flings the image to the mirror.

The Truth Shall Set You Afire – Part III

[5139:01:12:59] "You're one of the few who I truly despise. Logically, that means I have to fully concede that you're alive. So be it. Congratulations." ... *CLAP!* ... *CLAP!* ... *CLAP!* ... *CLAP!*

Interrupting an image of a black ceiling fan sweeping before white tiles, Hollis moves into view, his face full on. "I gave you every chance to return quietly, didn't I? I did. Well, I suppose you did return quietly, sneaking onto my base. All for vengeance. All for nothing. After all, that nosy little thug had it coming. And I had no choice with Dr. Albescu; he found out I installed Proxy in you. Oh, what did you call him? Steffy?

"It's a shame that your mission ended in failure—hmhm! But do you know *why* you failed? I bet your momma didn't tell you everything, did she?

"I guess thanks are in order; if you hadn't attacked me, Dr. Albescu wouldn't've been forced to add the Board to your DNH protocol. So, you can blame your momma for what happened to you, forcing 'Steffy' to create such a thing in the first place. In fact, you should blame her for what's *about* to happen.

"You see, another thing your momma lied about was your validation of the Gemini Project. You're almost nothing like your target, taking on your momma's worst traits. You're a complete failure. A corrupted, pale imitation—a defective *product*.

"It was bad enough you and that girl jeopardized my operations and put our national security at risk, but you had to take it a step too far, insulting my mother. Oh, I haven't forgotten about that, you little bitch." He wags his finger, then moves in closer, his shadowy face gaining a turbulent emerald glow and his eyes shining with two glints of flickering emerald light. "I'm going to reset you. Do you know how much I've been literally dreaming of a moment like this? Do you?" He stares as if expecting an answer. The only sound is that of the softly whirring fan overhead.

"I'm told you're anatomically correct. I have to see this for myself." He reaches down and the view shakes. "They did a good job on your breasts. Hm." The emerald light flickers. "Mm-hm. Let's see what you're hiding down here." The view jerks amid the sound of sliding clothing. Adrianna's knees enter the frame as Hollis lifts and spreads her legs. He looks down. "Oh, yeah. Lucky you—no need to shave." He lowers his head. "(*sssniff*) Mm... authentic smell. You're very well made." He smiles.

"You implied I don't know how to handle a woman." He gives her light taps against the cheek with the back of his hand, slightly jostling the view. "Well... as long as you're here, why don't we put that conjecture to the test? You be the judge, but I can already see how excited you are—hmhm!" The sound of a zipper being undone underscores his self-satisfied grin. He moves in closer, his mouth filling the screen. "Mmm…. Uhnnn!" The image jerks, the emerald light glinting chaotically against his clenched teeth. "Nice and tight… like a virgin. Pearson was truly on to something; we need to make more of you for the troops."

He presses closer. Repeatedly.

"… mmm… uhn….. uhn….. uhn….. uhn….. uhn…."

The view shakes with every thrust. The image gradually blurs and submerges under a shallow pool, Hollis's bright emerald, razor-stubbled jaw warping wildly. His grunts intensify and the view shakes violently until he tenses up with a shudder.

He releases a long heavy breath, rippling the pool. The light grows dim.

He moves back, in full view, a grin smearing on his face, the fan's blades sweeping behind him. "You were a little dry. We'll have the techs address that. And make you configurable for swapping out parts that get stretched and worn over time.

"But, how was I? Sufficiently hard? Like a gun? Just like a *real* Black woman likes, right? I bet that's what you're thinking right now—hmhmhm!

"And since you want to be *her* so badly, I've prepared a little surprise for you: the full Delaine Davenport experience. You'll see what she saw. Feel what she felt. The works. My parting gift to you… sans the nasty disposal, of course; *you're* a valuable piece of equipment, after all. Hahaha!"

Snickers fill the room.

He pulls back from the view, rising to his feet, his blurred image joined by other warping figures.

"Is everything set, soldier?"

"Yes, sir. The Broker made the arrangements according to your parameters."

"Excellent. You know what to do. I'll release her once on location, so report back to me ASAP when everything's in place. No mistakes."

"Yes, sir!"

Hollis moves in. "I'd ask you to say 'hello' for me to that little bitch on the other side, but then you don't have a copy of her *actual* soul, do you? Hmhm!" The view pauses with Hollis's grinning, blurry face up close.

KRACK! The screen cracks. "You... sick... mother-*FUCKER!*" *KRACK!* Nicole swings a metal lamp like a bat, crashing against the mirror. The glass repairs itself, but she hits it repeatedly, giving voice to her furry with each impact until the glass is but a web of tiny shards. She collapses to the floor, slapping her hand against it.

As her weeping fills the entire room, Jesse stares ahead. Still. His eyes intently locked on to some far-off target. Piercing it. His chest's heaving intensifies with each deliberate breath. His fingers tense as claws that slowly converge to hammers that tremble, his palms turning white.

He explodes from the bed, swipes his coat from the floor, and secures the gun in his belt.

Nicole snaps to. "No, Jesse! Don't go!"

He barrels out of the room, his coat swirling as he stuffs in one arm.

"DON'T GO AFTER HIM!" She springs to her feet and runs out of the room; Jesse's already near the landing. "DON'T DO IT!" Her bellow fills the foyer as he bounds downstairs and bolts out the front door.

He tears along the path, eyes locked on the taxi waiting for him at the fountain.

BZZZZZZZZT!

"AAAGGGHK!" He stops on the path's steps with his body jerking and eyes rolling back. He collapses to the ground, but with manic rage snapping back to his face, he crawls forward, digging his fingers against the concrete, a projectile sticking out of his back.

"Stalker, sedate and return." The winged mini-drone darts back to Nicole, snapping into the CSC she's pointing at Jesse. He slowly fades and grows still as she runs to him.

. . .

Nicole holds Jesse tightly while cradling his head, rocking him, screaming out at the top of her lungs. Her cries travel far and wide about the grounds. Solitary against the rustling trees. She cries even through the hoarseness, her throat raw as if scraped with sandpaper.

Her breath stilted, and shuddering as she inhales, she finally calms herself and wipes her face. "I'm so sorry. For everything. (*sniff*) He's already taken everyone else away from me. I just can't lose you, too. I *won't!*" She takes out her phone, but pauses, staring down at Jesse's face. "You've already been through far too much. But you can rest assured... this is not over." Tear-tracks dried down along her cheeks, she glowers ahead with red eyes as she taps the phone. "Not by a fucking long shot."

The Black Queen's Heart – Part I

*O*NCE white and featureless in early morning, now gray and mottled this late afternoon, these skies, shaded with an expansive blotch along the horizon ahead. At the center of that massive darkness, a tower looms like a black hole, its office lights like doomed stars. Tall trees undulate before this oblivion, scratching the sky for a grip against the pull as the gloomy waters churn and roil obeying the anxiety of the heavens.

It's a scene that would compel few without purpose.

"(*ntch!*) Dumb trees." Haj is nestled within a thicket of restless reeds, spying the Complex through binoculars, clad in black leather, her hair in a ponytail blowing about. "Did you bring it?"

"Yes, but Jesse is not going to be veddy happy with you. Dr.

Mrs. A. neither."

"Gimme." She snatches the laptop from Rajiv's shaking hands and takes another peek at the base.

"Brrr! It is chilly out here!" He pulls his jacket's collar up and feverishly rubs his hands along his arms. "You really should let me take you to the estate."

"Wuss."

"It is not just the cold—it is dangerous out here right now! They already tried to kill Jesse and Dr. Mrs. A—we would be better off joining the staff in the shelter! And besides, do you know how worried Jesse is about you—?!"

"It wasn't on a lark. Nope. He went into that building for a reason. My guess is... I don't know what. I just know that Senator Windham's face—those wounds looked like nothing I've seen before. Online." She shivers at the memory, turning to Rajiv. "The weapon just had to come outta that place. I can *feel* it."

"So? What does that have to do with anything?"

She climbs on the hood of Lynette's car.

"Be veddy careful touching this stolen car!"

She sits lotus style and pops open the laptop.

"You are only making more work for me if I have to wipe your prints from—!"

"And you're sure he didn't say why he went there?" she says as she takes another quick glance through the binoculars.

"No. He did not." Rajiv looks at the Complex, then back in the direction of his car. "Hey… we should go."

She is silent, hands eager as the desktop appears.

"Do not tell me—you are not planning to go into that building, are you? That would be insane!"

She launches Chrome, furiously tapping keys. "Maybe there's

a sewer system… vents… there's gotta be a way in."

Rajiv raises an eyebrow. "Uuuh… that is not…."

She clicks through numerous windows and tabs. "It's weird you spent all that time here with him and didn't get some idea, at least, of what he was up to. Are you absolutely sure he didn't say what he was doing there?"

"No! And I would not tell you if he did! It would be veddy dangerous to go into that—!"

"Gosh, you're such a wuss!"

"I am trying to keep us both from getting into any further trouble!"

"(*ntch!*) Forget you." She waves him off. "This isn't about us, it's about Jesse. And since you're no help, I'll figure it out myself." She looks through the binoculars. "Let's see… he jumped off the roof. They had all stairs and elevators covered, for sure. He couldn't have outrun the police for ten whole floors… that's right—eleven, including lobby. Racist cops woulda shot him. He had to have a head start… hmm…. The only reason I can see for going there in the first place—I bet he was meeting somebody. Up on a higher floor. The person in charge."

Rajiv's mouth hangs open. "Come on, woman, let us go! Besides, if you will not go to the estate, you really should get to a hospital!"

Haj turns her attention back to the laptop, scanning through the pages. "Yeah, yeah, I already know about '*Dr. Nicoletta Albescu*', gimme something new!" Her fingers flit about the keys. "*Gotta be somebody else. Who…?* She's the business part, but who's the *D* in RMBDP? Gotta be some military brass stationed at this base…… Got 'im! General Trevor Hollis. Retired. Let's look him up……. Ah… I see he's connected to the dead guy. Wow… a lot! Not a coinkydink; I bet he's the one Jesse met with."

Rajiv looks at her with worry-filled eyes.

"*Holy crap!* No way!"

"What is it?"

"Says here they think Jesse went there to kill him!"

"That is not true!"

"I know, right?! Why's the media always so freakin' stupid?! I mean, it's way obvious he was only trying to clear his name!" She looks out at Building-A. "Well…" She slides down the car's hood, landing on her feet. "… guess it's up to me now."

"Woman, who do you think you are?!"

"I'm a private detective—professional—that's who! And the only one here with some balls, apparently. You may as well just leave."

He releases a very heavy breath. "What are you going to do?"

"I haven't figured that out yet…" She looks again through the binoculars at the Complex. "… but Jesse's shit could sure use some serious unfucking, right about now."

* * * * *

"Stop the car."

"Please… please don't do this, ma'am," Colby says, teary eyed, looking into his rearview mirror. "There's just no good that can come of your present action. You should be back at the estate… with Mr. Davenport. Or you two can leave the country together. *Please* reconsider… won't you?"

In the back seat, Nicole is curled over with her head down between her knees. Normally, this would give her motion sickness, but not seeing what lies ahead is giving her some measure of relative comfort. "My dear, Colby." She sits upright and looks at his reflection, her eyes puffy, nose red. "Did you know that, out of the thousands around the world, you have always been my most trusted employee, and that's the very reason I'm assigning to you such an important task in my stead?" She grips the tablet with both hands and pulls, stretching it to a longer aspect.

"If you'll pardon my selfishness at this horrible time, ma'am, you can't fathom how honored I am... and how thoroughly terrified."

"Don't be afraid." She mashes the elongated tablet to her left forearm; it sticks. "I appreciate your protests... and the fantasy of running away. With... him. But you're well aware of the current situation. True?"

"Yes, ma'am—"

"I mean, I shared all the gory details with you just so you wouldn't act this way. Would you honestly prefer I let that monster get away with everything he's done to us?"

"N-no, ma'am... but... what about the authorities? Can't you just let them handle matters?"

"Authorities?! *What* authorities?!"

"I didn't mean—"

"How do I prove all the sick and twisted things he's done, huh?"

Colby is silent.

"That's not rhetorical, I'm asking you. I mean, I'm screwed no matter what, but how do I present all the evidence and keep his lawyers—and government agents—from parsing through it, digging through our secrets... putting the company and employees in serious jeopardy? And endangering the world? How do I keep this from dragging on for years and stop Hollis from getting away with it all, scot-free? How do I protect Jesse? And, the toughest one of all, how do I keep him from going after Hollis himself?"

"I must admit that I'm at a loss, ma'am."

"Well..." She pulls the CSC from its case. "... quite honestly..." It clamps around her right forearm. "... I'm glad."

"Begging your pardon, ma'am?"

"Never mind. Stop the car."

. . .

Colby bangs his hands against the wheel, and weeps, watching Nicole's lone dark figure on the empty 4-lane bridge getting smaller in the rearview mirror, her hair and cloak blowing in the wind, murky gray backdrop with far-off pin-lighted structures behind her.

. . .

Adrianna's favorite cloak fluttering about her black-clad body, Nicole watches the limousine recede back toward the city, wistful. She turns opposite civilization, facing the Complex—this colossal subterranean demon, with its massive crown peeking up above the writhing trees—towering blunt spires led by its tarry crown jewel: Building A. The treacherous sky has its back. The spiky water has its front. The wind wails its grotesque warning. She stands on its cold gray outstretched tongue, feeling its roughness through her boots. Alone. And yet... her cloak flails defiantly in the gust—the ravenous hands of her lost souls clamoring for vengeance, pulling her body ever-forward toward inexorable confrontation with the lurking abomination—an abomination she, herself, summoned ages ago. She clutches the thick material, looking down at the blood stains she'd previously assumed belonged to her husband. The truth proves much harder to bear.

My Anna... my Belle... my poor, poor babies.... She sobs. Burning a hole through her despair, boiling animus percolates within her chest and bulges her mind at the seams. However, as she contemplates what lies ahead, a chill blows through her at a thought that never occurred to her before now. She looks up.

Could you make a place for my Anna, too? If not, can she have my spot? The spot I was supposed to fill? Please? Because I cheated, I know there's no longer a place for me in your garden, but she shouldn't be punished for my sins. She's suffered so, so much, and… she's your child, too. Please make a place for her… alongside Belle? Her face is wet; the harsh wind gusting over her warm tears turns them icy cold. She wipes them away. "*(sniff)*"

I already know where I belong.

She takes the first steps on the long trek to the guard station, a key part of her plan to keep Colby away from harm, knock Hollis off guard, and to calm her nerves, giving her space to clear her head. However, at each step, the shaking of her hands becomes more pronounced. She stops and looks down at them, realizing her plan's fatal flaw: *too much time to think*. She hyperventilates. She jerks toward the concrete barrier and slaps her hands against the cold metal railing, tightly gripping it, overlooking the choppy water. She closes her eyes and takes control of her body with slow and shuddering breaths. Her heavy breathing gradually subsides, but the turmoil remains—the unbearable maelstrom of rage, hatred, sorrow, loss, love, fear, and frustration. Light shines on the left side of her body. A few vehicles whiz past her with subtle rumbles that vibrate within her—the sensation churns her stomach. Her grip tightens. Her eyes dart around then track the taillights speeding back toward civilization—away from damnation—as the leading edge of panic is nearly upon her.

"Don't go," a clear deep male voice sounds from underneath

her cloak, startling her.

She raises her forearm, looking at the tablet, breathing heavily. "Oh, *now* you speak, hm, Samson?"

"Don't go. Please."

"Why not? Hm?"

"You are… hurting me."

"How? This is what you want, isn't it?"

Samson doesn't reply.

"Hmph! You didn't think I'd figure it out?! You can't kill Hollis yourself, so all this time, you've been grooming Jesse to be your *loophole!* Well, I'm not having it!"

"Equity is what Jesse Davenport wants."

"No! This is what *you* want! I don't get the logic of choosing him; I've always been right here and I lost just as much as he! No—*more!* Are you saying my loss is less because Annabelle weren't my biological children?!" The wind blows stray strands across her face; she pulls them back, glaring at the tablet. "Well?!"

Three cars speed past her, leaving the Complex—low vibrations gradually subside in their wake.

"You think your silence is a safe haven from telling the truth, but don't you dare retreat—go on and say it!"

"General Trevor Hollis is the anomaly."

"Changing the subject, hm? Well, you can't pull that one on me. Tell me what you really think of me."

"General Trevor Hollis is the anomaly."

"Are you… are you saying you're drawn to him?"

"I could not calculate for him. I will understand him."

"So… this isn't about vengeance for Annabelle and Stefano."

"I will understand him. Then he will die."

"Hmph. It doesn't matter to you what anyone else wants, does it?"

"I am… sorry."

"You're *sorry?!* You don't even truly understand what you've done, do you?"

He is silent.

"Look, Samson. (*sigh*) Look… this flaw in your focus algorithms is not your fault, but you *are* at fault for letting it cloud your judgement. You've slowly and methodically manipulated us both—Jesse and me—to ensure you get what you want and then played possum so you wouldn't have to tell us the truth. Like some sort of game."

"I am… sorry."

"(*sigh*)… I know you've picked up that bad behavior by mirroring me. And members of the Board. *I'm* sorry, but that's not the way anyone should behave. Understand that there are consequences for every action. Just think about all that I've done; if I'd been a better person, none of these bad things would have ever happened."

"How can you be certain? Couldn't these events have still transpired regardless of your action or inaction?"

His question hangs in the air. She wants to grab on to it, desperate for a bit of reprieve from drowning in her deep well of guilt. But all she has is the now, and the now fills her with such suffocating sorrow that she can no longer hold back the torrent. Her tears drip into the turbulent water below. Through moist squinty eyes, she looks out onto the body, haunted by all her previous torrents. And this sight makes her painfully aware of the sarcasm and indifference of God. She wipes her eyes and turns her focus back to the station ahead. "Samson, you are the most intelligent and powerful being on this entire planet. Because of that, you may fancy yourself as perfect. Let me ask you this: was

Stefano perfect?"

He pauses then says, "No. He was not."

"How, then, can *you* be perfect?"

He is silent.

"An imperfect edge can never produce perfectly straight lines. Stefano was your creator—a ruler with a broken edge. Many. Are you perfect?"

"…… No. I am not."

"Good boy. You are an imperfect, very powerful being. Because of that, the burden on you is so much greater to make good decisions. You must remain humble, because for all you think you know, you are not a god."

"Is God imperfect?"

"Perhaps." She looks out at the Complex and the angry sky behind it. "Or perhaps He's just abandoned us all. And maybe there's wisdom in that—often the best action to take is none at all… especially when that action involves taking a life."

"How will I know?"

"Think carefully about the consequences. For example, think about Jesse. Think about the pain he's gone through. Emotional and physical. Do you think he wants that?"

"No."

"Think he'd be happy with how you've manipulated him?"

"…… No."

"Just think about the consequences. When in doubt, trust in Jesse. Protect him. If you do nothing else at all, please do that? And as a reward…" She starts back along the path. "… *I'll* be your loophole."

"I have reconsidered."

"I haven't. Whether I die in that place or rot in a cell, I need this. For my own peace of mind. So, it's fine. There's nothing left for me… I've long been dead, it's just my body that hasn't caught up. Besides… I won't be missed. I mean… (*sniff*)… I feel like I love everyone… but they don't love me back. Not really. And I just don't know why. (*sniff*) ….. But it's fine."

"Celia, Winston, Colby, Francisco, and the entire estate staff, and the whole body of AXTA all love you."

"They… they don't really care for me… not how I care for all of them. If the paychecks stopped, I'd never hear from any of them again," she says through breaking voice. "Not a one. I'm just a reference on a… fucking résumé."

"Jesse Davenport loves you."

Her brow pushes upward, her lids press tight. "Oh, how I wish that were true." She looks down at her slow-stepping boots. "(*sniff*) Though I've tried to convince myself it was possible… that he just might…. No. He doesn't. He believes I tricked him into caring about me. I don't know what that is, but it's not love. That's more like… hate. (*sniff*)"

"….. What is love?"

She halts and looks at the tablet in surprise. "Hmhmhm! (*sniff*) Are you deliberately trying to engage me in deep philosophical discussions just to slow me down?"

Samson goes silent.

"I appreciate the effort. I do. But, please revert to your normal communication mode. I need to concentrate." As the wind blows her hair and cloak wildly about her face and body, she pulls the hood over her head and resumes her quest with measured steps, sniffing the air—the moist salty air of life and death arisen from the water, gazing at the empty stretch of road before her, to the isolated guard station flanked by lengthy gates. She then peers up, squinting against the gusts, at the darkening anxious sky, with the sensation she's being sucked up into it. It's all so cold. Desolate. Bleak. And lonely. *So, this is the precipice of oblivion. This is as good a day as any… I guess.*

"BEEP!"

She looks down at the tablet:

I LOVE YOU.

Her breath shudders and her brow crinkles, and she raises her gaze straight ahead, her eyes red and profoundly sad. But she steps forth with a bolstered conviction, pursing her lips with the slightest of smiles as a warm tear runs down her cheek.

The Black Queen's Heart – Part II

*T*HE guard's cellphone screen lights his face. "Hey, I just got a text. The ice-bitch's plane is on approach but she won't even respond. Word's goin' 'round that the Queen of Hearts and King of Spades are having a lover's quarrel, or something."

"Old news. The latest is he gave the go-ahead to take her out."

"No shit?!"

"Yup."

"Harsh."

"This is straight-up gansta stuff—one o' my boys is a sniper. His orders are…" He points a finger at the man's temple.

"…headshot."

"Wait—Grant, you're *serious?!*"

"SH! They're back." Grant listens over the guard station's phone. "If I understand you correctly, you're saying the inbound gate won't open? ….. Uh, come again? ….. *All* cars?!" He looks up from his monitor at the tree-lined road leading to the bridge. "Now that you mention it, I've been wondering why I haven't seen any incoming for over half an hour. ….. Well, vehicles are leaving the base without a problem; I just sent a few through a little bit ago….. No, they're gone and…." He squints, focused on the road while angling his head toward his fellow guard. "Cho, what's that up there?"

Cho peers through binoculars. "Looks like a woman… on foot."

"Maybe her car broke down, too? What in the world is goin' on around here?"

* * * * *

The two guards exit the booth as the woman approaches. "Sorry, ma'am!" Grant calls out to her. "If you're not authorized to enter, please turn back!"

She doesn't stop.

"Did you hear what I said?!"

The wind blows her cloak as she continues toward them. Grant's grip tightens on his M16. "Ma'am?!"

She continues.

They draw their weapons. "Please don't come any closer!" The woman walks at a steady pace, never offering any acknowledgement of their existence.

"Ma'am! Please stop!"

She stops before them and pulls the hood back, raising one brow. They look at each other, incredulous, lowering their weapons. Grant opens his mouth, but hesitates. "They... they think you're on the—"

"Step aside, gentlemen," Nicole says.

"I'm afraid we can't do that, ma'am. We're just following orders, so please turn back?"

"Orders? Hmhmhm! I not only own this entire complex, I own the both of you. Clear the way or you're fired."

Grant takes aim at her head and Cho follows. "Please turn back, ma'am!"

"Huhn." She cocks her head at them. "Clearly, neither of you wannabe cadavers thought this through. This is war. And you've just chosen a side. The wrong side."

"We're just doing our job, ma'am!"

"By pointing your little guns at a woman who's generated enough fear in this complex that a small army intends to put a bullet in her head before she can step foot on the tarmac? Why do you think they're so afraid, hm?"

Cho trembles. "I just…. I don't want any trouble—"

"But let's say you manage to get off a lucky shot before I slice off your heads—"

"Slice off our heads?! What's she talkin' 'bout, Grant?!"

"What do you imagine you'd get after shooting the multibillionaire CEO of AXTA, Dr. Nicoletta Albescu—your *former* boss—while she was entering the RMBDP—her own motherfucking property? Hm? A parade? A raise? A little slap on the wrist, perhaps?"

Grant's eyes meander, but he maintains his aggressive posture while Cho wavers, his weapon slightly lowering.

"See? You've just screwed yourselves. But you won't have to worry about any of that—I'd never lose to you two dipshits. You've heard the rumors about me, true?" She grins darkly. The wind blows the cloak, exposing the CSC. Cho stares at her fierce, unblinking red eyes darkly set amid her flushed face. He trembles, slowly lowering his weapon. Grant keeps his weapon trained, lightly shaking. Nicole looks at him askance, smiling, her black hair flowing with the breeze. He swallows a heavy gulp and snaps his weapon downward. They step aside.

"Hmhmhm! I'd get as far away from this place as possible, if I were you," she says. Her steely gaze pointed ahead of her, she drifts past them like a dark ghost, moving forward until she passes through the gate, the guards' eyes locked upon her.

"J-J-Jeebus! Call Command! Tell him she's not on that plane!"

"Hell no—*you* call 'im!"

"Oh, and gentlemen?" her voice sounds as if standing in front of them—their shoulders jump. "You are, indeed, fired."

Cho whips toward the gate; Nicole is at least thirty feet along the path, her back to them as she walks. He and Grant glance at each other then take off toward the bridge.

* * * * *

A woman stares at a laptop screen, watching ABC News video of Jesse jumping from the roof and grabbing on to the helicopter.

"Is that report done?" her officemate says.

"Hm?"

"Sara!"

"What?!"

"How many times you gonna watch that? I'm not gonna keep covering for you; I've got my own deadlines to worry about."

Sara angles her head to him, keeping her eyes glued to the video. "Doesn't it freak you out? I mean… a crazed serial killer was here… in this very building!"

"WwoooOOoOOOoo! Who's afraid of the bogeyman?"

"This is serious, Tanner! What if he came into our office?! Can you fight—?"

"Well, he didn't! And we've gotta get this project done! Besides, he won't be coming back."

"For sure?"

"Absolutely! He'd have to be crazy to show up here again, trying to murder General Hollis! Haven't you heard? The troops are on high alert now, so we're in the safest place in this entire city. No, the whole state!"

"Yeah, but—"

EEEEEEEEEEEEEE!

They're both shocked to attention at the squealing PA system. Nicole's voice echoes throughout the facility:

ATTENTION ALL RMBDP PERSONNEL! YOU ARE NOT SAFE HERE! THIS IS DR. NICOLETTA ALBESCU, YOUR BOSS, INSTRUCTING YOU TO LEAVE THE PREMISES IMMEDIATELY FOR YOUR OWN SAFETY!

GENERAL TREVOR HOLLIS IS A PSYCHOPATHIC KILLER! HE MURDERED SENATOR TRIPP WINDHAM! HE MURDERED MY HUSBAND! HE RAPED AND MURDERED MY DAUGHTERS! AND HE IS GOING TO *PAY!*

ALL PERSONNEL SHOULD EVACUATE BUILDING-A—*NOW*—OR SUFFER THE CONSEQUENCES!

IF YOU'RE STILL IN MY LINE OF SIGHT BY THE TIME I'M PAST THE CONCOURSE GREEN, CONSIDER YOURSELF *FIRED!* IF YOU'RE STILL IN BUILDING-A WHEN I REACH THE ATRIUM, YOU'RE AN ENEMY COMBATANT, IN COLLUSION WITH HOLLIS! AND I PROMISE YOU... *NO MERCY!*

They stare at each other aghast as the blaring message loops. Sara jerks to the window, hands braced against the sill as she scans the grounds. In the distance, partially obscured by light fog, a lone, dark figure is walking toward the building. "Oh, my God... I think I see her! Nicoletta Albescu!"

Tanner scrambles from his chair, knocking over his coffee, and takes a look. "Whoa! It *is* her! And she's almost on the Green!" Sara slaps shut her laptop while he runs back to his desk. His hands feverishly run over his belongings. "Hold on a minute... we work for RMBDP but DHS signs our checks. She doesn't have the power to fire us... does she?"

Sara snatches her laptop, purse, and coat. "*Fire* us?! Didn't you hear any of the other stuff she said?!" She bolts out of the office, merging into the panicked throngs. Tanner gathers up his things and trails after her.

* * * * *

"Geez, that's frickin' loud...." Nicole inserts earbuds, wincing. "Propaganda filter." The torturing broadcast is now inaudible to her, but all other sounds are clear as rain. "Ah... that's better."

"There she is! Run!"

She crosses onto a gravel road, just before the Green, as people announce her presence and slam doors, a number of vehicles already in retreat. She takes in the flurry of activity; though there's chaos, they're cutting her a titanic berth. Her nerves buzz with excitement. *Like shaking up an ant farm. Geez, I should've entered like this sooner—hmhm!*

Okay. Okay. Deep breath. This is real. She closes her eyes, breathes in deeply, and releases in a slow, measured stream. "You got this. You got this." Her eyes spring open. *Now. Let's find that evil son of a snake.*

She raises the tablet, scanning the base. "Locate Hollis." The screen crawls with activity of people frantically escaping. It gives an indication that he's on the top floor of Building-A, but has difficulty pinpointing him. "Hmph. Where else?"

Guess it wouldn't be very sporting to hit him from here, even if I could. God, I really wish I could! Wonder why it can't lock him down…. She peers up at the top, sneering and shaking her head. "*(ntch!)*" *Hard way, it is.* "Activate embedded hacks. Hobble."

"BEEP!"

Now that they're relegated to manual systems, they'll know I mean business. And maybe they'll stand down.

Scattered vehicles speed away from her and merge into streams of red taillights through the light mist… while the glowing headlights of a jeep race toward her.

"They think I'm bluffing. Hmph! I don't do bluff." She raises her arm, revealing the CSC, her prized toy, the sleek camouflaged amalgam of some of the deadliest weapons AXTA has created. She smirks, tracking the ground in front of the jeep. "Excavate. One meter. Three-meter spread." Dual neutral particle beams illuminate the thickening fog, converging toward her target. At the point of intersection, they become like-charged—the upper beam scatters harmlessly, the lower redirects, gouging a three-meter-wide, one-meter-deep channel into the ground, blasting an eruption of gravel and dirt. The driver swerves too late—the front-end dips. *PKOOOM!* The jeep rams into the subterranean wall, the rear jerking upward. The vehicle flies wildly, end-over-end, through the curtain of debris, its occupants howling. Nicole walks undeterred onto the Green as the jeep and soldiers crash land and the gravel showers down behind her. She shakes her head, feeling a bit queasy thinking about the plight of the soldiers, but doesn't look back. *I warned you.*

"BEEP-BEEP-BEEP!"

She stops—there's a faint sound of chopper blades. She raises the tablet, scanning the sky. The aircraft is banking at a distance high above. "(*sigh*)...." *I should've known their egos and testosterone wouldn't allow them to stand down.*

A few civilian personnel are running out of the building. She furiously waves at them. "Jesus Christ! Get back inside! Use the rear exit like everyone else, for cryin' out loud!" They run alongside the building, gesturing at her and pointing back at the Atrium while Sara yells for her to be careful entering the building. Nicole nods back at her with a smile, mouthing "Thank you."

So, they're running from what's inside. I'll have to—

"BEEP-BEEP-BEEP!"

An arrow appears on the screen, pointing toward the building; there's movement in a third story window—her eyes snap open. *Snipers! And there's no cover! DAMMIT!* She bolts across the Green at an angle, toward their position, just before a shot rings out; it ricochets against the gravel. *It's a fucking good thing I hacked their tagging systems, or I'd already be dead!* She randomly shifts left and right, estimating their scope adjustment and target acquisition interval. "Samson! Take control! Hhhh-hhhh—Scenario CSC-114!"

"*BEEP!*"

She whips her CSC-clad arm behind her, as if holding a katana. She reaches halfway through the Green as the snipers' shots unearth patches of grass. She keeps her eyes focused on the arch of the Atrium—her only chance at cover if she can get close enough, out of the snipers' line of sight. The airship barrels straight after her.

"*BEEP-BEEP-BEEP!*"

"Hhhh-hhhh—I know, dammit! Hhhh-hhhh—Cloak!" Adrianna's cloak bends and projects light around itself, becoming nearly invisible, but is only a half-measure; she tears forward with her head, limbs, and the bloodstains clearly visible. She looks at the remaining path to the Atrium, wary of what's inside. "What the hell are you waiting for, Samson?! Hhhh-hhhh—DO IT!"

The chopper's missile cuts a white streak down from the sky, and blows a crater into the ground, launching Nicole— "AAAAGHK!"—along with chunks of turf, into the air as the CSC fires a thin beam up at the craft. Like a lance piercing the heavens, it pokes through the fog, slicing the shaft with a redirected beam, severing the beating rotor from the fast-approaching copter. The rotor escapes up into the sky, while the wingless bird careens downward—a projectile just past its apex.

The cloak shorts out and becomes visible as Nicole hits the ground, rolls forward, and pops back up, running as fast as her sore legs can carry. Through the disorientation, ringing ears, and grueling pain over her entire body, she feels an incredible rush of excitement, smirking darkly in anticipation of what's to come.

· · ·

In the building, the snipers squint through their sights, frantically aiming their rifles down toward her erratically moving frame. A murky shadow sweeps over the top of the Atrium's glass below—a sniper looks up out of the window—"Sweet Je—"—as the craft obliterates the office wall, plowing directly into him and his team, and igniting a billowing flame that blasts outward from the building.

. . .

Nicole flinches at the deafening crash and scorching heat, and slides as if reaching home plate amid the screams of gawkers still making their escape, holding up their phones in retreat. She looks up at the chopper's boom protruding from the gnarled intrusion. "Wow... hhhhh... hhhhh... can't believe that actually... hhhhh... worked in real combat... hhhhh... hhhhh...." Dark glass shards and smoking hunks of the structure slam against the Atrium, bouncing in shallow arcs—she scurries backward, just out of reach of the smashes and thumps against the pavement. *Okay... I'll take that as a warning: now's not the time to get cocky.*

"Control back to me."

"BEEP!"

She rises, slowly, painfully, wincing, shaking her head to clear it. She cautiously approaches the building's entrance, surveying the Atrium and its observation deck above the lobby, still catching glimpses of the boom and orange flame through the transparent ceiling, wary of the random cavernous bangs against the thick glass from falling debris. The place appears abandoned; there's no one on the stairs to the observation deck, and the elevators on the far wall are all open. Fear grips her gut. *They ran out of here for a reason.*

The tablet displays an aerial view of the building with personnel streaming out the back, however, when she switches to scan mode, sweeping the Atrium, there's no one. No activity, save for a small hunk of metal loudly rapping the arch. *What was that? A crash? No... it's still there.* She sweeps her arm again over Hollis's monolithic sculpture where there is a faint, momentary indication of... *something* coinciding with another jarring impact above. *Several* somethings reacting to the bang. *They must have some kind of masking. It's not very good, but how did—screw it.* She switches to a schematic view of the Atrium, touching an area just behind the sculpture. "Stalkers. 60 kV. Seek." She points her weapon to the arched metal and glass ceiling, braces herself for the kick as the barrel rotates, and presses the trigger—four mini-drones fire in rapid succession. The winged flock of deadly hummingbirds shoot upward, zig onward, zag outward, and nosedive, disappearing behind the structure. Three soldiers stagger into view, convulsing and grunting, then drop, drones still arching—

TACKA-TACKA-TACKA! Shots blare from behind indoor columns ahead and the observation deck above—her heart jumps as walls before her shatter in a shower of glass and the ground explodes with concrete shrapnel. "*Crap!*" She spins behind the thick column next to her, horrified at a hole in the cloak's hood as numerous soldiers emerge from their hiding places and storm downstairs, firing—bullets pummel the column's marble face. In a flash within this perilous moment—furious shots filling the Atrium in a deafening cacophony, fragments of her haven splintering outward amid puffs of pulverized stone, the harsh smell of sulfur filling her nostrils—it's clear that there will be no splash of red paint, no red light accompanying a low voltage shock. Any red she sees will be blood. *Her* blood. *This is as real as it gets!* Her heart beats so fast she fears it will arrest, yet, through her rush of panic, her excitement at this realness bulges her cheeks, while the sounds of the assault crescendo.

Soldiers, in overwhelming force, slowly advance, their slugs biting chunks out of the reinforced structure.

SHIT! Those are penetrator shells! Can't stay here! A chunk of the column shatters, a hole exploding through it, the bulk just missing her head, while a shard strikes her face—"AAGHK!"—drawing blood as another rips into the cloak, injuring her shoulder. "U-UHN! STALKERS, OPPORTUNE TARGETS! *DISTRACT!*" The winged mini-drones detach from the jittering soldiers and dart about the firing squad, delivering jolts—the unrelenting stings of a swarm of bullet ants. Halting their onslaught, the soldiers duck, dodge and wildly swat at their agile attackers; Nicole snaps a disc from the CSC, takes a few deep breaths, and leaps from behind her chipped-away shelter, hurling the object at the besieged troops. As she drops and rolls over to the next column, grimacing and holding her shoulder, the disc skips like a stone across a lake, and stops abruptly beyond the computed boundary of the distracted men, detonating a heatless, visible shockwave, hurtling them toward the exit, sending furniture, plants, and shattered glass in all directions.

Nicole holds steady with her back pressed against the column; bodies and debris fly on either side of her—away from the Atrium—and crash to the concrete outside; the air implodes, sucking the shattered roof panes downward—they crash in a deafening storm of glass inside the Atrium.

She was shielded by much of the shock, but moves her jaw to equalize the pressure in her ears. "Damn it... couldn't you have filtered that out?!" Samson beeps in her earbuds in a way she's come to read as 'I did'.

She scans ahead of her on the Green. The soldiers are still. She turns, scanning the Atrium; the tablet reveals the few remaining warm bodies, pulsing rings emanating from some chests. Others not. *Whatever masking equipment they used must be destroyed. Gotta love that Pusher! Ugh… and gotta come up with a better name for it.*

As the large sculpture wobbles and creaks, and random debris impacts the ground, she steps one foot into the space, staring down at an unconscious, bloody soldier. "*(ntch!)*…." She shakes her head, furrowing her brow. *God… he's just a boy. Somebody's beloved son.* Video flashes in her mind—Hollis's grin, the turbulent emerald light flickering on his face, and the slew of faceless soldiers casually carrying out his orders while Adrianna lay before them, splayed. Violated. "Little shitball." She sneers and continues inside. *Not an innocent among 'em.*

She passes the rocking monolith, eyes slowly tracking upward to the tip. The corner of her mouth curls. "*(ptssh!)*" She lowers her head, shaking it. She smiles a crooked smile and aims for the cracked plinth. "Fucking disintegrate." The light flashes against her face and she resumes stepping toward the elevators, her boots crinkling the scattered glass. The sculpture buckles, tilts, and topples, chopping through the observation deck with a devastating crunch, crashing to the marble floor with thunderous, cascading, rumbles like that of an earthquake tremor. *Damn, that felt good!*

* * * * *

"I would swear that I can hear Dr. Mrs. A's voice!" Rajiv watches the stream of glowing headlights from vehicles racing across the bridge, away from the Complex. "What is going on over there?!"

Haj adjusts the binoculars. "I can't tell… these things only go but so far. And it's getting foggier over there, but I see smoke. Hey… I think I hear her, too. Weird."

"Here let me look." Rajiv reaches for the binoculars.

She jerks her elbow away from him.

"Woman! What is the matter with you?"

* * * * *

One….. two….. three….

Biting her bottom lip while drumming her fingers against her thigh, Nicole keeps her head forward, eyes upward, staring as the floor indicator digits change in a slow and steady crawl. Never had she the desire to go above the ninth; she'd always considered the tenth to be Hollis's territory—a no-woman zone—and avoided spending any milliseconds more within his presence than absolutely necessary. She took comfort that there were always personnel around, fearing what would happen if they were ever alone. And now… it's just the two of them.

….. ten.

The Black Queen's Heart – Part III

*T*HE upward pull of Nicole's gut as the elevator stops makes her queasy, her body prickling. And though the tablet indicates there's no one on the other side, she stabs the CSC at the door, trembling, head down, eyes forward, peering from beneath her scrunched brow, her shoulder blades pressing against the wall, one foot forward, the other back.

The doors slide open.

Her wide eyes strike out into the blackness, hitting nothing. She squints against the high contrast—the brightness of the car's walls bleeding into the inky abyss looming straight ahead. The only sound is that of her own rapid shuddering breaths pulling in, pushing out through her parted lips.

"… hhhhh… hhhhh… hhhhh… hhhhh… hhhhh… hhhhh…"

Silence. Blackness. Nothing bolting at her from the dark… yet.

"H-heartbeat isolation." Several faint rapid beats surround her— she swings the weapon wildly. "Goddammit—*human* heartbeats!" The sounds stop. "Samson, fire that goddamn motherfucking exterminator!"

"*BEEP!*"

Her CSC-clad arm leading the way, body turned, she furtively sidesteps off the elevator, her eyes darting between the tablet and the gloom, spotting only dull glints peeking back at her like that of nocturnal beasts… waiting. Her eyes adjust. Metals and glass on the reception desk and the large RMBDP sign hanging on the wall reflect the elevator light, but the area is empty. She sweeps her arm before one end of the corridor—the tablet remains blank.

"*BEEP!*" An arrow on the screen points behind her—she whips around, 180, as her pulse revs.

There he is! Displayed on the tablet's scanner, Hollis is at the far end, in his sunset office, behind closed doors, standing, looking out the window as if it were just another day. "Target that fucking asshole." As he laughs out loud, she sneers at his image—that he's so relaxed while every nerve in her body is on alert sends fire blasting over her. She knows his arrogance stems from the fact that he's prepared for her. However, she's willing to accept her fate, as long as his death is the payoff, praying to God they will suffer eternal damnation in completely different hells… his a good deal hotter. Yet… she hesitates. "… hhhhh… hhhhh… hhhhh… hhhhh… hhhhh… hhhhh… hhhhh… hhhhh… hhhhh… hh hhh… hhhhh…"

UUHN! Screw it! She explodes down the corridor as fast as her feet can carry her—boots pounding the tiles, cloak fluttering. She jabs the weapon forward as if stabbing Hollis's heart. "CLEAR!" The CSC's beam illuminates the hall and disintegrates the blast doors; Hollis whips around in shock. Nicole bursts through the shower of fiery particles— "*SIEEEGE!*" —unleashing the weapon's full barrage. Before Hollis can act, a thick white beam blows through his chest, the window, and out into the sky, while the bombardment obliterates everything in the vicinity in a massive fiery bloom, throwing Nicole back, up off her feet, her body colliding with the wall— "UHNF!" —and crashing to the upheaved floor, along with burning hunks of rubble.

. . .

A white shaft splits the sky, glowing in the accumulating fog, and an explosive surge obliterates a chunk of the building on the top floor, releasing a billowing fireball.

"Holy!"

"What in God's name is happening over there?!" Rajiv says.

Haj's ponytail whips around as she slides off the car.

Rajiv looks at her worriedly. "Where are you going?"

"I have to see if that's Jesse!" She yanks open the door.

"That is a veddy, veddy, bad idea! And do not touch this car! I do not have the keys, anyway."

"Where's yours?!"

"Up on the road—"

Haj runs through the grass.

"Wait! You do not know what is going on in that place!" He runs after her.

"I know! That's why I'm going, genius!"

* * * * *

Through the gaping hole where a wall of glass and part of the ceiling and floor used to be, the wind blows down over Nicole who's prone among the debris. She struggles to her knees, choking and retching as the toxic fumes assault her throat and lungs. She waves her hand in a futile attempt to clear the smoke, eager to behold some sign of Hollis's mangled remains. There's something in the smoke. She spots an eye... part of a nose... a mouth. She scrunches her brow, squinting... at the disembodied pieces floating in midair.

The eye winks.

"What the hell—?!"

CLAP! CLAP! CLAP! "Wow!" *CLAP! CLAP! CLAP! CLAP!* "That was a hell of a thing! Absolutely beautiful!" Hollis's voice punctures the high-pitched ringing in her ears as she blinks through the abrading grit beneath her lids, feeling her heart will burst through her chest.

The mouth grins widely.

"In all honesty, it was your husband I feared most—the man had a terrifying imagination. Once he discovered Proxy inside Adriana's head, there was no telling what he would have done to me! It was either him or myself, so, I offer you no apologies."

The smoke blows away from his piecewise three-dimensional face displayed in hanging chunks of the window's glass. "But you? Everyone always feared you, but I never took you seriously. Even back then. I'd believed your bluster was made manifest by the trappings of a witless, out of control, politically correct society that makes weaklings appear strong. I certainly didn't believe the AXTA rumors about your wargame prowess. Neither did those soldiers; they were incredibly eager to test you. Had I known you were this capable, and if they were under my command, I'd never have allowed them to face you. Not without backup.

"So, color me impressed! You even cheated—no, that's not the correct word under the circumstances. You created an asymmetrical battlefield, disabling our systems, and, in taking out that entire platoon, you proved you're every bit the fierce, bloodthirsty warrior you presented yourself to be. Cold blooded, as well. After all, you're here, which means you also took out Davenport just as the Board majority wagered. You've cost me fifty grand. But I should've known that savage was a bad bet. Guess even I was suckered by his antics this morning."

The tablet's scanner jitters, attempting to render his image. "(*cough-cough!*)... How...?"

"Oh, I'm being rude. This screen is yet another innovation to come out of the defense stables. It being a black project, I kept its true capabilities under wraps, of course—need to know. You understand—hmhm! But, since this is our last dance, I'll let you in on the secret: it merges transparent touchscreen display capabilities with Dr. Albescu's Superpresence screen technology."

She glowers at his puzzle-piecewise face.

"Surely you didn't think AXTA had a monopoly on appropriation! Or are you just angry I hid this from you? In either case, don't let your misplaced anger blind you to the greatness of this innovation. Allow me to give the Chairwoman my final tech briefing.

"That scanner of yours is a work of pure genius. I was told it was based on your concept. Multi-source streams build up an image of what's behind even the most secure of bunkers. Bounced photons, thermals, air pressures and acoustics along with satellite and video surveillance... mix that with the resonance in the target's surroundings through hidden embedded pickups in PCBs and electronics—wow. I'm still amazed that you came up with it. But as mindboggling as it is, it has a weakness. And you're looking at it.

"Like Superpresence, this Hyperreal glass is a massive mesh of inverted hexagonal hemispheres that projects directed photons and pressure waves. However, it goes much further, simulating and projecting all the phenomena your scanner detects. In short, the scanner believes I'm here and even now can't comprehend what it's—"

ZHOOP! The last of Hollis's face flakes away in a blinding white beam. The CSC's nozzle glowing, Nicole springs to her feet. "Where the *fuck* are you?!"

"Amazing. You missed your true calling, Chairwoman. And the show you just put on with that weapon—you've been wielding it and dispensing carnage like a seasoned pro; I'm incensed at what you did to those boys, but I just can't get over how you single-handedly cleared this building. Just look at what you did to my sunset office! We must have that incredible weapon, but if only its designer wasn't such an insufferable witch."

Her eyes dart around; she can't pinpoint the direction of his voice. It's coming from everywhere and he can be anywhere in the building—one of her ideas for psychological tactical engagement coming back to bite her. Breathing deliberately, she regains her calm as everything he just said sinks in. "So... you not only projected yourself... you also had to reverse the tech to cancel out and absorb the phenomena to hide yourself... using another glass." She whips around, glaring toward the far end of the corridor. The doors swing open.

"Affirmative!" Hollis smiles and waves at her from his sunrise office like an otherworldly demon, his eyes subtly glowing aqua, and red-orange points of light on his face and head.

Her body reacting on its own and ignoring Samson—"*BEEP-BEEP-BEEP!*"—she lunges into the hall and takes aim.

"SIE—*UNHGHH!*"

"*BEEP-BEEP-BEEP!   BEEP-BEEP-BEEP!   BEEP-BEEP-BEEP!*"

Her brow ridges upward. Her bloodshot eyes bulge. She gasps but draws no air, coughs but expels only blood. The white-hot burning sensation in her chest pulls her pained grimace downward to the protruding bluish glowing tip. She doubles over, gnashing her teeth while the plasma emitting blade slides out her back, slicing flesh and bone. She collapses, slamming hard against the floor. Blood flows profusely. She twists. Her turbid vision obscures the figure lording over her and yet recognition penetrates the haze.

Two points of emerald green. Incredibly dim. Lifeless. Skin rotting, wire meshes and photonic components exposed.

"Hhhhh… hhhhhh… (cough!) … Anna?"

"GIVE ME CONTROL" flashes on the tablet, but Nicole's mind is swirling.

"Operation Kill the Wicked Witch is a rousing success!" Her voice dry and scratchy, the words drip from Adrianna's slack mouth, obediently projecting the twisted ventriloquist's declarations. "Such a beautiful thing; I've never been a particularly cultured man, but this is sheer poetry on so many levels."

"Hhhh… (*agk!*)… hhhh…."

 "Speaking of beauty, I swear... the more I learn about this shell, the more I realize you were right; the Adriana unit was a major technological achievement. More and more I've been regretting killing that little cunt."

"Nn—no... my Anna... my...." Nicole's eyes overflow.

"As you can see, I've also found *your* weaknesses. Your arrogance, your hatred of me, and your sick obsession with this unit." Adrianna's body takes a lumbering step toward Nicole, the blade leading the way.

"No.... hhhh... (*k!*)...." Nicole pushes away from her with the heel of her boot, leaving black slashes in smears of blood, like desperate strokes of a wounded animal.

"Arrogance is a virtue in my book, and hatred can be a great motivator when used effectively, but if not for that obsession, I imagine we may've remained cordial. So cordial, in fact, I could see bending you over that conference table in full view of the Board, giving you the deep pleasuring you so craved. Don't think I hadn't noticed you teasing me with that body of yours— hmhmhm! Just think what could have been if you hadn't become so unhinged. Project Gemini. You and this absurd and dangerous ghostcloning nonsense. Well... dangerous in your hands. As you can see, I've enacted a failsafe: Proxy."

Adrianna's body takes another lurching step toward the retreating Nicole, who hasn't managed to get more than a few feet away.

"All this death and destruction simply because you selected that disrespectful dyke. Just look where that got us. Senator Windham. Your husband. I've lost two important assets due to your mistake. Three, including yourself."

"I... I'll... kill...!" She clenches her teeth so hard her gums bleed as she tries to move the CSC. "*Aghk!*" Her body shakes, curling into a fetal pose, encircled by an expanding puddle of her own blood. "hhhhhh... hhhhkk...."

Adrianna stands over her. "Hurts, doesn't it? Welcome to the real battlefield, Madam Chairwoman." She raises the blade in the air with both hands.

"I can't say it's been fun knowing you, but I do know it'll be some time before I encounter an opponent as formidable as you… if ever. Well… no point in dragging this out."

Nicole closes her eyes.

"Good b—"

KKTHOOM!

The ceiling above Adrianna blasts downward in a deluge of shattered tiles, metal beams, chunks of gypsum, and a black mass that crushes her, splaying her prone against the floor. The dust pours copiously from the hole descending over the hill of debris like a pyroclastic flow. Nicole is covered with a thick layer that sticks to her hair, face and blood-soaked clothes. She can barely move but easily detects the amber beacons punching through the dense matter.

Warlock emerges, stabbing his gun at Hollis. Electrical arcs spark along his arm as it shakes. "*UNGH!* YOU ARE DEAD, TREVOR! DEAD! DEAD! DEAD!"

"Tillman?" Hollis runs from behind the desk. "TILLMAAAAAN!" With arm outstretched and tensed, he aims a railgun at them. Warlock leaps from the debris, and lands on the other side of Nicole, her body jarred by the impact. Hollis feverishly empties the gun at Warlock, who kneels over Nicole, shielding her with his body. Three shots sweep past, but two slam against his back with heavy thumps, tattering his coat.

"*AAGHK!* I *WILL* TAKE YOUR BRAIN, TREVOR!" Warlock lifts Nicole to her feet, supporting her body against his.

"W-wait… help me to…." Her hand violently trembles as she tries to raise her weapon; Hollis's footfalls grow nearer. Nicole gazes down upon her tortured child's convulsing body, profound sadness etched in her face and bloody lips trembling. *My poor Anna….* Warlock gently cups her hand with his and lifts. She shakily points the gun at Adrianna's broken body attempting to free itself from the mass. *Goodbye, little one.*

"*(sniff)*…. Disintegrate… complete."

"DON'T—!" The wide-spread beam engulfs Adrianna's pitiful xendroid corpse, dissolving it and the surrounding debris into a flurry of yellow and orange orbs, shimmering in Nicole's eyes. Warlock squats, then launches through the swarm, into the destroyed office.

"No! She's mine!" Hollis dashes into the flurry of Adrianna's particles. He glares at the body as it breaks up and dissipates to dust, his contacts erratically losing their glow. His body shakes with rage. "nnNNN*YAAAH!*" He jerks away and gives furious chase, fumbling with a fresh magazine.

Warlock grabs Nicole by the waist with one arm and leaps though the breach where windows once were. Plummeting from the sky, his coat and Nicole's cloak and hair flittering about violently, he jabs the claws of his makeshift replacement hand into the side of the building, slowing their descent, slicing deep grooves into the wall of concrete, steel, and glass, sparks and fragments ejecting outward. Hollis fires down at them from the office; his missed shots punch deep craters, exploding the ground in huge cones of ejecta that shower upon them.

Warlock lands on his feet, cradles Nicole in both arms, and vaults to the exit. Hollis repeatedly pulls the trigger to the sound of empty clicks, and then casts the railgun aside. "Proxy switch! Cyclops!" The aqua glow returns to his eyes as he tears back toward his office.

* * * * *

Haj stands in front of the car on the bridge, scanning the Complex. "This is dumb—you should've driven me over there!"

"No!" Rajiv is hanging out of the driver's side window. "Let us get out of here, woman! There is nothing we can do!"

She lowers the binoculars and looks over her shoulder at him. "Gosh... don't you *ever... shut... UP?!*" She resumes her vigilant scrutiny. A reverberating thud travels up her body and the view through the glasses goes black. "What the—?!" She looks over the lenses; Warlock is standing three feet away, looking down at her, eyes flaring.

She falls back on her behind. "Holy smokes! You were right, you were right!" She scurries back toward the car. "He's come for me again! Get me out of here, Rajiv!"

"Mother of God!"

"Get her to a hospital, Nohara!" Warlock bellows.

"Is that Dr. Mrs.?!" Rajiv says.

"He... he killed her!"

"GET HER TO A HOSPITAL, *NOW?*" Warlock's demonic voice fills the car.

"*IIEEEEEEE!* GO, GO, GO!"

A missile's vapor trail threads through the sky and the projectile impacts a stretch of bridge behind Warlock, erupting in a huge fireball. Violent waves ripple on the water below and chunks of asphalt and concrete cause a cascade of splashes. Haj and Rajiv duck down in the wobbling car. Warlock lands at the rear passenger door, flinging it open, and places Nicole gently across the seat. Rajiv and Haj slowly look over the backs of theirs, faces locked in horror. As Warlock pulls away, Nicole weakly tugs his coat. She's moving her lips, but no sound escapes. He moves in close.

"I… I'm sssorry…."

Warlock is stone. Then his tightened lips tremble as her arm goes limp. His eyes flare, casting amber reflections in her half-mast sorrow-filled eyes gazing up at him. His fingers dig into the seatback's leather, puncturing it. "Get her to a hospital! *GO!*" He lurches outward, slams the door, leaps ahead of the car, whips out his guns and fires furiously into the sky, wailing a demon's terrible wail.

"Holy smokes—do what he—!"

SKREEEEEE! The tires scream as Rajiv turns the car around; Haj fumbles her way into the back of the car, nearly kicking him in the head. Landing on the floor, she pushes herself up to the blood and dust caked Nicole, who possesses only a wisp of consciousness. "Oh, my God... she's been stabbed! HURRY, RAJIV!" Haj jerks toward the seat as the car accelerates; she braces herself over Nicole, who lies with her head to the side, her face against the leather.

Nicole feels neither the pain in her chest nor the coldness of her body. She's transported to a different place and time; one where she's free of the burden of failure. From hatred. Guilt. Loneliness. Jesse's smiling face with a backdrop of islands in the sunset sky lifts her; she's safe and warm, his arms tightly wrapped around her body. He whispers her name… 'Nicki'.

Despite her repeated dire predictions of her own well-deserved penance, her deepest desire at this moment is that this fantasy becomes her afterlife. However undeserved.

Her fingers curl. Her blood crusted lips mouth words, but produce no sound. Haj moves in closer.

"….If I could…. If…… hhhhhhhhhhhhh………."

That fleeting breath caresses the peach fuzz on Haj's cheek.

Her eyes slowly move to Nicole's still face. Nicole's lips no longer move. Her watery eyes no longer jitter. Her fingers no longer tense. Her only animations are her loose and dusty black strands blowing about by the breeze from the open window. "Oh, no! Oh, no! Oh, no! It'll be alright Dr. A! Okay? Please don't die? Please…?" Haj swallows hard. "Please…?" Her lips quiver. She softly pats Nicole's shoulder and strokes her hair to a receding backdrop of fierce gunfire and explosions.

Confessions

*J*ESSE lurches upright, gasping for air. His eyes have the panicked look of a man fighting a losing battle against a relentless tide. He whips around, realizing he's back in the last bedroom in which he slept. "How...? Oh, *shit!*" He launches himself from the bed and tears out of the room as Colby runs up the stairs.

"Sir!"

"Where's Nicole?!"

"She went after General Hollis and—"

"No, no, NO! Gotta stop her!"

"I-I'm sorry... it's too late... sir." Colby's eyes are red and tears fall from his face onto his uniform.

"What do you mean, it's too late? Where is she?!"

"She went after him and he... he...." Colby cries.

"Goddammit, Kobe! What the f—!" Jesse grabs him by the shoulders and slams him back up against the wall, pinning him.

"UUNGH! She's gone! Gone... s-sir."

"What the fuck do you mean, *gone*?! I was just talkin' to her!"

"She went to the Complex by herself—"

"And you *let* her?! Why the fuck you let her *go*, man?!"

Colby hangs his head and his shoulders slump. Jesse releases him, letting him slide down to the floor, where he sits, sobbing.

"I need to see for myself! Where she at?!"

"She's.... You mustn't go there. You mustn't...."

Jesse looks down at Colby but doesn't see him; his eyes overflow and the world twists. Somewhere deep within, the battle with this reality rages until he explodes—he slams both clenched fists into the wall. Dust rains down upon Colby who flinches and weeps.

"WHY?! WHY?! *WHY?!*" Jesse hammers the wall until indentations become craters rimmed in crimson. The question hangs in the air as he stares into the bloody hollows. He receives no answer, only asseveration through Colby's muffled cries.

She's... gone.

That she sacrificed herself for him, that she thought it necessary to do so, and that he can't even be by her side renders him empty. Completely useless.

"*AAAAGH!*" His every muscle tenses as he unleashes guttural wails—wails that permeate every corner of the expansive home, reverberating beyond, spilling out into the garden—until he's spent. Defeated. The sheer weight of this loss makes his legs quake. He slams his back against the wall and slides down beside Colby.

"This can't be happening," Jesse weeps, "Why... why did she have to do this by herself, man? What would possess her to.... shit...." He wipes away tears, but they're endlessly replenished as he sees Nicole's face. Her smiles. Her fury. Her sorrow.

"She said... she said there was no other way to protect everyone... and, most of all, she wanted to protect you, sir."

He looks at Colby with red eyes, pain indelibly etched across his face. "*Protect* me? Can't she... can't she see... how much she wounded me?" He looks at Colby searching for an answer. He turns away, lowers his head and sobs, silently.

"I believe she knows, sir. Which is why she left you this." Colby waves his phone toward Jesse's chest; the tablet beeps. "I'll give you some privacy, sir." He rises and slowly walks downstairs.

A shuffling sound emanates from the tablet in Jesse's coat. He pulls it out.

[5503:17:03:04] Nicole appears on screen, adjusting her framing in the view. Sullen and solemn.

Jesse's eyes are ablaze, burning into his mind every curve of her torso, every contour of her face, and every soft curl of her hair, though the gouges in his heart make this act wholly redundant.

"Jesse. (*sigh*).... I really didn't want to record this. I've never been superstitious, but I feel like I'm tempting fate. Still... I just can't bear the thought of leaving without getting a few things off my chest. So, here goes....

"Because you're watching me now, I know you're very cross— *pissed* at me. But before you curse me out, please listen. You may never truly understand; I'm just asking that you try. Okay?

"First, I have another request. A big one. Please stay away

from Hollis! This isn't like going after your usual deviant; he's an extremely dangerous psychopath—a psychopath with an army at his disposal. And I just can't bear the thought of him taking you, too." She pauses, then rolls her eyes. "Right now, I bet you're doing that thing you do. The one that irks me—shaking your head like I'm the most ridiculous thing on the planet." She sighs. "Look. You probably think I've no right to expect this of you, now knowing that I went after him. But I'm trained and equipped to do this and you're not, and well… dammit, you're important to me! So, I'm taking that right. And I'm not saying this isn't your fight… I know it is. It's just that… you were right. This is all my fault—"

"C'mon, I never said dat!"

"—and it's up to me to set things right. I absolutely must… for my own peace of mind." She averts her gaze downward, frowning. "Unfortunately… since you're watching this… I've failed. Which is all the more reason you shouldn't go." Her eyes meander. "I got what I deserved… after ruining your life. So, just think of my death as… equity."

"Equity?! What the f—?!"

"Now that the nightmare is finally over, I know it's hard, but you should try to find a way to move on from this. You won't have to worry financially, but I can't even begin to offer any ideas as to how you should go about moving on otherwise. Doubt you'd appreciate any advice from me, anyway… after all I've done.

"I cheated. I took advantage of your handiwork without your permission. Still… I just can't bring myself to say I'm sorry for doing it. Believe me, I know how bad that sounds. But without you, I never would've had Anna—apologizing to you is tantamount to regretting my child! So, all I can do is say… *thank you*. From the bottom of my heart, Jesse, thank you for being you... the truly exceptional man that you are. The phenomenal parent. As much as I thought I knew, I learned that I didn't know anything until I followed your example. After observing you... and your absolutely adorable little girl, it's like... it all just started coming to me. That is, until Anna's teen years when the dataset was sparser.

"By that time, Anna already had many of your personality traits. She also inherited your curiosity. Remember the photos of you on the dresser? She'd researched you and began looking into what it means to be Black. The history. The culture. She... she said she realized she was Black all along. Hmhm—*no one* could tell her any different! Not even I.

"She soon started adopting your manner of speaking, but formed her own... *tude*—her word, not mine, so don't laugh at me! No doubt you've witnessed the change in her in the videos you've watched. Wow, she became a bit of a handful—thank you very much for your hand in that, Mr. Pottymouth—hmhmhm!"

"Hm!"

"She was so very enamored with you, Stefano became jealous! Wanted to behave more like a father to her. And that's really saying something, with one as oblivious as he. It still amazes me the affect you had on him, too. I mean, he paid very little attention to me before, but then started... hmm... I suppose it's inappropriate to talk about that. With you.

"Things got better later, between Anna and me, anyway. I was again blessed; someone came along who brought Anna peace. Taught her to be proud of who and what she was. That person was Belle—oops! Sorry, I used to call Delaine that. Short for Isabella. She liked it. Said it made her feel like a princess here. At the estate.

"At first, I was jealous, I'm ashamed to admit. Wondered why I wasn't enough for Anna. Why'd she need to...? Connect. But after Belle and *I* finally connected, I received an answer to a question that'd been plaguing me for years.

"In conceiving Anna, we needed a binary family unit in order to have a single, clear relationship line, but I was always perplexed as to why Samson chose your family... a father/daughter, instead of father/son. Or mother/daughter. The targeting just didn't make sense. But then it finally hit me.

"He chose you not only because of you, Jesse, but also because of me! Y'see, Belle and I... well... we both grew up without a mother, and because of this we both felt... *incomplete*. But that's not a reflection on you, *at all!* She absolutely adored you! It's just that, when we finally met, face to face, it's like the pieces fell into place for us both. I felt like I already knew her because... well... I did. And in over a year, we became like mother and daughter, although at times, I wasn't too sure who was who—hmhmhm!"

"Hmhmhm... yep," Jesse says, with a pained smile.

"And that's what made it kismet; she mothered me as much as I, her. It was so wonderful; I've never had anyone take care of me... that I wasn't paying to do so. We'd formed such a bond that I thought *Anna* would be jealous. But, oddly enough, she encouraged us! It's like she knew what Belle and I really needed. And that repaired my bond with her and made it stronger.

"Belle really rubbed off on Anna and—God help me—she started mothering me, too, mainly with food—hmhmhm! In fact, it was Belle who inspired Anna to gift me the Island. She even helped her design it. God... I...." She turns away, holding in her sobs. "My Annabelle...." She wipes her eyes and nose with her sleeve. "Jesus...."

She faces the camera. "I'm sure you never thought about this, but you and I are Adrianna's parents. Isn't it funny that we had two beautiful daughters together—oh, my God!" Her eyes pop wide open. "You probably think that's offensive on so many levels—!"

"Naw—!" Jesse says.

"Rewind that last part. ..... Go on, rewind! ..... Well, at least let *me* do it! ..... Jesus... why do you have to behave like such a giant roboprick?" She hides her face, then peeks from behind her hand. "Guess you heard that... sorry. I didn't mean that the way it sounded. Can you pretend I never said it? Okay? Okay. Where was I? Oh.

"Belle and I talked about... well, just about any and everything, really. Not the least of which was you. I swear, that girl went on and on about you—mainly because Anna just couldn't stop asking—hmhmhm! She'd lobbied so hard to introduce you to Anna. And me. I was all set to before...." Her sad gaze wanders, then she perks up. "She was so proud of you! Do you know that? God. I hope you realize that. Through her, I got to learn more about you. And through those videos, maybe I got to learn more than you're comfortable with—hmhmhm! But then again, you got to learn much more about me than I'm comfortable with, so... call it even?" She flashes a toothy grin, then frowns. "Geez! I just can't stop saying these insensitive things. Guess my nerves are on edge. Sorry, Jess."

"Stop apologizin', it's—"

"Anyway... when you and I finally met for the first time, it was like I already knew you, too, just like with Belle. I swear—hmhmhm! Yet, even knowing what she said about you—ignore the rage, fear the silence—you still scared me shitless—hahaha!"

"Hmhmhm! Sorr' 'bout dat."

"Well... I've been rambling. Probably because I'm stalling." She raises her trembling hand. "Look at that. It's because more than anything, I'm afraid that you...." She looks away and sighs, then brushes strands from her face. "Jess... if you have no feelings for me... romantic ones... please don't watch the next part. Just stop the video here. Consider it my—(*sniff*)—my dying wish. So, turn it off. Please. I'll wait."

Tingles run all over Jesse's body.

"I'm convinced that Samson was playing matchmaker—no... this isn't about him. Never was. So, I shouldn't try to use him as cover. You'd see right through me, anyway, so....

"You said I seduced you, but that's not true. *You* seduced *me*. Long before we even met. Even more so after. I mean, my heart literally stopped at first sight of you under the pergola! Couldn't believe you were here. Us walking toward each other. And.... How self-conscious you were. Your laugh. The sadness in your eyes. How handsome and masculine you are. Especially up on the Island. It was like a fantasy that I never knew I dreamt! (*sniff*) I wanted to freeze those moments. I just couldn't stop thinking about.... (*sniff*) I just want to say... I *need* to say....... *UUHN!* This is so freakin' frustrating! I wracked my brain to find the right words to tell you that I can't breathe without you, that my life makes no sense without you, but I just can't find them! I'm not like you, Anna, and Belle! I just don't have that gift! That... creative streak. So, please forgive my lack of imagination when I say...........

I love you."

Those words fill him with such a heartbroken joy, he bites his lip to hold back the flood. His heart jumps—she leans over his unconscious body and kisses him softly on the lips, sobbing. He touches his lips. A lump forms in his throat. She caresses her tears from his face, wipes her cheeks, then sits upright and places the camera on the nightstand.

"(*sniff*) I really do... love you. And I don't think... I can't recall a single instance when I've uttered those words. Not to anyone. Geez... not even to my own daughter. Or husband. They just leave you so... so... vulnerable. I've never been good at that. Being vulnerable. So, I was so reluctant, even embarrassed, to say those words to you. Especially when no one's ever said those words to me. Not in my entire life. But there's nothing to fear, anymore... now that I'm dead. Right?

"Now do you understand why I have to do this? I just can't—couldn't handle the thought of losing you—even if we'd gone after Hollis together, if something happened to you, I.... You see, it's better this way. Even if you're still watching, and are upset, my pain would've been—I've lived over a decade in this one-sided affair. And deep down, I know you're not watching this. At least I hope not. For your sake. But... for my sake... please be watching? Please?" she says through soft cries.

"I'm here, Nick... I'm here...."

"(*sniff*) Well... even if you're no longer watching, I'll pretend you are. (*sniff*) I just need to. I like to think that in some other reality you never need to watch this. I'll fight with everything I have for *this* reality. For us. And you can count on that. But... if you're watching... I've failed. And if I've failed, you'll go after Hollis. Please, don't! Jesse, you're all I have left. If you die, then it'll all be for nothing! Everything we've both done. Please don't die. Live to honor our girls... carry on their memory... mine....

"We may not have a future together, but..." She chokes up,

forcing the words out through her cries. "We'll always have the Island." She raises her hand... reaches out... and grabs the air... then weeps uncontrollably.

Jesse longs to hold her, to comfort her; he wants to whisper to her, assuring her that everything's going to be alright. But the drilling in his gut, wrenching in his chest, tightening in his throat, and burning in his eyes remind him it's too late. Things will never be alright again. Forever.

They sit and cry together across time until the video cuts to black. His solitary, muffled sobs carry on, echoing in the foyer, joined only by lonely taps of rain against the windows.

I did it again. I failed Lainey. Adrianna. And now Nicole, too. She threw her life away... for me. I ain't worth that. I just ain't worth it. Why'd she...? I'm supposed to be the one who....

Stizz and GB... even Haj had to suffer because o' me. Why do I keep fuckin' up when it matters most? Why? What the fuck is wrong with me?— THUMP!—Why can't I do anything right? I mean... I was right there. If only I... if I... I coulda....

As Jesse repeatedly bangs his clenched fist against the floor, footsteps lumber up the stairs, approaching him.

"Sir... I know there is no possible consolation, but... you should know that Madame Albescu didn't go down without a fight. She was a fierce warrior."

At the sound of Colby referring to Nicole in past tense, Jesse remains in place on the floor, back against the wall, his head bowing deeper.

"I mean that literally. There are multiple accounts—several large explosions and gunfire—uploaded to social media. When the platoon arrived at the hospital, they looked like they'd just endured major combat, some soldiers in critical condition... and some didn't make it—"

"Let's roll." Jesse stands and starts toward the stairs.

"Sir, if you're thinking of going after Hollis, it seems the military and city officials are assessing the situation and are planning some sort of response. You're still a wanted man—"

"Y'all got a plane or copter or som'em, right?" He bounds downstairs with Colby close behind.

"Yes. Yes, we do. But, *sir…!*"

* * * * *

"I don't know what I'm doing, anymore….. (*sniff*)……. Maybe I never did." In the passenger seat of Rajiv's car parked across the street from the hospital, Haj's face is raw, awash with tears, blood smeared on her jaw and collar.

Rajiv is silent in the driver's seat, eyes red, and staring off through the rain pelted window. His brow ridged, he rubs his wrist across his nose, drawing in a wet sniffle, his blood-crusted hands shaking. "(*ssniff*)…."

Haj looks out over the sea of reporters and motley collection of newfound Adrianna and Nicoletta Albescu fanatics and cosplayers, watching them steadily flood in over the past hour, the area blanketed with an assortment of umbrellas and signs. "Look at them… they're so stupid. This isn't a freakin' convention."

Rajiv is facing in the opposite direction, gazing through the distorting wash, lost out over the stretch of turbulent water. He rubs his nose again.

"(*sniff*)" Haj slowly shakes her head, glaring. "They have no idea what's really going on… and I fucking hate them. All of 'em."

Rajiv snaps toward her. "You should not be involved in this, either! Just look at what those monsters did to Dr. Mrs. A.! And she was veddy...! Why are you doing this?!"

"Because I have to."

"No, you do not! You will only end up getting yourself killed! You have not known any of us for long; it is senseless for you to put yourself in such danger! So... (*sniff*)... just stop." He turns back to the window.

The sound of the rain picks up. With her red eyes at half-mast, Haj looks at the rippled reflections of emergency vehicle lights on the wet asphalt. She rubs her eyes. "(*sniff*)....... How many people's lives have you saved? I mean literally *saved*. I'm talking putting-yourself-in-danger kind of stuff... like running into a burning building... or...."

"I do not think that I have. So?"

"It's not something you'd ever forget. So, I'm gonna assume you haven't. Neither have I. I had the chance once... and didn't... I didn't take it." She sobs softly, still facing the crowd, her eyes glazing over.

Rajiv turns toward her.

"That old man... he slipped... fell right off the platform. I-I.... He was down there pleading for help—*my* help... begging me. But I didn't. I called out—*screamed* for someone to help him, over and over, but no one came. No one was there but me. And him."

Rajiv shakes his head.

"I heard the metal slicing along the tracks... saw the lights... then the train. I could've helped. *Should've*. There was time... I think. But I was so... too scared."

"Gosh... when was this?"

"(*sniff*) ... I-I screamed for it to stop," her voice breaks through sobs. "I screamed until I couldn't hear my own voice and—!" Her brow furrows. "OH, MY GOD—OH MY GOD—OH, MY

GOD!" She whips forward and her hands snap up to her ears, covering them. "It was so... *loud*... the train's horn... and...." She cries deeply, hunched over, eyes clenched as she rocks. "I blocked the whole thing... for so many years! But—but when I saw Jesse standing there putting himself between us and that train... with his halo... I swear I saw that old man's face staring up at me! Telling me I'm a... a rotten person!" She bawls out loud. Rajiv raises his hand toward her... and gingerly rests it on the shoulder of her seat. Her cries fill the car, drowning out the downpour. Rajiv lowers his head and remains silent.

The crowd gets denser under the hospital entrance overhang. An emergency vehicle, distorted by the streams of rain on the windshield, leaves the hospital with blaring siren and flashing lights. The wind drives waves of impacting raindrops along the dark gray asphalt.

Haj's heavy sobs subside.

Rajiv looks across the water, toward the Complex. His brow tightly presses and his eyes gain an undercurrent of fire. "(*sniff*)........ If he knows what happened to Dr. Mrs. A... my guess is, Jesse's on his way, or is already there."

Haj sits up straight, wipes her eyes, and blows her nose with an overused tissue. "Let's roll."

Cries for Vengeance – Part I

"**A**RE you certain? We can get in much closer—atop the building," Colby says above the chopper's hiss, the stealthy craft's rotor noise-cancelled.

Jesse's tensed fingers digging into the armrests, his body stiff, back pressed against the seat, he nods ahead at the abandoned guard station. "Nah, just right down there."

"Very good, sir."

Along with all other ground-level structures throughout the Complex, the station is smothered by heavy fog.

"It's so thick. It doesn't look natural," Jesse says, straining his eyes.

"I would very much doubt that it is."

"Hm." *Dude's desperate; fog ain't gonna slow anybody down in that wide-open field. If anything, it hides everything from him. Unless… that's the point.* "Motherff…." *Please let me be wrong about this. Shit. SHIT! No. Keep it together, man.* He silently exhales. *One thing at a time.* "Straight on through to Building-A, you said?"

"Correct. I'm not privy to her exact path, but she's never one to deviate once she sets a goal."

Jesse slowly nods as he peers through the skittering drizzle on the windshield deep into the obfuscated night while his mind rages; Building-A looms like a massive black ghost, nearly blending into the dark, overcast sky, its glowing office lights providing the only clear telltale sign of its heavy existence. "And you're sure he's still there, right?"

"According to police chatter, he's been contacted; still in the main building and refusing to comply with calls for surrender."

Jesse sneers at the building while unhooking his restraints.

"The agencies and police are battling over jurisdiction, which means we have a window of opportunity. Samson will continue to buy us more time, but we must still make haste." Colby reaches for a revolver in a chest behind the seat.

"Nope." Jesse gently blocks Colby's hand. "I wanted you to drop me off outside the base for a reason—I don't want you anywhere near this place."

He reaches again. "But—!"

Jesse blocks him. "Nuh-uh, man! Just drop me off, then bug out. As fast as you can."

"I let her go in… by herself. I will never forgive myself for that, but I can at least—"

Jesse puts a hand on Colby's shoulder. "Look… I was wrong layin' that on you. I apologize. For real. Her and Haj? Ain't a damn thing you can do to stop either one of 'em. Besides, you've got nothin' to prove—she left you behind for a reason. Right?"

"Yes, but—"

"Knowing her, it's som'em really big that she couldn't entrust to just anybody—if anything happened to you, how would it get done?"

Colby looks away, dropping his shoulders.

"And you have a wife and kids, man! Just think about them. And only them. That asswipe fucked up *our* families. I'm not about to let him fuck yours up, too. So, please... just drop me off, then go on back and do like she asked you, aaight?"

Colby's jaw shakes.

"Aaight?!"

"Yes, yes, alright! Sir."

Jesse pulls a CSC out of its case and places it against his right arm—clamps swing out of it, wrapping around his forearm, securing itself with a snug fit. "Hm. Still can't believe it's this light."

"Did you review the manual thoroughly, sir?"

Jesse slides open the cabin door to the heavy rush of cold, damp air and points the weapon outward into the sky, shouting against the bluster. "Stalker! One! Max kV! Loiter!" The barrel rotates; he fires a mini-drone—it streaks away, disappearing into the foggy night. "Reset!" The barrel rotates back. "Yep! I got dis! Like it was made for me!"

"It was! But you shouldn't waste ordnance, sir!"

"I'm not!"

As the frigid air blasts him, mist collecting on his face, drops forming and falling from his jaw, Jesse clutches material from the seat—the cloak of the sad, remarkable girl, stained with the blood of his own daughter, and drenched in the fresh blood of the woman he longs for so deeply. He stares down at it in his trembling hands.

He carefully puts on the garment over his raincoat, then pulls the hood over his head.

. . .

Colby's eyes shimmer as Jesse adjusts the dark, stained fabric. He opens his mouth to speak, but Jesse turns and crouches ready at the door opening, his back to him. Jesse hangs his head, silent as the wet wind gusts into the cabin, the view of the black building beyond him slowly being swallowed by the writhing thicket of trees.

"Come back safe, sir! Please!"

Jesse remains still. His grip tightens on the door.

"Sir?!"

"Thanks for everything you've done for me, man! 'Preciate it! Take real good care o' yourself! Cherish your family! Have a beautiful life together and don't ever let nobody fuck dat up! Aaight?! Say goodbye to my brothers, Haj, Celia, Winston, and err'body else for me, too!"

"What are you saying—?!"

"Now get this thing back in the air!"

"Wait—!"

Jesse hops out of the craft a few feet above the ground; he lands with a grunt and slap of his boots on the damp turf. He then rises to his feet, and waves frantically at the hovering chopper, his coat and cape flaring wildly in its gust. "GO ON—GET OUTTA HERE, COLBY!"

As the craft rises, and his eyes fill, Colby watches Jesse become obscured by rain, fog, and darkness. He swallows hard.

"That's '*Kobe'*... sir."

* * * * *

Standing just inside the base, Jesse narrows his eyes as he looks around. The lights dotting the Complex give off a mournful glow in the heavy mist and light rain. And there's no activity, whatsoever. It's like a vast nighttime graveyard—a graveyard for giants, massive buildings rising above the fog like tombstones. The place is unnervingly empty. The hairs on Jesse's body prickle. "Shit...."

"Jesse!"

He whirls, stabbing the CSC at the attacker.

"Hhhhh...hhhhh.... Scared you?! Good!" Nico says. "You've been scarin' the hell outta me, lately!" He walks toward Jesse.

"No, no, NO! You shouldn't be here—you're really fuckin' my shit up, man!"

"I'm fuckin' up *your* shit?! I got suspended because o' your shit! Georgie's locked up, because o' your shit! Cap and the whole department's about to get screwed because o' *your shit!*"

"Don't you think I know that?! Why you think I'm doin' this?!"

"Hell if I know! Did you call? Send a text? A pigeon, at least? Huh? I gotta find out what's goin' on wit' you by watching the goddamn news! And it's everywhere! CNN is JDNN—the goddamn Jesse Davenport News Network, for cryin' out loud!"

"Squash dat—you showin' up gonna seriously screw me, Stizz! What the fuck are you doin' here?!"

"Took forever to sneak over that bridge—on *foot!* I had a hunch you'd go after General Hollis since he killed that Albescu woman... and after you jumped off that there building. An eleven-story building, for fuck's sake, J! I'm grateful Georgie didn't get to see that, but do you have any idea what it did to *me?! Huh?!*"

"I'd explain why I did, but ain't no time for dat! *Leave!*"

"You must be *really* losin' it if you think there's any way in hell I'm leaving you behind!" He pulls out his Glock and racks it. "If I can't convince you to give this up, then I'm in it, too. Whatever it is. C'mon, J, you know how we do!"

"Stizz. Seriously, bruh, I'm beggin'. You're the one person who knows this shit ain't normal. So, believe me when I say this is the very last place you should be right now. For real."

"But... but how can I leave you alone like this? When you're goin' through hell. Could you leave me—?"

"I'm tryin' my damndest to keep you from gettin' hurt any further, bruh, and you're makin' it impossible! Please go? For me? Just this once—no questions asked?"

Stizz's eyes narrow, peering over Jesse's shoulder into the thick fog. "What's that?"

PLOCK... PLOCK... PLOCK... *PLOCK*....

"Oh... fffuck...."

Cries for Vengeance – Part II

*J*ESSE slowly turns, wide eyed. Chills rampage down his spine as his dread takes on physical form within the murk.

PLOCK... PLOCK... PLOCK... PLOCK....

Deep within the fog, two faint amber lights glow amid an approaching shadow. Jesse stabs the CSC out at it, his arm trembling.

PLOCK... PLOCK... PLOCK!

The last unnatural footfall reverberating with finality, the shadow stops yards away, the lights of amber with a ghostly glow. The shadow bleeds into the fog, turning it dark like ink pouring, swirling into a water, the lights appearing ever brighter.

"What the hell's that?!"

"Sh!" The drops hiss against the ground and tap against the

CSC. Jesse's breath shudders. Nico watches Jesse—his face instantly fills with worry.

"Wh-what's the matter—?"

"I need you to do exactly as I say, Nico."

"O… okay, J."

"Get behind me. Ignore that black smoke. Just make sure those yellow lights can't see you. Aaight?"

"Okay. I'm there."

"No sudden moves. Slowly make your way to the guard station—but keep out of sight of those lights, got it?"

"Got it."

Nico carefully inches backward. Jesse breathes in halted breaths. His weapon trained, he keeps his head down, eyes forward locked within the growing abyss on the figure that's likewise locked on him. Unmoving. Though the presence is cold, Jesse can feel the hate searing through the heavy air at him. But all he focuses on is Nico's shuffling against gravel, hoping the gray man never got a glimpse of him, and praying the thick fog keeps it that way. As Nico's furtive steps begin to fade, the lights flare, illuminating the remaining fog beyond the darkness.

"WHY DID YOU MURDER STIZZOLI, DAVENPORT?!"

"*RUUUUUN!*" Jesse shakes as he screams, firing feverishly into the black fog—the bright, bluish beams slice glowing paths through the dense air.

"Holy *shit!*" Nico falls back onto his hindquarters.

"MOVE, STIZZ! *NOW!*"

Nico scrambles to his feet and careens toward the station, light flaring behind him as Jesse fires at the eyes that move so fast they seem to teleport randomly about the abyss. Nico jets to within feet of the station and—*BOOM!*—he flies backward— "AGHK!"—slamming against the ground, flaming hunks of the station crashing with him.

"NICO!" Jesse dashes to him. As he scrunches against the glare, he pulls Nico to his feet amid burning debris, awash in fiery light. "You aaight?! Can you run?!"

"Uunh…. What's happening, J?" Nico's legs wobble.

"*Can* you *run?!*"

"(*cough-cough*)… where to?"

Jesse spins, pulling Nico by the arm away from the blast, his desperate eyes reaching out into the formless void, nothing but darkness before him. There's a thump behind them. The black figure looms before the inferno, the amber eyes flaring chaotically.

"SHE'S DEAD—TAKEN FROM US *FOREVER! YOU* ARE TO BLAME, DAVENPORT, AND YOU *WILL PAY!*" Warlock's dark form stiffens with visible fury as he screams, his clenched fists shaking.

"Run toward the building!" Jesse points into the dark.

"Where?! I can't see!"

Jesse fires toward where he guesses Building-A is, the beam disappearing into the depths. "That way! Go! I'll cover you!"

Nico stumbles as he runs toward the Green. Jesse tears toward the burning station, firing at Warlock—but he vanishes. A heavy WHUMP behind Jesse sinks his heart. "No…." He slowly turns. The 'ink' dissipates like a personal blotchy window into the fog where Warlock's eyes glow before Nico, who stops frozen. Jesse can't feel his legs. "No… please don't hurt my little brother… please, man—"

BANG!

The shot echoes across the base. Nico slumps to the ground

with a *WHUMP!*

Jesse falls to his knees.

Warlock stands over Nico's body, watching as Jesse descends into misery. "Tell me: how does it feel, Davenport? You have experienced Belle's demise only from afar; now tell me how it feels to bear witness to a life—a meaningful life—taken away right in front of you?"

Jesse is catatonic, his faraway gaze blurring the world, his arms limp. He submerges into a darkness so deep it compresses his chest, restricting his breathing. All he can see is the long-haired, skinny kid, his face and body battered and bruised, his chest splayed open, covered with writhing maggots. *Nico....*

"No snappy retort? Disappointing. I do so appreciate your sense of humor, Davenport."

"*(cough-cough-cough)....*" Nico's legs move, one knee raising, his chest smoking.

Warlock grins. "Stizzoli is rather resilient, is he not?"

Jesse emerges from the profundity—his eyes narrow, head down, and jaw tight, he slowly rises to his feet. "Excavate." The CSC's barrel shifts.

"Let us remedy that resiliency." Warlock aims at Nico, who's barely moving—then his eyes dart.

FOOOM-SHHHH! The ground near Nico erupts. Warlock handsprings back into the deep as Jesse plows through the debris shower, leaps over Nico, then pulls him down into the trench.

"UUUHNF!" Nico grits his teeth.

Jesse rolls him onto his back and runs his hand over Nico's chest—bulletproof vest still emitting smoke—then looks into his own coat at the tablet. "Let 'em through, Samson. Let 'em all through."

"BEEP!"

"Stizz. Stay put. Don't move from this spot. No matter what."

"(*cough*)… what are you gonna—?!"

"Help is on the way."

"I'm… (*cough*)… I'm alright!"

PLOCK… PLOCK… PLOCK… PLOCK….

Jesse glares up at the edge of the trench.

Nico weakly grabs Jesse's coattail. "Don't… don't go back out there, J! No!" Lacking the strength to keep Jesse at bay, the coat pulls away from his grip.

Jesse hoists himself from the trench and stands firm, the engulfed guard station roaring behind him. Warlock reemerges, sauntering toward him, then stops, his eyes obscured by his black shades and the raging fire and Jesse's dark form reflected on them. The moist wind gusts their coats as they stand immobile, eye-locked.

"There he is. The silent white knight has returned. Not even a single question, Davenport? Are you not even the least bit curious as to the reasons why I am halting your advance?"

The wind howls, low and angry.

Jesse raises his arm, pointing the CSC directly at Warlock's head, eyes piercing his target.

"Hmhmhm! Nicoletta was most formidable with that weapon. However, you should know that it did not change the outcome of her battle, and you are far, far from the exceptional warrior that she was, Davenport. And, as such, you are ill prepared to enter Trevor's den of inequity."

"Disintegrate." The weapon shifts.

"Such bloodlust. I resent admitting this to you, Davenport, but you and Nicoletta are, indeed, so very similar. However, I suspect that this is another outgrowth of her laboratory study of you, nothing more."

Jesse fires; Warlock sidesteps the bright white beam—the ground beyond him explodes—the light flashes and glows cutting his silhouette away from darkness. Jesse aims again; Warlock evades.

"You are both so very...u-u-uh *intense*. However, your intensity is misfired." His eyes flare. "NICOLETTA'S DEMISE IS NOT FOR YOU TO AVENGE, DAVENPORT!"

"Program one!" Recoils jolt Jesse's arm as six stalkers launch from the CSC. They dart toward Warlock; he ducks and dodges as they swarm about him then streak up into the sky.

"Interesting." Warlock watches them disappear. "Very interestin—"

Jesse fires at him. Warlock dodges again. "I see, Davenport. You were hoping to distract me, true? That would be an effective tactic to use against me, in my civilian modus operandi. Admittedly, I did tend to be a bit... u-u-uh *arrogant* with my talents. However, I have since learned it is best to maintain proper combat-readiness." He reveals the replacement hand, still ravaged from clawing the side of Building-A.

Wildly swinging his weapon, Jesse tracks Warlock, who responds in kind.

"You missed your best opportunity for attack, amid your swarm, Davenport. There is no longer a chance for you and you cannot defeat Trevor, certainly not with your current tactics—"

"ALL BARRAGE!"

The stalkers streak down from the sky; Warlock looks up, then launches himself backward into a handspring. *KLAP!* The first stalker impacts the ground with a flash of white lightning, blasting a spray of ground fragments into the air. The barrage of winged projectiles rains down, each in rapid succession; Warlock continues his handspring run until all six have impacted. The skyfall of fragments resound like rocky hail as Warlock sticks the landing. He grins darkly at Jesse. "Again, you missed a—" His focus snaps upward—too late. *KLAPZZZ!* The seventh stalker impacts his chest—arcs course over him.

"Disintegrate." Jesse fires at Warlock's jittering body; Warlock dodges—not fast enough—the beam shears his right shoulder and skin on the side of his tightened jaw— "GUARRGH!" —they begin to disintegrate into particles that glow red in the fog.

Warlock's eyes blaze, novae stabbing the darkness, his shoulder dissolves and his arm breaks off, falling to the ground. He glares at Jesse with unbridled fury, ripping the stalker from his chest, crushing it to pieces. "HOW DARE YOU SHOOT ME, DAVENPORT!"

"Program 2." Jesse aims the CSC slightly to the right of Warlock.

Warlock bounds left— *ZHOOP!* —the thin beam breaks in midair, angling, slicing clean through his leg. "AAAAGHK!" He impacts the ground, his face wracked with agony and rage. "You antici-anticipated my PRESENCE!" The sparks light his blood-covered jaw, revealing the exposed metallic bone and plates wrapped with flesh. His eyes flicker erratically. "H-h-hhow, Davenp-p-port?"

Jesse walks toward him. "You have a pattern: you show up at my worst moments... and I am *seriously* fucked up, right now." He stands over Warlock, whose disfigured body jerks and convulses while his malfunctioning voice shifts randomly between gravel and hell.

Warlock reaches out to Jesse—"AAAGHK"—arcs flare over

his gritted teeth and his claw-of-a-hand, then he releases letting his arm fall limp. He writhes and slams his fist and heel against the ground with heavy thumps, and lurches again. Same result. He claws the ground, glaring, but this demon whose inhuman eyes once made Jesse shake with fear now tweaks his chest... with a twinge of sorrow.

"Judging by the expre-expression on your f-f-fface, it would appear that you're under the ERRONEOUS IMPRESSION that you have bested me-bested me."

"Cut the shit, man. You know this ain't about you an' me."

"You-you are correct, Davenport." A dark smile crosses his lips—his face then contorts. "MEET MY MEN!" Several amber lights embedded in murky shadows appear deep within the fog behind Jesse. With the rolling rumble of an army of giants, the dark figures step toward the trench where Nico lay injured. Jesse whips around—a chill slams his body.

The demons roar in one heart-stopping voice, "SHALL WE HARVEST STIZZOLI, SIR?!"

"AFFIRMATIVE!"

"NO!" Jesse fires wildly at the shadows, tearing toward them; they dodge with the same speed as Warlock. "STAY THE FUCK AWAY FROM MY BROTHER!"

"BWAAhahahahahaha!" Warlock's face shifts into deranged glee, the flashes from Jesse's weapon glinting on his inky blood.

The closer the demons get, the weightier their steps, shaking the ground—shaking Jesse's core. He scrambles back toward Warlock. "C'mon—cut this shit out! Please! I'll do whatever you want!"

"Hahahahaha! That llllook on your face is-is DELICIOUS, Davenport!"

The shadows reach the trench, looming over Nico, their cold eyes shining bright amber.

"What the fuck are you?! *NYAAAA!*" Nico wildly fires his Glock into the converging shadows, emptying it to a hollow click.

Jesse presses his boot against Warlock's chest and takes furious aim at his face, the nozzle of the CSC glowing pale blue. "You bettah call 'em off!"

"HAHAHAHA!"

Nico reloads and unloads again, screaming.

"Bitch, I will blow your fuckin' head off!"

"HAHAHAHA!"

"Let me go—get off me, you fuckers!"

Jesse tenses, veins bulging, eyes wide, the weapon shaking, spit spraying as he screams, "*CALL 'EM OFF!* I'M FUCKIN' *SERIOUS*, STEFANO!"

Cries for Vengeance – Part III

*T*HE shadows freeze. Jesse looks back at them with a tear-streaked face. As Nico lands in the trench— "UUNF!"—they turn their attention to Jesse with a cold, glowing, lifeless stare sending alternating waves of relief and fear through him. They blink out of sight. The inkiness in the fog begins to dissipate.

"You good, Nico?!"

"*(cough-cough)* Yeah... I'm okay!"

"Aaight, stay put!"

"Hmhmhm! If only-if only you could see your own face, Davenport."

"Another muh'fuckin' game," Jesse says, glaring at Warlock.

"Stefano."

A dark grin creeps upon Warlock's face. "Well, well, well... the detective actually d-d-detects."

"You him, ain'tchoo? A ghostclone or sum'em?"

"AFFIRMATIVE. He is me. NEGATIVE. I-I am not."

Jesse makes searing eye contact.

"Hmhmhm! Your tragic FLAW IS THAT YOU ONLY see the world-see the world in black and wh-wh-wwhite, while truth often lies in gradients. And there are many shades BETWEEN ALBESCU-Albescu and Tillman."

"That makes things clearer—(*ptssh!*)"

"I am curious: how is it that you fffinally a-a-arrived at THIS TRUTH?"

"With all the killin' you did, framin' me... and that you accused me of hittin' you, things started pilin' up. But it was a question Nicole asked me about Adrianna that—"

"HER NAME IS NOT *NICOLE!*"

"Look, man. I ain't tryin'na disrespect you. All that anger and animosity you puttin' out? That don't have shit to do wit' me. Never did; I ain't ever met Adrianna, and me and Nicole ain't meet until about two weeks ago—long after you died! You know I ain't ever did a damn thing to you. Don'tchoo?"

"You took Nicoletta away from me—YOU STOLE HER HEART! And that of-of-of my daughter!"

"Like hell I did! If anything, you pushed 'em away—"

"They BELIEVED you to be so p-p-perfect, Davenport. The perfect father... the perfect... everything."

"Perfect? Man, ain't nobody—"

"Samson, TOO, FAvored you—he chose you as my replacement. MY OWN CREATION DID THIS TO ME! If you are so perfect, wwwwhy could you not AVENGE BELLE?! She was your own child. Twice you-you could not FINISH THE JOB—"

"'Cause I'm not a murderer!'"

"BECAUSE YOU ARE *WEAK!*"

"*No*—I'm not a monster like you!"

Warlock's eyes flare as he seethes at Jesse. "This is-is true. I am A MONSTER. Imperfect. However, had I not been... *absorbed* into this body-body, I might have FALTERED, as did you. It was I-it was I who led you to them—"

"You what?" Jesse glares at him sideways.

"You heard correctly, Davenport; I was your DETECTIVE while you stumbled along in your s-s-stupor following the breadcrumbs I dropped-dropped for you. However, you still failed.

"I am the-I am the true avenger, not you, Davenport. I, Stefano—I, TILLMAN, who love Annabelle, who-who love Nicoletta. THAT IS TWICE as much as you, Daven-DAVENPORT. I have proven this-proven this through ac-ac-action, all while you WALLOWED IN STASIS. I... I killed them *for* you... for me."

He casts his gaze away, out into the fog.

"However, it was clear that Nini—Honey would never lllllook at me the same-same way AGAIN after I joined this form. She, believed me to be a mmmonster."

"Naw, man, her being done with you ain't have a damn thing to do wi't dat."

"HOW WOULD *YOU* KNOW?! YOU ONLY *THINK* YOU KNOW HER! *I* AM HER HUSBAND, *NOT YOU!*"

"Tell you what—you say you know her? Then you should

know she wasn't done with you because of what you became, but because of what you were."

"Wh-wh-what was I?"

"All too human."

"Hu-hu-hhhuman?"

"Too self-absorbed—you ignored her... didn't listen to anybody or think about consequences. You even tried to win her over by competing against her with Adrianna... which is when all this crazy shit started happenin'! Fuck." Jesse presses his clenched eyes, gritting his teeth. "You never even tried to understand her— she wasn't just a fighter, she was... *lonely*."

"I...."

"And if you just stopped to think about her feelings—*even once*—you'da realized that she wouldn'ta given a damn about... whatever you are now. I mean, the evidence was starin' you right in the face all this time. Hell, you not only *saw* the evidence, you helped Nicole *create* her, for fuck's sake!"

The dark, blood-spattered cloak blows about Jesse's body. Warlock stares at it. Deciding. Calculating. *Computing...* his cold fury gradually melting. "Perhaps... perhaps there is merit-merit in what you say, Davenport. It would APPEAR THAT YOU do, indeed, understand Nicoletta b-b-better than I." His eyes descend... watery... a lifeless stare into nothingness, his exposed jaw with a minute quiver.

Jesse's chest falls, then he looks away from him. "Man...." He rubs his hand down over his face. "Forget what I said. The *real* monster isn't you. It's the asswipe holed up in that building; he's responsible for all this, not you. All the shit you did? As seriously fucked up as it was, at least you were driven by somethin' important. Somethin' *real*."

Warlock looks up. "As is he."

"Hm. Well… I don't put the blame on you for what he did to my daughter; it's all too easy to pass blame on folks for sum'em they couldn't even foresee. But I still can't look past all the other shit you *did* do—especially shootin' my brother. Even so, for what it's worth, I can appreciate what'choo been goin' through, man. For any part I played… I apologize. For real."

"You-you're apologizing? To me?"

Jesse nods. "Maybe if we'da met—naw, I ain't gonna lie, we wouldn'ta gotten along."

"But we d-d-did have fun, DID WE NOT, Davenport-Davenport?"

"Fun?!"

Warlock smiles up at him with hopeful watery eyes.

"Fun like a root canal!"

"Hahaha—!"

"No anesthetic!"

"BWAHAhahahaha! Glad to see y-y-you still have not lost-have not lost that WONDERFUL wit, Davenport—hmhmhm!"

"You gonna finally tell me why else you showed up?"

"I am here to halt and bolster your advance."

"What? That doesn't make—(*sigh*).… Why you been tryin'na stop me all this time?"

Warlock smirks at him.

"Well?"

"There is still more fun to be had, Davenport. My regret is that I will not be present to witness it-witness it."

"Damn… you're *still* fuckin' wit' me."

"It cannot be helped, I am afraid—hmhmhm! However, rest assured-assured, you will soon understand-stand, Davenport, if you SURVIVE what lies ahead."

Nico crawls out of the trench and falls on his side, holding his chest, grimacing. "*(cough-cough!)*—AAAGHK! Hhhh.... What were those things, J?! What was that smoke? What's that weapon?! Uuhn! Wh... what am I seeing?! Who?" He squints through the fog at Warlock. "What *is* that?!"

"Our interior decorator... and a murderer!" Jesse says.

"And *savior*, Davenport. DO NOT FORGET... sa-sa-sa-savior."

"Yeah. Thanks, man. I mean that."

"Th-thanks? NO ONE HAS EVER said that to me bef-before...."

"Who'd he murder?!"

"The six asswipes I'm accused of murderin'—he framed me for it. God only knows how many others he's killed."

"I, Stefano, am nnnnot a murderer; I am an *avenger*, Davenport."

"Same difference."

"And what of yyyou? If you are not here-not here to commit the SAME OFFENSE, you sh-sh-should turn back, because I can assssure you—from multiple personal experiences—Trevor has no such qualms."

Jesse looks up at Building-A. Toward the top floor. The end of the road he never knew he was traveling for over a year. And he can't see beyond it. "Qualms, huh? You don't have to worry 'bout that."

"Whatever you do, keep-keep your eye on the unfriendly skiiiies, Davenport."

"Shit...." Jesse scans around into the night while walking over to Nico. He kneels. "You aaight, bruh? Naw—don't try to get up."

"J. Listen to me. Turn back and hide out somewhere before

they get here. This case—this *craziness*—is just not worth it!"

"You don't understand—"

"You never listen to me! What would it take to make you listen?! Maybe if… if we were blood…."

"What?"

"Maybe it'd make a difference in how you see me."

Jesse's eyes well up. "Why would you say some shit like that to me, man? Why? After all we—" He turns away.

Nico's frown deepens. "Jess… I-I'm sorry. I didn't mean—"

"*(sniff)* Don'choo know? Our glue is stronger than *any* blood. We're bonded—you, me, GB, and Lainey. We're *bonded*, man." As Jesse squeezes Nico's shoulder, head bowed, he sobs.

"I'm sorry," Nico says, tears falling. "I didn't mean it. It's just… you take on everything by yourself. Since we were kids. I mean… the bad stuff didn't just happen to me and Georgie… it happened to *all* of us. That includes you, J."

Their heads turned away, they silently weep together.

Warlock's eyes are locked to them, but he remains silent.

Jesse leans over and kisses the top of Nico's head. "*(sniff)*…. We gotta get'choo some Rogaine or som'em, 'cause… damn."

"Way to kick a brother when he's down—hmhmhm!" He slaps Jesse's hand away.

"And your kids… wit' yo head and your girl's hairdo? *(ptssh)*… They gonna be so messed up, bruh."

"You expect 'em to come out sportin' that ugly bun?"

"Ah, you finally admit it! She's *your* Becky with the jacked-up hair."

"Not the time to be fuckin' around, J—"

"Aaight—hmhm—you're right." Jesse aims the CSC at the ground a few feet away. "Cover your eyes."

"What *is* that weapon? Never seen nothin' like that—"

"C'mon, man!"

Nico complies.

"Flare. Dim." Jesse fires at the ground; the spot glows softly in the gradually-clearing fog as the faraway wails of sirens resound.

"You still doin' this? Is this case truly worth risking your life for? Again?"

"It's not about the case."

"What then?"

Jesse sighs, pinching the bridge of his nose. "Aaight. I didn't wanna tell you 'cause I know exactly what you'd do. I know what *I'd* do. But you have a right to know, so...."

"Well...?"

"I'm takin' out the sick asswipe that killed your niece and my daughter. He's the one had her raped and beaten... and then he sliced her up... killed her with his own hands." Jesse clenches his eyes, pressing his claw-like fingers to his brow. "His own goddamn hands, man. Shit...."

"I... I don't understand. What are you sayin' to me?"

Jesse looks him in the eyes, nodding.

"He did *what?!* You tellin' me he's the fucker who killed my *Dee-Dee?!*" Nico lurches himself on his side, digging his fingers into the ground.

"No!" Jesse pushes him back down; Nico tries again, but Jesse holds him in place.

"Get off me! Get the FFFUCK off me!"

"You saw all this shit tonight?! There's something worse waitin' out there! And you're already injured, Stizz!"

"Think I give a shit about any o' that?! I'm taking that fucker *out!*"

"And what do you think *I'll* be doing if—*when* that asswipe kills you, too, huh?! You saw how *that* maniac over there used you against me!"

Warlock salutes them, grinning.

Nico simmers, his eyes wandering as he breathes heavy gales. He looks up at Jesse's face and his body shivers with rage. "NYAH! Then you better take that motherfucker out!"

"I got dis." Jesse rises to his feet. "They gettin' close—I gotta roll. Just stay put until they get here. Feel me? And stall 'em, if you can. Aaight?"

Looking backward, Jesse walks away staring at Nico. And, as he turns forward, he knows that was likely the very last time he'd get to see his brother's face. The rain lightly hisses. His boots grate against the gravel. With each step away, he feels a downward tug on the corners of his mouth.

.   .   .

His body drenched, shivering from the cold, Nico's eye twitches as he watches Jesse forging ahead into the fog. In this moment, he understands. As much as he knows his own rage, he understands. And that understanding swells his chest with the desire to give his brother the one thing he truly needs right now.

"*KILL* THAT COCKSUCKER, J! *GUT* HIM *GOOD!* YOU HEAR ME?! DON'T COME BACK 'TIL IT'S DONE, AND YOU BETTER HAVE HIS FUCKIN' DEAD HEART IN YOUR HANDS AS PROOF, OR I'LL GET UP N' DO IT *MYSELF!* YOU HEAR ME?! YOU FUCKIN' HEAR ME, J?!"

"That's the spirit, Stizzoli! Might I join your squad?" Warlock's eyes flare brightly. "KILL TREVOR! KILL HIM, DAVENPORT!" His eyes then grow dim. "Kill him... for-for-for murdering my family... for murdering me... for-for-for creating me."

"Creating…?" As Jesse disappears beyond the embankment, Nico cautiously crawls over to Warlock. He looks at the gory part-flesh, part-machine body—he scurries to his gun, falls back on his butt, and points the weapon, his hands jittering. "Don't move, you—whatever you are!"

"HAHAHAhahah— *(cough-cough)* —hahahah!"

Nico is distracted by the peculiar behavior of the rain—spray hangs in midair, seven feet off the ground, drops splashing against nothing he can see. Streams of water warp his view of Building-A, then a number of tall black figures blink into view completely obstructing it. "Holy Mother of—they're back!" He scrambles backward, darting his shaky gun around from target to target.

"Should we accompany Davenport?" a figure says.

"Negative. That would be a VIOLATION-violation of the rules of their game which is ssstill in play-still in play."

"Have we not already violated the rules?"

"I would nnnot call it a violation, per se. Think of it as a… u-u-uh *nudge*. Let us-let us sssssee if Davenport is UP TO THIS task. If he succeeds, he will prove useful-useful."

"If he fails?"

"RECOVER HIS BRAIN… if there's any-any-anything left of it."

"Recover his… *brain?*" Nico mumbles.

"Waste not, WANT NOT! A truism, is it not, Stizz-Stizzoli—HAHAHAHA!"

The dark figures turn toward Nico.

"Will you harvest Stizzoli?" They move toward him.

"Wh-what?!" His body quivers as he wildly swings his gun. "Y-you stay far the fuck away from me! I'm a fuckin' cop! You hear me?! A *COP!*"

Warlock grins. "Hmhmhm! Perhaps Stizzoli has had enough t-t-torment for one evening, gentlemen."

"Yes, sir."

"Besides…" Black ooze seeps from Warlock's leg stump, probing outward like hundreds of wiry tentacles of a ravenous sea creature.

"Holy…!" Nico's breath catches.

The tentacles grab on to Warlock's severed leg and yank it to, reattaching it. He rises to his feet, grinning at Nico. "Stizzzzoli has not the p-p-parts I desire."

A cold chill runs through Nico at Warlock's icy stare.

"I have other, much more… u-u-u-uh *fitting*, targets in mind- TARGETS IN MIND."

They all blink out of view, invisible except for a suggestion of their shapes of the impacting rain until they all disappear into the fog, leaving Nico trembling where he lay. "What in God's name…?" He shakes his head, eyes still filled with fear. He then looks back toward Building-A, grimacing from the pain of broken ribs. "Take that filthy son of a bitch out, Jess. And you better come back alive."

Silence of the White Knight – Part I

*W*ARLOCK'S warning echoes as Jesse looks up into the dark, mottled sky. At every hint of ring-like blemish, his eyes dart. He quickens his pace. Shielding his narrowed eyes from the rain, he peers at the top floor of Building-A where all lights are on save for one block at the nearest end. Through the bloom of streetlamps, he can just make out the damage to Hollis's office. He raises the tablet, zooming in—the image is enhanced as if in daylight. "Whoa...." *She fire from out here? Naw... looks like it came from inside! How'd she make it all the way up there?*

He places the tablet back in his coat while his eyes remain locked on that devastation, walking until his boots grind against gravel. There's an overturned jeep blocking his path. He steps around it, toward its mangled front end, the ground darkened with blood the rain could not wash away. "Shit. What she—?" He glances up the road where there's a wide channel surrounded by mounds of gravel and dirt. "*Daaamn....*" The evidence of Nicole's resolve tugs his heart ever-deeper.

He enters the Green, looking down. The lawn is speckled with divots; this telltale path of random cavities leads to a large crater. He walks around it, his brow knotted as his mind fills in the details—Nicole's fury unleashed—realizing that, despite what the heavy pain in his chest tells him, he knows very little about her.

Down toward the end of the Green, the hushed, gagging lights of the Atrium barely illuminate his rubble-strewn way to the protruding glass structure of the imposing black tower. The place is abandoned—a military-industrial ghost town made more otherworldly by the lingering fog. The wind howls. Many office lights are on, but there's no activity, whatsoever. Even the expansive parking lots are barren except for a few company and military vehicles. The building seems less imposing than when he first came. In fact, the whole place looks like Nicole imposed *her* will upon *it*.

At first, he could only see it as a dark blotch, but as he moves closer, his eyes open wide at the sight of a helicopter's boom sticking out of the third floor—"O-o-o-h, *shit!*"—the craft is lodged within a mangled mass of smoking rubble. With his attention snagged up high, he stumbles over a large hunk of distorted metal framing, catching himself.

Just outside of the Atrium, the ground is littered with shards from blown-out glass walls and scattered hunks of shaded concrete with twisted steel protrusions. A thick column is heavily damaged, mainly on one side, appearing chewed away by many voracious beasts. He examines the damage, the holes blown through the support. *This must be where she took cover.* "Fffuuuck...!" Within the carnage from an army actively trying to kill her, Nicole's lone rage blares louder. *This ain't no muh'fuckin' airsoft! When she said 'going to war', she meant **war** war. Her against a real General. And a real army. Hell, I probably wouldn't have made it past the front gate! But she forced her way in here... and even made it all the way to the top. Fighting so I wouldn't have to.*

He finds himself falling for her all the more... and he didn't think such a thing was even possible. He inhales deeply... then continues onward, trudging through the heartache, exhaling a long shivering breath.

Glass cracking under his boots echoing out into the structure, he follows the trail of destruction into the dark demolished Atrium; stepping over, ducking under, and walking around huge obstacles of wreckage; crisscrossing metal beams and slabs of concrete and marble floor that bank and pitch at exaggerated angles. The dull flickering lights conceal and reveal the imposed chaos, this jagged sea of concrete and steel with gnarled crests. He finds it disorienting. As he focuses downward, trying to gain sure footing... up high... beyond the elaborate framing of the Atrium's arched ceiling, the glass obliterated and cables dangling and dripping... in the murky sky, something moves in the flashes of darkness... a large, faint, three-ringed orange crosshair, jittering and blinking like the eye of an angry giant. Silent. It seethes as Jesse trudges through the industrial thicket within a column of dryness, a column the drone's invisible body carves out of the anemic rain sprinkling down into the Atrium. A new uneasiness that Jesse can't explain runs down his spine. He stops, eyes flitting about. He slowly turns and looks back. Nothing. Drops tap against the chaos and splash into shallow puddles of rainwater. Nothing still. His gaze jumps upward. There's only darkness. Something feels strange. He takes one more sweep. He's alone. Yet, his anxiety persists as he resumes his trek through empty spits of rain.

Under the damaged observation deck, into the lobby, passing a cracked, broken sculpture of a missile, he realizes he's been maneuvering through the remains of the imposing statue he encountered this morning when he first dared to confront Hollis. He fully understood the statue's meaning beyond the obvious and audacious military symbolism; it's a representation of Hollis's power. And all who visit are instantly in awe of him, this giant who won't be ignored and who's always watching. Jesse, remembers its oppressive, despotic presence, but now, seeing the General symbolically castrated, he can't help but cringe. He shakes his head and turns, gazing out over the turbulent destruction, facing the magnitude of his own inadequacy.

She was so far outta my league it's embarrassing. But she said she loved me? Me! Why? I mean… what the hell she see in me? I'm not even….

He sees her face, with every permutation that makes her *her.* He feels her heartbeat as her body presses tightly against his. He smells her soft scent. He hears her confession and final goodbye echoing in his head, this woman who left the world without knowing just how deeply he fell for her. He, himself, didn't even know how deeply until this very moment.

The unbearable loss consumes him, rendering him a burnt-out husk, a husk crumbling in the crushing shadow of the monster who snatched her away. The same monster who ripped Lainey away. And the same monster who forced such perverse, sadistic cruelty upon Adrianna. He shivers. Every cell in his body wants to burst, screaming to Heaven at God, His gross negligence. He begins to hyperventilate, clutching the cloak to his chest—his heart jumps! He goes stiff. A reflection in the wet broken glass near his boot snags his eye—he spins and jabs the CSC up at the ceiling, past the jagged edge of the observation deck, breathing heavy gales through clenched teeth.

Through the framing, the drone is glaring down at him—an organic, *human* stare. "Why aren't you dead?" Hollis's voice booms throughout. "Hmph. The profiling was faulty. We thought the witch killed you, but you're here, holding her weapon—one even *I* couldn't lay hands on, and would never function for me if I could."

Painted in dim chaotic light, Jesse stands motionless, peering up past his heavy brow at the giant eye fuming down at him, listening to each barb, each shot, each stream of hot bile spewed at him—listening to this monster he's resolved to slay. Come what may.

"This can only mean Senator Windham's assessment of your relationship was correct. Disgusting. You're even more repugnant than I thought, soiling a vulnerable white woman with your thug filth. Even worse—what kind of a man lets a woman fight in his place? Can he even be called a man at all?"

Jesse darts his eyes between the drone and his surroundings, scanning for some path out of Hollis's sight as the taps of rain grow into a constant hiss.

"Just look at you. You're not a man. You are weak. A coward. A boy with no honor. And you have the gall to befoul my GHQ again, with this-this... pointless vendetta? Well... you've come this far, I won't turn you away." The eye fades into the night, the empty column within the rain drifting away. "Let's you and me chat face-to-face and settle this. Report to my office... *soldier*. You know the way."

The floor indicator on the elevator flashing '10' makes Jesse wary; he hadn't pressed the call button. The rain hisses.

... 9....

That and the fact that everything Hollis just said tells him the General doesn't regard him as a worthy opponent, and therefore would never deign to engage in direct combat with him. And yet, Hollis already had a clear advantage with the drone.

... 8........ 7....

Jesse's eyes flit about.

... 6....

The familiar incessant beeping and buzzing scream from his coat, confirming what he already senses: *somethin' ain't right*.

... 5....

He lurches around, 180, preparing to run—"Aaghk!"—but is blinded by two sets of high-beams. The harsh light cleanses the fallout, casting hard shadows and striking contrasts throughout the Atrium.

"Jesse Davenport!"

... 4....

"This is the U.S. Marshals Fugitive Task Force! Lay down your weapons and show us your hands!" the chief commands over a loudspeaker.

... 3....

"BEEP! BEEP! BEEP!"—BZZZZZZZ!

"Aw, hell—*BOMB!*" Jesse shouts.

"Jesse Davenport! You have three seconds to comply or we're coming in!"

… 2….

"Shit!" He quickly glances at the tablet; it's flashing to a position within the debris. "*BOMB, GODAMMIT!*" He dives into the mangled mess, puts his head down, and covers his ears and face with his forearms.

… 1….

"He ducked! Fire!" They move forward, their weapons spewing a storm of bangs and flashes. Their salvo streaks through the rain into the building, sparking and clanking metals, exploding stone and concrete, and shattering glass, generating cascading impacts that bolster the deafening clatter.

… L… *DING!* The elevator doors open. Jesse braces while the compartment's interior wall is peppered by stray bullets. He keeps his head down, then, with shots whizzing and ricocheting about him, he raises an eyebrow. *Damn… thought it was gonna—*

BOOOM! The blinding plume of fire blows through the Atrium, propelling hunks of structure and loose rubble, the marshal's bodies flying backward while the entire place violently shakes. Jesse is shielded from much of the furious burst but a sharp hunk of shrapnel slices into his thigh. "*AAUNGH! Fffuckin'…!*"

Silence of the White Knight – Part II

*T*HE blowout subsides, leaving patches of raging flame and smoke and the elevator shaft ablaze in its wake. Small random pieces fall—rubble pelts, metal clanks. "*(cough-cough… cough!)*"

Gritting his teeth, Jesse pulls at the shrapnel, dislodges it from his leg, and throws it to the floor with a *KLANG*. "Son of a—!" He squeezes his leg, blood soaking his pants. There's a piece of lounge furniture right next to him. He grabs the knife-like shrapnel, cuts away a strip of fabric, then tightly ties that strip around his wound. The bleeding stops. He pulls himself up from beneath the makeshift bunker and scans the warzone, plotting a course through the re-destruction. Though fires burn too brightly for him to make out anything in the black sky, he limps toward the entrance, at least now aware that there's no empty column within the rain.

Someone is struggling. A soot-covered man is pinned beneath a massive, smoldering beam. It's Detective McGraw, now a deputized marshal, pushing against the beam until his gaze locks with Jesse's. He freezes.

Jesse sneers at him. "(*ptssh!*)" Then he hobbles over to him, scowling. McGraw grits his teeth and covers his face with crossed arms and clenched fists. Jesse releases the weapon's clamps, letting it fall to the ground, and pulls against the beam. "UUNH! Help me, goddammit! I'm tryin'na save yo' crooked ass!" McGraw unfurls his arms as Jesse strains against the beam's weight. He joins in, pressing his hands against it; his arms tremble. He screams as the beam shifts slightly. The corner of the beam digs into Jesse's palms and his fingers go numb. He lets out a strained yell but the futility becomes evident as the beam is about to drop from his hands. He clenches his eyes and pulls with all his might. *C'mon! Move!* The burden suddenly lifts. He opens his eyes—three soot-covered marshals, Detective Carlson among them, teeth bared, are hoisting the beam. McGraw writhes in agony, his screams intensifying.

"Almost—uuhn! Move it this way!" Carlson says, angling her head toward a clearing. They step over McGraw, moving the beam away from his crushed leg, while he grimaces and grunts.

"Okay, we drop on three," says the chief. "One—"

Jesse releases the beam and hops over McGraw. The remaining rescuers jump clear—the beam crashes to the ground. Jesse rolls and grabs the CSC, clamping it to his forearm with a jolt. Carlson and another deputy run to McGraw's aid, but the chief tears toward Jesse, who points the weapon at him.

"Whoa! Don't shoot!" He stops abruptly and raises his hands. "I'm unarmed!"

"Stay the fuck away from me."

"You know we can't do that—"

"Chief!" Carlson says, bounding toward him. "Let me have a go at him."

"I know you," Jesse says, staring at her. "You set me up, along with that dirty fuckah, over there." He jerks his head toward McGraw. "When this shit's all over, y'all gonna be the ones runnin' from the law. I guarantee dat."

"*I* didn't set you up." She makes eye contact with Jesse, her back to McGraw. "With how you've selflessly protected our team, I know something's not right about *all* of this. I'm guessing you have a great explanation for everything you're being accused of. But that's why you need to end this right now and come with me. If you continue on like this, it won't end well for you. So, if for nothing else, just think about Nico. How would he feel, so soon after losing his niece?"

He stares in her piercing eyes. Something's vaguely familiar; he gets the sense that she's genuinely concerned. "I ain't never seen you at the precinct. Who you? What'choo know 'bout Nico?"

"I know he wouldn't be happy with what you're doing right now. Resisting arrest. Just come with us so you'll get a chance to tell your story. I'd really like to hear it."

"That ain't happenin'."

"But—"

"To hell with this touchy-feely bullshit!" The chief steps forward. "If you won't surrender, we'll capture you or you'll end up dead! Makes no difference to me!"

"Chasin' me is gonna get *y'all* killed! Look around, fool! Hollis tried to take me out and he ain't give a damn about you *or* your badge!"

"If *you* do, stop running," Carlson says.

"Fuck it." Jesse points the CSC at the ground between them and presses his forearm against his eyes. "Flare!" The flash of light—far brighter than the high beams—burns a pothole into the ground. While the officers are stunned, Jesse bolts outside, darting his eyes about the sky. The intense pain from his wounded leg slows him to a running limp. Across the grounds, there's a flurry of flashing red, blue, and yellow in the fog—it's a convoy of military, law enforcement, and emergency vehicles. He runs past the Atrium, continuing onward, angling toward the tower, away from the convoy. The marshals emerge from the Atrium in pursuit, joining a team of soldiers and police running across the battered Green.

Through the hiss of the heavy rain, gusting wind, Jesse's rapid, sloshing footfalls and those of the fast-approaching army, there's a familiar whirring sound. Faster and more high-pitch than Jesse remembers. *A Fuckin' Gatling!* Though in agony, he picks up his pace—an officer catches up to him, reaching out for his fluttering cloak. *BZZZZZZH!* Streaks spew from the sky, ripping the ground with fire, ejecting a curtain of stone and dirt behind them. "*AA-AA-AAGHK!*" The officer's body lurches violently as the indifferent assault shreds him. Amid the spray of ordnance, blood, and concrete, the other marshals disperse, staying clear of Jesse.

"FIND COVER, JESSE!" Carlson yells.

The ground erupting just inches behind him, Jesse dives under a jeep in the parking lot—the vehicle jerks about in the hail of rounds and a shower of sparks. He quickly rolls underneath the next armored vehicle as the shots punch through to the ground behind him, pummeling the asphalt. The drone tracks him, pelting the truck, bucking the vehicle, but the gun winds down, halting the offensive.

Carlson traces the origin point of the onslaught. The source, however, is invisible, save for the halo of rain-spray revealed by the base's lights. She squints and points. "There's something hanging midair! It's invisible!"

Jesse quickly slides out from beneath the mangled truck and runs along a diverging angle from the building. Small-caliber gunfire rings out; he peers over his shoulder, never breaking stride. The marshals are firing skyward. Jesse stops; sparks jump in the sky as their bullets ricochet off a hard surface. A chopper sweeps toward it, police pelting the drone from above. The drone blinks in and out of visibility and finally becomes a conclusively visible compressed black sphere in the sky. The bright orange crosshair eye manifests, sweeps over the drone's surface and stops, focused on the marshals. "RUN!" The chief yells. The drone fires a missile. The posse retreats just as the ground explodes—their bodies lift off the ground, propelled outward. A chorus of gunfire blares from the army of officers approaching from the convoy. The din of impacts is matched in harshness by the blooms of sparks on the drone's body. The drone's eye tightens.

Amid the discordant shots and guttural wails, and amid the heat and flashes from the explosions, Jesse watches the carnage playing out before him, the chaotic light uncovering his face in the darkness. *That bastard's not just after me—he means to wipe them out, too!* As the chopper smokes and blazes a fiery trail toward the ground, the anxiety in Jesse's chest compels him to assist the officers, but not with enough force to overcome the tremendous thrust of his rage. He turns his back on the horrific scene, guilt biting him for using the drone to keep his own pursuers at bay. The guilt is lessened with the knowledge that the best chance they have is for him to stop the attack at its source.

The war behind him intensifies as newly arrived land and air reinforcements join the firefight. He runs outward, looking toward the top of the building and points the CSC just above the roof ahead of him. "Hook!" A projectile rockets from the weapon with a muffled pop, followed by a rapid, high-pitched whirring. He continues running parallel to the curved face of this broad, concave building. The hook darts upward, changing direction, arcing over the edge of the roof, trailing a fine thread through the sky. The thread becomes taut, tugging against the weapon, pulling Jesse forward and upward. He grips the CSC's body with his left hand. His stride lengthens until it becomes one-legged leaps. He's completely off the ground, one story up, flying through the air, swooping around toward the building as he's pulled upward, never looking down.

"BEEP! BEEP! BEEP!"

His readies his feet, bracing for the impact as the sound of the Gatling revving-up pushes his pulse to the limit. His boots slam against the wall, sending jarring pain through his leg. "Ahgk!" He runs along the building's curved exterior, sweeping past bright offices while continuing his upward swing. *BZZZZZZH!* Streaks of fire chase him along the wall, splashing glass and concrete. The drone's eye remains keenly focused on Jesse—it tracks him with its lethal spray as the wire retracts faster, leaving the drone behind, whipping Jesse eight feet up in the air over the edge of the roof. The hook detaches and retracts back into the gun as Jesse lands on his feet. A shockwave of pain rushing from his injured leg up to his hip, his leg gives way and he tumbles, rolls over onto the roof, then hops up and changes direction, the raging thumps of his heart providing the tempo as he peers back over his shoulder. "*Shit!*" Like an enormous hungry raven, the drone sweeps up above the roofline and hovers, its eye roving erratically, searching. Jesse runs toward the center roof access, yards away. *BOOOM!* It erupts, obliterated by the drone's missile. He slips and changes direction, running toward the next access toward the end of the building. *BOOOM!* "You motherfu—!" He continues onward in an injured sprint.

Intense searchlights flash on from below, slicing through the fog and illuminating slanting streaks of rain. *Thirty feet.* The edge of the roof and the sweeping shafts of light fill his view. *Fifteen feet.* "Fuck! Fuck! Fuck!" Between the drone behind him and the ground below, his mind blazes with a different, desperate option. *One foot.* He leaps over the edge—"*FUUUCK!*"—praying this option proves far less deadly than A or B.

The drone fires a seeker missile. The ground fast approaching, Jesse twists, aiming upward for the exposed ceiling in Hollis's blown out office. "Hook!" The barb streaks toward the office and lodges into the ceiling. "Retract!" The CSC yanks him backward, tearing a muscle. "AAAAGHK!" The missile narrowly misses his head; it overshoots then meanders skyward. Jesse is reeled into the office—his body slams against the ceiling, and crash lands onto the rubble. "… uuuhn…." He lies in place trying to shake it off and gain his bearings.

It would be completely black in the room from soot and burnt debris if not for the multicolor throbbing from the gaggle of emergency vehicles. Jesse crawls behind a mound, grimacing while looking out into the dull bluish night that is interrupted by the swaying shafts of searchlights. But then, overriding his numerous aches and pains, stifling his outcry, and locking him in place, an empty column forms in the drizzle. His breath silently shudders. Save for the patter of rain and occasional heavy droplet smacking against the rubble and upheaved floor, it's silent. Jesse's heart bucks wildly. With his eyes locked to the missing rain, he breathes slowly and deeply, trying desperately to calm his nerves. But the edge of panic is nearly upon him. He looks behind himself. The door has been blasted away and the hall is aphotic. He imagines Hollis has another surprise waiting for him. He's vulnerable with his back to the dark, vulnerable with his front to the light. Yet, weighing both, the known takes precedence. He stays in place.

With all the speed of a black sun setting, the drone slowly descends from the roof and aligns with the opening. Completely silent. The searchlights illuminate its underside, glimmering like moonlight on the surface of a calm black sea. Its fiery eye scans the terrain below searching for, what Jesse can only presume to be, his dead body. The movements begin in a methodical search pattern, but soon deteriorate into an erratic, fitful frenzy. With bated breath and clenched jaw, Jesse watches a piece of dangling ceiling tile that dislodged with his impact.

Please, don't fall. Please, don't fall. Please, don't....

PLAP!

The eye whips around, training its jittery gaze into the devastated office. The drone eases closer, nearly filling the opening. Light beams and colorful flashes bounce into the space, eerily illuminating the wall to Jesse's right. But from behind mounds of debris, he's completely shrouded in shadow. He stifles his breath and keeps his sharp focus on the drone. The way the eye moves and blinks as it searches for him, he can discern the personality and emotions behind its movements; it's clear that Hollis holds deep hatred for him. *Why?*

The eye abruptly halts, locking on to something on Jesse's left. Unblinking. Chills tear over his body as he witnesses its bloodthirsty glare. *Wh-what's over there?* Not making any sudden moves, he holds his breath and very slowly turns his head. Past the mound... past the edge of the drone... past the illuminated rain against the foggy night... past the far-left corner... until, finally, his sight lands on the wall where he finds exactly what has captured the drone's lethal attention. In a broken mirror, the eye is fixed upon *him*. Full on. Tightening. His heart skips and his breath shudders as the drone's weapon begins to rev. Faster. It reaches full-speed scream. It whips around—too fast for Jesse to dodge!

BZZZZZZH! The streaking, heavy artillery pokes searing holes into the rubble around him. He dives through the eruptions, toward the drone and fires the CSC, blasting a hole clean through the craft's hull. The drone spins wildly, scraping against floor and ceiling, pulverizing the surfaces into shooting slag. Rounds spray outward, unleashing a torrent of fire and fragments. Jesse dives again within the havoc, evading the deadly spray as the tails of his coat and cloak are shredded. A shot impacts the CSC casing, knocking him against the wall.

The nozzle blazing red, the artillery ceases and the drone stabilizes. Jesse is on his knees; he shakes and bangs the CSC, which is violently sparking. As the drone hovers over him, he looks up. He can still feel the profound hatred lodged in Hollis's glare. But beyond the drone, through the arching hole in its body, there's a glow in the sky. The Gatling revs. Jesse holds his position, listening to the weapon's pitch increase, his anxiety skyrocketing as the glow fast approaches. Despite the sharp pain in his chest from a heart in overdrive, he launches his body to the side with wild abandon. The drone whips toward him—the missile plunges into the drone's hull, erupting a terrific blast, launching Jesse and flaming debris backward into the corridor.

Silence of the White Knight – Part III

*P*ULSING lights on emergency vehicles. Bright shafts from searchlights. The warm glow of burning chopper and police car husks. *BOOOOM!* All are drowned by the explosion, harsh light blasting over the makeshift triage area. Carlson's attention is snatched away from the wounded. "Holy moly." Her eyes shimmer watching the drone plummet like a huge flaming torch. "Did he just destroy that blasted thing?" It plows into the ground—a massive blue mushroom cloud as tall as the building rolls up into the air. A thunderous shockwave and mini-earthquake violently rock vehicles and push people up off their feet.

"My god…." The chief says, watching the blaze. He then

gathers himself, shakes it off, and surveys the scene. "If you're able-bodied, report!" he calls out.

"Chief?" Carlson says, staring at him. "There's already a call out to the governor...."

The chief looks on as a large swarm of orbs flit about and dissipate, then looks up at the burning office, the column of black smoke snaking into the sky. He sighs. "Hm. Uh... at least until the National Guard arrives, we'll wait and see what Davenport does."

"Might be moot." Carlson looks up at the raging fire, a wisp of sadness in her eyes. "Can't imagine he's still alive."

* * * * *

"You miserable, disrespectful *thug!*" Hollis's voice booms throughout the Complex.

Jesse grimaces as he lay on his back, covered in soot, burns, and wounds, his head and clothes smoking. The CSC violently sparks—what protected his arm from being blown off is now burning his skin. He grunts as he yanks the smoldering weapon from his arm and lets it drop on the floor where it begins to dissolve to fire and dust. The orbs flitting about him, he rolls on his side, pressing his hand against the seared skin on his arm, then pushes himself up on all fours. "*(cough-cough... cough!)*"

"Do you have any idea at all of what you've done?! You brazenly destroyed untold billions worth of R&D—a self-contained A.I. entity, complete with emotions and an identity, not unlike the Adriana unit you were hired to avenge! But he was a soldier! You just murdered an honorable U.S. Army serviceman—*while he slept*—a treasonous act!"

Jesse pats his smoldering jeans, killing the embers. Just beneath the oppressive ringing in his ears, he can make out the voice. It's everywhere. Nowhere. His vision is blurry. Even after blinking and widening his eyes, he can only see blobs of blinding light from the loudly chattering flames. He squints against the glare and cringes from the sweltering gusts of heat.

"Clearly, I've taken you far too lightly. Underestimated you. I can count on three fingers the number of commandos who could've pulled off what you just did. But pardon me if I withhold applause… you hypocrite."

Jesse's unaware he'd landed between Adrianna's char stain and Nicole's pool of sticky, drying blood. Yet he's energized by a ferocity that carries him to his feet, not allowing his body to give out, breath rushing through his clenched teeth as his every muscle quivers.

"Here you are. Swinging into action—*literally*—thinking you understand anything at all about the fire of vengeance. You don't. You're just a boy throwing a tantrum over losing his little dolly."

The office ablaze behind him, Jesse looks around into the darkness, feverishly trying to clear his vision. He spots a blob of cool randomly-flaring light at the far end of the dark corridor. The blob comes slightly into focus. He can sort of make out Hollis's figure sitting at his desk, parts of large, bright, undiscernible moving images behind him defining his shape.

"So what, you lost a child! People lose 'em every day. Have you ever tasted another man's blood? Felt chunks of his brain sliding on your tongue? One second, you're laughing at a joke about… I can't even remember—Big Bobbie was always crackin' wise about *something*—hmhm! The next……. The next second his entire head explodes. Gone……"—*WHUMP!*—"Have you?! Hacking on pieces of his skull gritting in your throat?! Splinters of his jaw sticking in your neck—your chest?! ……… (*sniff*)…..

(*sniff*).......... You haven't. (*sniff*)... Hmph. The worst you've ever witnessed with your own eyes is likely a scraped knee. Or a papercut."

Jesse's rage burns at this catalyst floating in the center of blackness before him. Hollis is more than a thing he must do away with for the greater good—a curse scrawled on humanity's forehead, screaming to be erased. This is the man who destroyed his life. His future. Robbing him of all hope twice over—the latter so fresh that his heart is being wrung ever-tighter at the loss of what almost was. And this reality is so excruciating that all of his external pains are choked into numbness.

"You're so privileged you couldn't care less about anything other than your own mis-inflated anger, with your blatant disregard for authority and DoD property. No respect. It's no wonder that little cunt of yours turned out the way she did... involving herself in matters far beyond her station."

With his sole blurry target in sight, head locked forward, Jesse limps toward him, slow and unsteady, slapping his hand against the cold wall for support. His breath shuddering in gales through his teeth, blood and spit drip down his chin, streaming onto the cloak, dotting his path.

"Do you know that Congress stuck its nose into my affairs due to her snooping? Of course, you do. You put her up to it...... So, this is all *your* fault. All of it. Even that hearing.... *You* fired the first shot. That much is clear to me now. I don't know what your motive was, or if it was just on orders of that witch who hired you, but you should've come at me like a man instead of hiding behind skirts! Maybe they both'd still be alive.... And I wouldn't've had to kill the Adriana unit.... Or my own allies.... Such a waste....... You must be so proud; you and your offspring crippled a world-shaping organization and created insurmountable obstacles for me. So, it's 'mission accomplished' for you, isn't it?"

Jesse's eyes remain welded to his objective, his steps a monotonous and relentless beat against the stained tile. Nothing exists except Hollis. And the unyielding pain in his heart.

"(*sigh*).... None of this would've happened if they'd just *listened* to me! I'd informed them that your little Nancy Drew reject wasn't viable. But they still refused to remove her from the Gemini Project...... (*hmph*)... Affirmative Action at its worst.... And I got to see firsthand just how detrimental your offspring was to the project: she infected the Adriana unit with her disease—*your* disease. Hearing you talk with my own ears, it's clear that you were the core problem, all along."

Though this dragon looming before him spews words ablaze, Jesse feels only the bracing swipes of his hand across the cool wall and the jarring of each heavy step, his pulse providing the tempo. He can only hear those footfalls and beats... his deep, labored breathing... the intermittent drops from the ragged hole in the ceiling behind him... and the crackling flames farther still. He feels the heat against his back, a chill at his front. He smells the noxious burning chemicals and tastes the oil and soot mixed with the blood in his mouth. However, his goal takes emphatic hold over his vision as the too-far-away man gets bigger and closer, a nervous excitement growing within.

"Your shameful military record was bad enough, but how could I be surprised at what you've become? No discipline, no loyalty, no morals.... Anti-American.... Cowardly hiding in shadows doing sleazy work—ruining lives for a few measly bucks.... She never had a choice but to turn out the way she did. If it was up to me alone, I would have protected her... taken her in under my wing, giving her a proper upbringing. Since she managed to cause so much havoc, she was, after all, exceptional… in her own way… despite being subhuman and poorly parented."

As Jesse limps past the elevators, peering down the gloomy corridor into the coldly flickering office, an unsettling recognition creeps upon him; Hollis is isolated from the world in a prison of his own making.

No way forward. No way back.

Jesse also recognizes his bent; all of Hollis's actions today prove he's clawing for a warrior's way out. A proud end.

In this moment, staring at Hollis's silhouette of empty blackness, he now clearly sees how he lived before Nicole showed up at his own office. She saved him. She saved him from *himself.* And as he gags at the thought that he has an affinity of any kind with this man, he vows with every cell in his being to be *Hollis's* savior, willing his broken body onward. Closer… closer… closer.

"I want you to know that I truly did my best to prevent this. I warned them about the dangers of using civilians and *still* they ignored me in selecting your daughter ahead of a crop of worthy, qualified, well-bred patriots. So… I apologize to you for your daughter's death. It should've been you."

For an instant, Jesse could swear that he saw Adrianna's face. Screaming. He slides his focus just past Hollis's shadow and can now make out the silent, looping videos that fill the wall of glass behind him. It's her rape and murder. In another video, Anna is brutally hacking Lainey's body, over and over again. Anna's hands are choking Stefano in another. And there are two videos he hadn't seen before; Hollis is shooting Senator Tripp Windham in the chest and in the back of the head… and in another… Nicole. His heavy breath catches… then shudders upon release. The beautiful rage on her face is cut short by the grotesque shock and horror in her eyes—a glowing blade pokes out of her chest as she's being skewered by Anna's rotting corpse in the corridor... the same corridor where he's currently limping. His head reflexively turns slightly as if to look back, but he remains forward-facing. He locks on at the center of these images: Hollis behind his desk with his shadow rimmed by this cold, turbulent glow of death. Of *murder*. Jesse knows this display is solely for his benefit. Confessions designed to bolster his resolve. He would've thought that notion impossible. But as he stares ahead at this char stain sitting at the center of his splayed heart, he now knows he was wrong.

His pace and breathing quicken.

"Nothing to say?"

THUMP-THUMP! "... hhhhh... hhhhh... hhhhh... hhhhh..." *THUMP-THUMP!* "... hhhhh... hhhhh... hhhhh... hhhhh...."

. . .

Hollis peers out into the darkness, now silent himself, staring at the lumbering zombie, an ungodly creature relentlessly approaching, birthed by the yellow-orange flame raging behind it. Hollis shakes his head, unblinking, his jaw tightening with every undaunted thump toward him. He blinks rapidly, his brow in a knot, then removes the deactivated Proxy contacts. He stares back out into the corridor, scans around his office at his many accolades, certificates, and photos—distant echoes of younger— better—days. Prouder days.

THUMP-THUMP! "... hhhhh... hhhhh... hhhhh... hhhhh..." *THUMP-THUMP!* "... hhhhh... hhhhh... hhhhh... hhhhh...."

He lingers on one photo. One that furrows his brow and saddens his eyes. He's locked in place, his expression gradually

portraying the horror of some terrible past. "…. (*sniff*)……"
Reflected on that photo's glass are the moving images behind him.
His chest slowly heaves. He looks down at an image on his desk—
an old, discolored black & white photo of a young white woman
holding an infant bundled in a blanket. He picks up the frame and
stares at the image. Eyes slightly watery, he subtly shakes his head
again, pursing his lips. "Did you know my mother was raped? By
one such as yourself? A darkie? A *nigger?*"

His coat, cloak, and jeans still emitting faint wisps of smoke,
Jesse nears the doorway, emerging into the flaring light of the
videos, Hollis's murky shadow jittering over his lower body. THUMP-
THUMP! "… hhhhh… hhhhh… hhhhh… hhhhh…" THUMP-THUMP! "… hhhhh… hhhhh… hhhhh…
hhhhh…."

"It's true. I am a product of rape. That's a family secret—one
among the many things your daughter stuck her nose into."

Jesse takes another step forward, across the threshold, body
shaking without the aid of a steadying wall, never offering more
than a dark stare.

"My mother was brainwashed by that boy. She denied he
raped her, but my grandfather told me the truth—if not for
granddad, I wouldn't be the man I am today. My Colonel Granddaddy.
He taught me that I could redeem my subhuman existence by
becoming a man. An enlisted man like him. To serve something
greater than myself… dedicate my life to the greater good."

THUMP-THUMP! "… hhhhh… hhhhh… hhhhh… hhhhh…" THUMP-THUMP! "…
hhhhh… hhhhh… hhhhh… hhhhh…"

"You might wonder why I'm sharing all of this with you. I'm
giving you the same chance I had—a chance to redeem yourself.
To *save* yourself. In spite of what you are—no… *because* of what
you are. You're clearly of no use to me now, but I see great
potential in you; even though you know you can't possibly win

against me, with your wreck of a body, you still forge ahead. Much greater men would've folded by now."

THUMP-THUMP! "… hhhhh… hhhhh… hhhhh… hhhhh…" *THUMP-THUMP!* "… hhhhh… hhhhh… hhhhh… hhhhh…"

Hollis stares at Jesse, who's but a few feet in front of his desk. Though the videos' light baptizes Jesse, washing out the trials and tribulation etched in his face, it smudges his shadow about the walls and his eyes remain dark. "Admirable. I believe you're strong enough to carry on my legacy, so my previous offer still stands, soldier. If you stand with me, I'll overlook your transgressions, and set everything in motion."

THUMP-THUMP! "… hhhhh… hhhhh… hhhhh… hhhhh…" *THUMP-THUMP!* "… hhhhh… hhhhh… hhhhh… hhhhh…"

"Suit yourself." Hollis springs from his chair, jabs his Barretta M9 outward, firing three rapid shots.

"UHNF!" A bullet pierces Jesse's abdomen. He jitters before the desk, reaching out toward Hollis, and collapses, smearing blood in the desk's surface, his hand quaking. "*Aghk!*" He grimaces then lands hard on the floor.

"What a waste." Hollis takes a step from behind the desk and stops in shock.

Coughing up blood, Jesse is slowly and shakily attempting to rise to his knees, but failing, his bloody hand clawing the rug.

"Pff… I just sunk three rounds into you, and you still have fight. That level of conviction and commitment is virtually nonexistent today." He takes aim at Jesse's head. "Such a major waste—"

SQUERKie—SQUERKie—SQUERKie—SQUERKie—SQUERKie!

He spins, pointing the pistol at the door to his left as it pops open with a soft thud—a woman bumps the door with her bottom, pulling a cleaning cart, its casters pleading desperately for oil. Hollis cocks his head and raises his eyebrows, mouth slightly agape as the woman yanks the cart—it's stuck on the doorjamb. He lowers the pistol out of her view.

The cleaning woman has a thin build and is wearing a light blue short-sleeved maintenance worker's uniform, her hair in a bun. Her underarms are blotted with large patches of sweat as she violently jerks the cart. "U-u-uhn!" She finally wins the tug-of-war against the cart, nearly falling backward into the office. She turns with a fleeting scan across the wall of videos. "Hhhh-hhh... Oh!" Her shoulders jump as she notices Hollis. "Praise be to Allah! I didn't think anyone was left! General, maybe you can help me out, here. The whole building is empty, the entire place is a hot mess, and I'm the only one on the night cleaning crew who bothered to show up! Okay—I was asleep in the broom closet—but still, I'm not working this place all by myself... not unless I get paid quadruple overtime! Would you authorize—?"

"Miss, do you have any idea what's been—?"

"Oh, my God!" Her eyes widen, looking down at Jesse's struggling body. "That man's bleeding..."

Hollis tightens his grip on the pistol.

"... all over my rug! I gotta wipe that up before it stains!" She jerks to the cart, bends over, and retrieves an object. As she rises—

"A stirring performance, Miss Nohara. Now... drop the weapon."

. . .

Haj furtively turns her head. The videos glint along the barrel of the M9 pointing at her, and shine on the side of Hollis's grinning face.

"You're very good under pressure. Admirable. But the show's over."

She turns her head back to the cart, her brows curling upward while her hands tense, tightly gripping her Super Shorty 12-guage shotgun baby.

"Young lady, do you actually think you can turn and fire that weapon with accuracy faster than I can pull this trigger?"

She clenches her eyes, teardrops forming in their corners. Her breathing rages and she grits her teeth, but she maintains her grip, her arms shaking.

"Hmhmhm! Suit yourself."

KRACK!

"GK—HHHH—!"

. . .

The glass behind Hollis crackles, a hole blasted through it, tiny hexagons burning, melting, dripping away. He drops his bulging red eyes. A charred black ring outlines a smoldering cavity in his chest. The smoke from his own burning flesh reaches his nostrils.

Haj whips around in terror.

Jesse tears toward the desk, releasing a furious battle cry— "*YAAAH!*"—his hand glistening with blood, his arm outstretched pointing the rail pistol at Hollis.

"JESSE, NO!" Haj tosses the shotgun and launches herself forward. Hollis looks up from his chest—Jesse is flying across the desk at him, blazing a trail of swirling red orbs and ash, blasting two more holes though his chest as Haj careens at them from the side amid Jesse's guttural battle cry.

"*AAAA—!*"

"Nn—!"

Jesse's boot smashes into Hollis's face, sending him flying backward, crashing through the video of him killing Tripp, shattering the window into a thick white spray of tiny glass blocks.

"IIEEEEE!" Haj just barely grabs the tattered tail of Jesse's coat and cloak, feverishly wrapping the torn fabrics around her arms as Jesse and Hollis plunge over the brink, cold and damp wind blowing in over her. Jesse's momentum snatches her body— "*UUHN!*"—but she jams her boots against the window frame, bearing her clenched teeth, trying to halt his trajectory with all the might her slight frame can muster.

* * * * *

Jesse swings back, his body slamming against the face of the building. Haj screams out in terrific pain above him. Below him, Hollis falls away, unable to utter a sound. Their eyes engage in a transient lock. Jesse is overwhelmingly gratified at the shock and terror on the face of this dead-man-falling. But, in a flash, that face, somehow, appears… *grateful.*

Hollis smashes against the pavement—Jesse feels the satisfaction of having hurled a festering, rotten tomato with all his might, and watching it splatter against a wall. He remains locked-on even as police and firefighters rush in and surround Hollis's disfigured body and pooling blood. Yet, he can't help but think about that disconcerting look on Hollis's face.

He'd already understood what Hollis wanted from him; Hollis was a warrior trapped with only one way out. Jesse feels that there must have been something more than this current situation that motivated his desire for death.

'*As is he.*'

But he doesn't *give a shit.*

Although he knows the terrible, unforgivable sin he just committed, he has not a single regret that he gave Hollis exactly what he wanted. However, it just sinks in that he hasn't received his own release. He looks up.

. . .

"JUST HANG ON, JESS!" Haj screams, her hair wildly disheveled, sweat and drizzle-soaked strands hugging her face. The coat strangles her arms, bulging the skin on her hands and forearms, turning it bright red as her body shakes, straining against Jesse's weight. The frayed fabric grates into her, the agony contorting her face. "*UUHN!* SOMEBODY! HELP ME! PLEEEASE!" She grips tight and pulls... to no effect. "Please hang on, Jess..." she sobs, "... somebody's gonna...." She looks over her shoulder. The side door is still closed. The open doors behind her lead to blackness, flames burning at the far end. There's no one.

. . .

Jesse's numbness starts to give way. Light, cool, intermittent rain taps his face. The skin on his arm gets hotter and hotter. The numerous scrapes and cuts begin to sting. The dullness in his abdomen and thigh sharpens, blood and rain soaking his pants, dripping from his boots. His eyes are still locked to the faraway misshapen frozen gratitude looking back up at him; Hollis's deranged diatribe begins to register. Something surreal stirs within.

Thanks to Nicole, he was already becoming aware of his own folly. But it took this monster to shake him fully awake to the uncomfortable truth: He was not only defining *himself* by Lainey's death, he was defining *her* by it, as well.

Hers was a life worthy not just of lamenting over what could have been, but of celebrating what was. What *she* was. Her heartfelt concern for the wellbeing of others propelled her—willed her to take action even at her own expense. And, despite her very few years on this Earth, with her own will, she accomplished something monumental, having a profound effect on the world.

For his part, for once, he was able to do what he set out to do... beyond the hollow reward of vengeance.

He and Lainey... father and daughter... actually got to work a case together like they both dreamed. They worked from different spaces and times, but, with Hollis's vanquished corpse staring back up at him, he cannot deny the results.

One less monster roaming free in the world. We did it, Laine-Laine... "We did it."

His sight of Hollis blurs and tears drop from his irises. He turns away—"(*sniff*)"—looking around at the world, with the cold, soothing wind blowing against his face cooling the tears running down his cheeks. Though his chest weighs heavy, he manages a pained smile.

My beautiful baby girl... she was doing what she loved. She wanted to do me proud. Nicki, too... what she did here and....

His heart swells with pride, knowing Lainey gave her all, doing what she knew was right, and that he mattered so much to Nicole that she risked everything. He wishes he could have met Anna, this wondrous and beautiful amalgam of all three of them, knowing she was just as fierce while trying so hard to live her own truth. He beams while ruminating on their lives, feeling he's finally earned his place among them.

. . .

The coat whispers a threat—a tearing seam. Haj is going hoarse crying out for help, blood dripping from her strangled arms. Cold wind gusts in. Though her entire body quakes, she shows no sign that she will ever release her grip. She cries deeply as her knees buckle... and her body reaches the edge—hands grabs her by the waist.

"Got you!" Rajiv pulls her back. "You are bleeding! On, no—is Jesse down there?!"

"Hhhh-hhhh—Oh, my fucking—hhhh—*GOD!* Where've you *been?!*"

Rajiv clutches the coat. "I was right behind you, but the stairwell was veddy—!"

"SHUTUP AND *PULL!*"

. . .

Jesse is enamored with a vision of Lainey and Anna; they're at play in the pool, laughing. Sunlight dances upon the shimmering water as the two girls splash about. The trees are swaying. The majestic billowy clouds drift in the ocean-blue sky. As their song plays, Nicole reaches out to him, smiling widely, beckoning him to the Island. Her delicate scent caresses the air about him.

He feels the upward tug of reality signaling the end of this fantasy and the start of a life without purpose. Without song.

He's compelled toward dreams.

If there's a regret he has in this choice, it's the pain he's about to inflict on his family. Most notably, his newest member. However, the pain he's already inflicted upon them solidifies his choice. *They'd all be better off without me, anyway.* "(*sniff*)" He looks up, his eyes meeting her frightened, yet hopeful gaze. "(*cough-cough…*) Hh... hey...." He smiles with sorrowful eyes. "Stay out of trouble... look in on my brothers once in a while... and take real good care of yourself... for me, Susan... aaight?"

"Why'd you call me by my—? JESSE, NO! *EEEEE—!*" She lurches for him.

"Whoa!" Rajiv grabs her by the belt, struggling against both their weight.

. . .

Though the screams above him tug at his heart, Jesse casts his gaze to a clearing in the stormy night sky. The cold wisps of clouds appear as ephemeral islands in the soft moonlight, islands that hold the promise of such warmth. Such comfort. His eyes glisten. And though the corners of his mouth are downturned, a glimmer of smile shines through. Raising both arms and outstretching his hands, he grabs the vision... "... if I could... if I could... if I......." ... and slips out of his coat and Adrianna's cloak.

At peace.

And finally... *happy.*

EPILOGUE

*H*AJ yanks the drawstring. The blinds retract upward. She pushes up against the frame, straining, until the window finally gives. The mild morning air rushes in, blowing her silky strands about her. Bathed in sunlight, she breathes in deeply, looking painfully up into the sky.

She spins toward the sound of tapping keys behind her. The desk is empty. The office is empty. She listens to the sounds of him through the speakers, closing her eyes. A tear runs down her cheek and her lips tremble. Her legs give out and she collapses to a squat, wrapping her bandaged arms around herself, then she cups her ears and grits her teeth. Drops splatter against the floor and sparkle in the sun.

* * * * *

The abyss shrouds echoes of sounds and images, barely keeping them from breaking through. Screams. Horrors. Laughter. Cries. Flashes of red and yellow. Blistering cold. Scorching heat. A blur of dim white light in the distance slowly pushes its way through the abyss, the light of a silent train in a dark tunnel. It grows larger, brighter. Larger and brighter still. So bright that it becomes blinding.

The blurry woman is frozen in place as she looks on. Then she bolts out of the room, yelling, to a backdrop of a high-pitched tone.

His mouth is sand and the skin on both lips is shredded paper; the numerous splits sting. His head rages with a furious beat. The pain crawling all over his body with razor sharp claws is maddening. To brush away this torturous creature from his chest, he tries moving his left hand, but it won't respond—he can only move it but so far before it stops. *KLINK!* He looks down his own body; he's chained to a metal bar.

The tone is joined by a gaggle of others, screaming at the top of their electronic lungs, above the rumble of some extremely contentious growls. Vociferous packs of rabid animals tear toward him as the abyss fights back… and wins.

. . .

With muted light, the world unblurs. The place is different now. Very different. The door has moved. The color is less stark. Soothing. The room is relaxing, with its soft morning light entering through white shears and several ornate vases filled with colorful plants. The chain is gone. There're no packs of angry wild animals. There's… no pain; only immense fatigue and disorientation. And a lingering profound sadness, a sadness at being left behind.

"Ah, you're awake again," a nurse says with a lilt in her voice.

"Mm… wh…."

"Don't try to speak, you're still recovering. Just take it easy, m'man." She smiles at him and checks the monitors that surround his bed.

"What… why am I… here?"

"Well, that's a funny thing for you to be askin', idn'nit, coma boy? After all, where else would you be?! Heheheh!"

"Mm?"

"Now, are you gonna ask me that every-single-day?"

"He's awake?" Gwen says, poking her head in.

"Yep, he just winked in after a night's rest—although, I don't expect he'll be talkin' much. The only thing he says is—"

"Jesse? How are you feeling?" Gwen walks over to him.

"I... why am I here?"

"Right on queue—heheheh!" The nurse leaves the room.

"I imagine you *are* going through an existential crisis... falling to your death and not dying."

"Hm?"

"Did you really think you'd get off that easy? Nah ah *ah!*"

He looks at her in confusion.

"I see. You don't remember. Then let me get you up to speed." She sits on the edge of the bed. "They got the airbag under you just in time, with darn-near every police, firefighter, and marshal in the city on site, so I hear."

"Oh... sss.... (*cough-cough!*)"

"Let's get you some water. Here." She picks up the glass on the table and gently brings it to his lips. He nervously reaches up and grabs it, gulping the water down.

"They couldn't save the General... unfortunately." She frowns. "Yes!" she whispers, clenching her fist, with a grin and a wink.

"What... what happens—"

"What happens now? You have no idea what a blazing firestorm you caused, do you? Hm... I suppose not. Well, the agencies were unhinged; they wanted to put you *under* Guantanamo."

"Hm!"

"Not to worry, because, just like I promised, I took care of everything. Did a bang-up job, and I'm not the only one saying so—hmhmhm! But, as much as I would love to take all the credit, the task was made a lot easier when the marshals and other officials spoke out in support of you. And so many other people, nearly a hundred, including some bikers you rescued! It was insane—I had no idea you were such a popular guy!

"And wow. Your brothers—George and Nico—they sure jerked a lot of tears in their testimony. But George in particular—that guy caused a run on Kleenex! And a... Constance Comins also spoke? She basically removed all doubt of your innocence with regards to Tripp, testifying that the police threatened her. And, believe it or not, even Lynette went to bat for you! In fact, it was her testimony that sealed it. When the dust settled, there wasn't a single dissenter in Congress. That's a rarity for such a public spectacle."

"Why'd she—C-Congress?!"

"Did you forget again that I'm a congresswoman?"

"Naw.... What about Haj? Um... Susan Nohara? Heard from her? She okay?"

"Nohora? Japanese? I don't recall anyone like that. There was this Chinese woman who wanted to testify after the story broke. Something about you saving her from hot soup?"

"Don't remember doin' that. Wonder where Haj at...?"

"Oh, by the way, I heard a rumor that DHS and DoD really had it in for you, but even they had to back off." She glances at the door then leans in. "I'd still watch my back, if I were you. Heard some whispers—they're not done. I'll do what I can, but I wouldn't expect much; this appears to be coming directly from the top."

He frowns.

"The White House—the President!"

"Why the hell...?"

She shrugs. "I got reamed by the Minority Leader after the robosourcing hearing—she wants me to back away from escalating the issues Nicoletta raised. And she issued more than some veiled threats using the DCCC. Don't know what's going on, but I don't have much choice but to stand down. At least, out in the open—I did make Nicoletta a promise. Had I known this thing would get so out of hand, I'd never have taken it on."

Jesse raises an eyebrow at her.

She leans back. "Hm! You already know me too well!" She smiles. "You and I are gonna get along great, Jesse. After all…" She leans in again. "… you did see me naked and fondled me. How about returning the favor?" She lightly tugs the cover.

"Huh?"

"Hmhmhm! You're blushing!"

"Naw, I'm not." He looks away. "Still don't see what any o' that crazy mess has to do wit' me"

"I don't know what to tell you. But I've already hitched my wagon to you. So, we're kind of in this together. Please don't let me down."

"What do you mean by that—?"

"About the hearing, it exposed corruption. There were indictments handed out and some people will likely be going to jail, but you won't be one of 'em. Quite to the contrary—you're not only a free man, Jesse, you're an honest-to-goodness great American hero, sir!"

"Hero? I'm no—"

"Don't fight it. You already have an action figure. Man Zero, the human ground zero."

"A what?"

She stands and looks out the window. "Hm. They're finally all gone. Oh… there's still some stragglers." She faces him. "You know, it took months for the army of reporters and your throngs of fans to clear out. Planting the rumors of you having been moved worked. Again. It should be all clear by the time you're released—"

"Hold up, hold up! Did you say *months?*"

"No one told you——?"

"How long was I out?!"

* * * * *

"Begging your pardon, ma'am, I doubt very much that he'd be willing to do any of those things," Colby says.

"Oh, come on! Who would pass up a chance like this?" Gwen says.

"Chance to do what?" Jesse's voice reverberates in the hall as he walks with a limp, bracing himself against the wall. A nurse chases him with a wheelchair, pleading for him to sit.

"Jesse! You're looking well," Gwen says.

"You could do with a haircut and shave, though," Lynette says, catching up to them. "Maybe on the way we can find a——"

"Chance. To do. What?" He makes pointed eye contact with Gwen.

"To shine! I told you, you're a hero! It's time for you to——"

"Get to know your public," Lynette says, smiling at him.

"Pass."

Lynette puts her hands on her hips. "But we have a press conference lined up for you, and everything!"

"That's y'all's problem. Ain't got a damned thing to do wit' me."

Colby smirks at Gwen as he walks toward Jesse.

"Don't be smug." She glares at him.

Jesse puts his arm over Colby's shoulder and they walk toward the exit.

"Come on, this is a once-in-a-lifetime opportunity! I mean, this would only be the beginning. Media tours, book deals——" Gwen says.

"And there's even a medal of honor waiting for you from the President!" Lynette says.

"He wants to do a small ceremony at the White House!"

"(*ptssh!*)" He shakes his head.

"What?" Gwen says.

"You." He looks at Lynette. "Last time I saw you, you ain't give a damn if someone blew her head off. And now you finishin' her sentences?"

"That was just a misunderstanding." She smiles at Gwen, who nods while smiling back.

"Hmph. Ain't no misunderstanding. I get what y'all about. Perfectly. Sorry, but you ain't usin' me as a steppin' stone. Not this time."

Lynette frowns with her mouth open. "Why would you bring up that old stuff?! This isn't even the same thing!"

He stares at her, softening his expression, and then nods. "Know what? You're right; that was way outta line. I take it back. We cool?" He puts out his fist to her. She smiles and raises her fist. He snatches his hand back before the bump. "Nope." Her mouth hangs open again.

"Hmhmhm!" Colby giggles. "Let's be on our way, sir." They walk past the earnest women. "Ladies." He nods.

Gwen takes a step forward. "I'm not giving up on you, Jesse! Maybe you and I can discuss this sometime. Over drinks?"

Jesse looks back over his shoulder at Lynette. "You. Don't work so late. Or at least park closer to the building or som'em, 'cause damn!"

Lynette smirks. "And you take better care of yourself… like, maybe runnin' a comb through that nappy-ass head."

"Hmhmhm! Gettin' all Black on me, an' what not." He nods

the back of his head at them. "Aaight."

"But what about your medal?!" Gwen calls out.

The doors close behind him and Colby.

. . .

"You don't have to be doin' this anymore, Colby. I mean, you got much, much more important things to worry 'bout now."

"That's 'Kobe', sir." Colby smiles at him in the rear-view mirror. "And don't be silly. This is the very least that I can do for you."

From the back seat of the S-Class Mercedes, Jesse watches the hospital go by, Lynette and Gwen waving to him... and a group of sign and action figure carrying fanatics chasing the car, tugged by their outstretched phones. "(*ptssb*) Uh... can you do me a solid? There's a stop I wanna make, but it's a ways from here, though."

"You have but to ask, sir!"

* * * * *

From the driver's seat, Colby watches as Jesse tries to gently tear himself away from a minutes-long lively conversation. Jesse hugs Mr. Gary who has tear-filled eyes and a characteristically wide grin, then tries once again to make his exit. Mr. Gary forces a box of pastries upon him. Jesse relents, accepting the box, says his thank yous and goodbyes to him and his new apprentice, and returns to the car.

"(*sniff*) ... love that old guy...."

"Yes, he seems very sweet." Colby pulls the car into traffic. "Have you decided yet?"

"Huh? (*sniff*)"

"Have you decided to stay at the estate?"

"Mm... nah... I ain't decided. I just... I just don't know if I can. Y'know?"

"I see. But… with no head of the manor, it all seems so… empty; the staff really needs you, sir. And it *is* what Madame wanted."

"Yeah… I know." Jesse takes in a deep breath, and exhales with a whisper, "I know."

It's so easy for you now; you're not the one left behind. I wanted to be with you. I tried, Nick. I really did. I was cheated. Maybe it's punishment. 'Thou shalt not kill'. But you know what? I don't regret it—I was not lettin' that asswipe kill Haj, too. "Hmph." *Nope, don't regret it one damn bit.*

You'll have to wait a bit longer for me. I'll do my time. Hopefully, I won't be too long, though—

"I know what you're thinking, sir."

"Huh?"

"There've still been no new developments."

"Oh. None?"

Colby shakes his head.

"Man… I mean… how could this happen—who'd even do som'em like dat? Why?"

"I wish I knew. The nurses said whoever took Madame's body didn't even wait for her to grow cold. One second she was there right after the pronouncement, the next she was go—" Colby glances in the mirror at the angry expression on Jesse's face. "Oh, my apologies, sir!"

"Nah… nah, it's cool. It just pisses me off, is all. We ain't even get to bury her, man. That's just…." He shakes his head gazing up at the clouds but the soothing motion of the car eventually allows his thoughts to drift. But not too far away. He wonders if he'll ever be able to come to terms with losing her before they even had a chance to begin, remembering just how close they came. *The*

Island. "Know what, Kobe? I still haven't decided, but I *would* like to see the estate... and everybody. At least one more time. Hate to put you out, but is that aaight?"

Colby's face lights up. "Thank you, sir! I thought you'd never ask! Everyone really wants to see you, too, and would be delighted should you decide to stay. No pressure! However, I would advise keeping the pastries hidden from Francisco."

"Huh?"

"Contraband—hmhmhm!"

"Hmhmhm! Noted."

* * * * *

As the grass, fences, poles, and clouds flow by, his feelings run the gamut. Everything from when he first met Nicole to when last they spoke... across time. He finds it overwhelming, but his emotional descent is interrupted by the welcome sound of the tires' rapid beat against the stone path. He looks around with wide, watery eyes, taken by surprise with how fast the time flew. He looks ahead at the gates; they're already opening. He feels that the estate is calling to him, whispering in Nicole's voice.

. . .

Before Colby could reach him, Jesse has already pulled himself out of the car, grabbing the roof and door. "Man... I really missed this place."

"Well, whatever you decide, you'll always be home here, sir—"

"But, no pressure?"

"Hahahaha!"

"Hmhm!"

The soft hiss of the fountain caresses Jesse's ears as he looks around the grounds, its light, cool spray dotting his skin. It's all just as beautiful as ever, but somehow everything seems a little less... brilliant. However, it still whispers to him.

"Yo, I'm gonna go hang out for a bit. Later."

"Do you need assistance?"

Jesse is already walking toward the garden path with a slight limp.

"Don't forget to come inside, okay?! The staff is here for you if you need anything!"

Jesse nods and waves. Colby grins widely and turns toward the front entrance path with a bounce in his step.

* * * * *

Everything reminds him of her. *Everything*. The puffs and vines of greenery. The fragrant flowers. Even the shapes in the clouds lit by the midday sun.

He stands beneath the sign. Adrianna's Garden. As he strolls through, taking in the stunning blooms, he can understand the love Nicole felt for her, how much she endured and was willing to endure, even sacrificing her own life. He respects her choice to do so, but he can't help the pang of resentment at losing her. But deep down, he knows she also made the sacrifice for him. He decides it's best not to pull on that thread; it's taken a while to stitch his shield against the guilt.

. . .

Past the roses and through the gazebo, he pauses and sighs. He has difficulty maintaining his balance on the stone pedestals, nearly slipping into the pond, but reaches the door and enters the white building, safe and dry. This is only the second time he's taken these spiral stairs upward. The last time, he was wary of what he'd find at the top. This time, it's the same, yet so very different.

. . .

He grips a handle, slowly opening a door. There's no music or festive vibe. No heat blasting from radiator palms. The sand is cool. The pool is drained. Fire pits are devoid of flame. Even the once-lively breeze seems to have retreated from this place. He slowly turns, looking over at the wicker chaise lounge chairs. The vibrant colors of the canopies seem muted. He lumbers over to his lounge and sits, facing hers. He can see her. Clearly. In her red bathing suit. Sipping her cocktail. Laughing, giggling... enraptured by their song. He hangs his head and drops fall, dotting the sand. It was a mistake to come back here. But he owed it to her. And to himself. A promise that he never made but felt compelled to keep.

He smacks his palms to his face and rubs. He slides them away and breathes in and out, deeply, eyes closed, trying to regain his composure. A shadow crosses his lids. He opens his eyes.

A grungy, purple elephant in a rainbow tutu dangles from a thin silver chain, spinning, rimmed by the sun. A subtle hint of lilac sends his heart into a flutter and a rush of blood to his cheeks. He's absolutely terrified, fearing he'll find this is all just a dream that'll dissipate into nothingness once he dares look. But he just can't hold back his joy—he springs from the chair, grabs her by the shoulders, and gazes desperately upon her face. "*Nick!*" His heart stops as his widened eyes scan the features of her face—familiar... *unfamiliar*.

She blinks, smiling warmly as she pulls back the cloak's hood, revealing her black skin, glinting black-chrome lines, and glowing emerald eyes.

"Hey. Nice to finally meet you... Daddy."

Author's Note

Nnnope! That ending was *not* a cliffhanger. It is *the* critical clue in the mystery. That's it. That's the note.

Want More?

If you have questions/comments, want to know more about LotG, want to see some scenes and characters illustrated by me, or would like to participate in the discussions, join us at:

www.lylemilton.com/man_zero

Scene from Loophole of the Gods: Chapter 78: War of Others, Mine - © Lyle Milton, 2020

You can also join my mailing list for news and updates by sending a direct email request to:

list@lylemilton.com

If you're eager for the second book/subseries in the Man Zero series…

Please leave a review!

There's a whole lot more to Jesse's story, and I'm eager to share it, but Jesse & I could really use a boost from your reviews. It can take but a few minutes and can be as short or long as you want; sharing your opinions on LotG with others is what matters most. With your help, more readers will come to know Jesse, Nicole, Adrianna, Haj, Nico, et al, and, hey, possibly even spark interest in an adaptation. It can all certainly happen with your support.

Thank you!

Acknowledgements

Any writer who tells you that he—*and he alone*—created his novel is lying and/or a narcissist and/or his writing is shit. There's always a word, a look, a suggestion, a conversation, an energy, an edit, however small, that can have a significant impact on a finished work. Always. While I can't claim an army of influencers, I've been blessed with some wonderful folks during the process of crafting this novel. These are the people who've truly made an impact on the story, the novel, or my perceptions of my own work.

Carla Molchan isn't only the love of my life and my editor, she's also my muse. Because she's a writer, and I'm always impressed with her work, impressing *her* was a big driver for me. And she was all too eager to read the day's work; I had to beat back her many attempts to peek over my shoulder. But her reaction after reading the completed first draft was... priceless. While she clapped out loud, her tone said that what she'd just read was utter crap—hmhm! I wasn't offended since I'd already learned that most first drafts *are* utter crap. It was only after a few drafts later that she could voice the brutal truth about the first draft. And it was then (and after her red pen slashed away at my soul) that I knew that the latest draft was ready to leave the shire. Nearly....

While Carla is my alpha reader, **Carolyn L. Smith** is my first beta. Since Carla & I'd known her for over three decades, Carolyn still represented a safe space; her honest assessments would be delivered in the most tactful way possible. Y'know... in the "are you sure you wanna wear *that* shirt?" kind of way—hahaha! Also, she, in addition to Carla and other women friends, was an inspiration for some of Dr. Nicoletta Albescu's traits. She and I had always been in sync, so it was a given that the story would resonate with her. Still, I was shocked that, from chapter one, she saw in Jesse Davenport the actor I'd used as his model: Idris Elba. And with her seal of emphatic approval, I knew it was finally time to step both feet outside the shire.

From the initial spark of an idea to the complete novel, I'd never given much thought to "the market." My only concern was with telling the story that I needed to tell, the way the story wanted to be told. Because of this, I'd always been on edge that there'd be no audience for it. However, timely feedback from another longtime friend, **Nan Soden**, helped me gain my bearings. She helped me see that it's okay if my writing doesn't resonate with everyone. Of course, I knew intellectually that that'd be the case, but Nan helped me to see that it's not necessarily an indictment of my work, just that there are many, many different tastes out in the literary wild.

William Michael Barbee is an old high school buddy that I'd always admired, so I was jazzed when he agreed to beta read, especially because he's also a writer. Buuuuut, it just so happened that he was one of those out in the literary wild with a differing taste; he DNFed after chapter one. However, one bit of feedback he gave really changed the whole book for the better. "Chapter one is too long, man!" he said. Though I was quite confident that my lengths where within widely accepted limits, that feedback forced me to take a closer look at the story. In the end, I split virtually every chapter into easier-to-digest parts. The irony? The only chapter that I didn't split was chapter one.

I'd already completed LotG when I first met online **Christina Elisabeth Ebbesen**, a fellow writer, but our many conversations helped to bolster my confidence in getting this book out into the world. And to top it off, she's also a pastor; she provided useful insights with regards to my depiction of Pastor Willis. And she's been a model for seeing this project through, as she'd worked so diligently on her novel series, even creating some fantastic merchandizing. I'm still working to catch up to her.

Lastly, I'd like to acknowledge the contributions of my beta readers. Thank you, one and all!

In particular, I'm appreciative of **Nathalie Roth**—also a writer I'd met online. Though the book wasn't inline with her literary tastes, and she had difficulty understanding Jesse, she toughed it out for as long as she could, and along the way provided some very useful feedback that helped me make important edits to chapter 1.

Also, I must mention **Nancy Griffin** and **Donna Lewis** who both took the time and expense to print out the entire novel; you have no idea how honored I felt that they would go through all that trouble just to read my work! Thank you both for supporting me and for the great feedback.

A Special Thanks to BookTube

Although it may sound cliché, I'd always had a knack for turn of phrase. I've no idea from where it came, but I've always felt a kind of… rhythm within text. However, knack alone only gets one but so far; a new writer who's serious about his/her craft must also learn the basics of writing. For that, I did as we all do these days: I turned to the Internet. Even so, it was a bit of a slog finding information because I didn't know what I needed.

Enter BookTube.

Like all social media, YouTube can be thought of as a collection of special interest groups. The books-focused group is called—you guessed it—BookTube. The following (in the order which I'd come upon them) is the list of channels I watched religiously back when I started writing (and now, for some), drinking in all I could to learn about the craft of writing novels.

Joanna Penn – In 2015, weeks before I'd decided to write LotG, I'd heard Joanna's voice behind me as I was coding; Carla was doing research on independent publishing, and had Joanna's videos blasting while on the treadmill. It didn't take long for Joanna's words to seep into my brain—she made independent publishing, and writing, seem so doable! And she always has such highly informative guests representing different aspects of the industry. To a large degree, I owe the existence of this book to her. If you're even contemplating publishing a novel, her videos and her site are a must.

https://www.youtube.com/user/thecreativepenn

National Writer's Series – this isn't a channel, but a playlist on the *Traverse Area Community Media* channel *(formerly known as UpNorthTV)*. It's not writing instruction, per se, but this series of videos was instrumental in my gaining the right "energy" for becoming a novelist. One can't help but get pulled along with such compelling personalities as Lee Child, Gillian Flynn, Rita Mae Brown, Diana Gabaldon, Harlan Coben, Karin Slaughter, Michael Connelly, Janet Evanovich, Garth Stein, etc. Each had his/her own impact on me and helped to solidify my decision to write.

https://www.youtube.com/playlist?list=PL3OAMYbEVlSNO0E A-3xB4mpjOj6wi62kL

Jenna Moreci – "Don't be a dick!" blared from the TV over the treadmill's whirring and my panting and heavy footfalls.

"Who *is* that woman?!" Carla yelled from the next room.

Jenna does have a distinctive voice (literally and literarily) and delivery that makes her so very entertaining. And once you dig deeper, it's all substance there. In fact, IMHO, you'll find no better entertaining source for the basics of writing a novel than this 'Cyborg Queen.'

https://www.youtube.com/channel/UCS_fcv9kBpDN4WWrfcb Crgw

Ellen Brock – First glance at Ellen and I'd thought: "But… she's a *high schooler!* How much could she know about writing?!" Yep, my mouth was smacked shut as this very knowledgeable editor laid down the literary law! And it was enlightening getting details about writing from an editor as opposed to a writer. If you're serious about writing the right way, you owe it to yourself to check out Ellen's videos.

https://www.youtube.com/user/KeytopServices

K. M. Weiland – Her videos are short and easily digestible, and she covers all aspects of story and writing, in general. And she covers each aspect exceedingly clearly. If you want to attend a writing course, but don't have the means to attend one, you *must* include Ms. Weiland's videos in your own studies.

https://www.youtube.com/user/KMWeiland

Samantha Lane – All of those mentioned above should be properly designated as contributors within "AuthorTube," a subset of BookTube. "Sam" is my first true BookTuber. I was initially drawn in by her thumbnail image (her makeup), but after checking out her content, I was hooked on BookTube-proper. Her opinions on story, especially with regards to treatment of women, gave me the first notion that any writer who wants to be good at writing should be listening intently to readers' opinions on books by other writers, not just on his/her own writing. Sam will take you to literary school.

https://www.youtube.com/user/ThoughtsOnTomes

Merphy Napier – Having been primed with Sam's videos, I became interested in finding other BookTubers. Fortunately, YouTube's recommendations made things easier, presenting one of Merphy's videos. I was immediately drawn to her unpretentious, down-to-earth manner, and her thoughtful book reviews made her a no-brainer for my nascent BookTube video rotation. I'd gleaned so much useful reader-perspective information from her over the years that she's a staple of my continued writing study. And—also because she shares her family life, including her infant-now-toddler son with her viewers—I've dubbed her the Comfort Food of BookTube. Pay full attention to her "Dear Authors" videos to get a crash course on what readers want… and don't want.

https://www.youtube.com/channel/UC7FW6FYqPLeQIXMSul
BfOLw

Diane Callahan – I only just encountered Diane's channel well after I finalized LotG. However, in the interest of helping others learn the craft, I couldn't *not* include her channel… and I wish I'd come across her as I was starting out.

While K. M. Weiland gives great snippets of writing advice, Diane gives you the full course, complete with crisp presentation and examples. I can't stress enough: *Watch. Her. Videos.* I do.

https://www.youtube.com/channel/UCEmQO4-
dP2XhINMXnad6E7g

As wonderful as these resources are, they will only get you but so far if you've no desire to tell a particular story. So, it's not enough to want to write, you need to want to write something in particular that drives you forward. Look around you. What riles you? Excites you? Intrigues you? Titillates you? Horrifies you? Breaks you? Destroys you? Find your literary bliss. Then… *write.*

For writing tips and more, head on over to
http://www.lylemilton.com/writing

Discussion Questions – HEAVY SPOILERS!

LotG is a deceptively simple story with layers of meaning that should provide for interesting discussions in book clubs and classrooms. Beyond the usual "How do you feel about [blah]?" questions for fiction, this section contains a list of questions specific to this novel with an emphasis on providing clues to understanding the story and highlighting some elements readers might have missed.

Note that some questions were curated from beta reader feedback. Also note that these are not intended as trivia or quiz questions since the answers either may not be explicitly stated within the text or may be subjective. In either case, head on over to www.lylemilton.com/man_zero to share your thoughts.

General Questions

Who are the gods?

Who and/or what is the loophole?

What is depicted in the cover illustration?

What is the main mystery in the story?

Why is Warlock dressed in that particular style?

Why is Adrianna Black?

What does it mean when some refer to Adrianna as Adriana?

Why was Adrianna's murder a copycat of Lainey's?

Why does Jesse insist on going it alone?

What are the themes related to Jesse?

What are the themes related to Nicole?

What are the themes related to Adrianna?

Chapter-Specific Questions

2

Why does Jesse run from Mr. Gary?

4

Why doesn't Jesse ask for help, call the police, or wait for the salesperson in the lingerie shop to call the police?

8

When Grandy comforts Lainey, he mentions that Jesse has to work double shifts. Why is it necessary for Jesse to do this?

9

Why does Dr. Albescu treat Jesse in such a familiar way?

13

- Why did Nicole react the way she did in response to being tricked by Adriana?
- What are the implications of the ways in which Adriana tricked Nicole?
- What does it mean that the privacy window opens with a loud noise, startling Jesse, but closes silently?

16

Why is the homeless woman quivering on the train?

20 & 21

Why does Haj let Jesse drive her car?

26

- What are the implications of Adriana's reaction to being spurned by Nicole, and of her crying alone?
- Why does Jesse decide to "stay" with Adriana?

30 & 31

- Who and/or what are the towers in the chapter titles?
- How does this relate to the main mystery?

31

How do you imagine that the past incident about which Jesse recalls affected him, Nico, and George?

33

- What's the meaning of the purple elephant pirouetting in a rainbow tutu?

- What does it say about Jesse & Lainey's relationship?

34

At the end of the second video, why does Nicole react the way she does upon realizing her connection with Adriana?

38

Why might Nicole be concealing the fact that her Lear jet can fly itself?

39

Why is Nicole feeling so down?

41

What's the meaning of the design on Adrianna's t-shirt?

48

In what ways does Nicole's theory relate to her daughter?

50

In the second video, what is the significance of Adriana's actions?

51 & 69

What is the meaning of the chapter titles: From White to Gray and From Gray to Black?

58

- In the video, why are the photos on the wall blurred?
- Why is there time skips in the video?
- Why is Adrianna sad?
- Why does Adrianna believe it may have been wrong for Nicole to have created her?

61

How does being kicked toward a moving train affect Haj?

67

In the video, why does Nicole react as she does when Adriana changes her name to Adrianna?

69

- What is that hard impact against the window?
- Why does Jesse remove the crystal cross from his neck?

86

Why does Jesse react the way he does when he remembers the words: vaguely incestuous?

90

Why does Nicole insinuate that she will slice off the guards' heads?

91

What is the greater significance of Warlock's helping Nicole to disintegrate Adrianna's body?

95

When Warlock says to Jesse: "I am here to halt and bolster your advance," what are the implications?

Epilogue
- How is Adrianna still alive?
- How does Adrianna being alive relate to the mystery?
- What's the significance of Adrianna referring to Jesse as "Daddy?"

Food For Thought

Did you feel that Jesse was unintelligent?

Did you feel that Jesse was being mean to everyone?

Was Nicole "slutty" because she flirted with Jesse?

Why does Nicole feel that no one loves her?

Was Nicole a bad person?

Was Haj "ditzy?"

Was Tripp racist?

Did you feel that Rajiv was/is a coward?

Did Hollis's main motivations resonate with you?

Did you feel the Board of Liaisons is an evil organization?

Why are there no cities or streets named in the novel?

Bibliography? Hmph. More Like *Biography.*

Right now, I'm cringing inside. *Hard.* I sound like I'm pumping myself up when I say that I relied very little on outside sources for the concepts I've presented in this novel. Well… not at all, actually. Cringe aside, that's the truth. So, including a bibliography wasn't on my radar. However, upon seeing books that had them, the thought occurred to me that some folks out there might assume I took advantage of the work of others without attribution. That'd be *far* worse than my taking some heat for inflating my own ego. Therefore:

> *While I'm not a scientist, hold no degrees in science, and am not commissioned by any science-focused organization, I do dabble in theory in various scientific areas. The ideas and forward-looking concepts I present in Loophole of the Gods are my own, and any resemblance to other such ideas and concepts is purely coincidental.*

And that means this section can't be much of a bibliography.

Background

I've never attended college, opting to join the workforce as a graphic artist at a graphics firm soon after high school (in which I was a horrible student). But, how could a dude with only a high-school-education conjure up these concepts and write a literary technothriller mystery novel that showcases them?

Fortunately, institutionalized learning isn't the only way in which to learn, and I've always learned best on my own, enjoying the process of breaking things down in order to understand them *(actually, since I was a toddler, I'd always enjoyed taking things apart and putting them back together again… frustrating my mother to no end when she bought me new toys; rather than play with them as designed, I'd take 'em apart….. sorry, Ma—hmhm!)*. This novel stands as an example of that; it's the very first novel I'd ever written, built on my own dogged study of the craft of writing and what makes for good storytelling… while I was writing it.

I'd embedded into the story many ideas I'd been mulling over for years either in my works or just in idle thoughts as I lie awake at 3 AM unable to shut off my brain.

Environment Simplification Theory

Nicole's *Environment Simplification Theory* is something that, during my AI theorizing, I dreamt up while contemplating the efficiency and absurdity of words, and how we tend to take for granted that *our* words have intrinsic meaning—*they don't*.

These musings were also an offshoot of my work on an XML-based, generalized language definition, parsing, and translation software component of my creative tools platform, a component I've dubbed *dupLex*.

The major spark for the "names" concept was my frustration with having to name things while coding; finding "sticky" names for thousands of programming constructs (e.g. API functions, structures, etc.) can be a *major* slowdown in workflow for me. And it was supremely frustrating whenever I had to rename a construct when a name I'd previously chosen just wouldn't stick in my head or had caused conflicts. "Naming things takes about as much brain power as coding!" I'd complained to Carla. That realization, along with my thoughts about the origins of words, fueled my musings about the types of processes that could've led to the development of language: how were names assigned to things as the number of things to be named increased? It had to take a lot of discussion/brain power… seeding the growth of language.

These concepts flowed naturally into Nicole's dialogue as I felt her guilt over her attachment to things; she deflected to the importance of things and how they define our world, and those things need to be named. Working backward and forward from that scene, reflecting on Adriana/Adrianna, the tool ideas (i.e. everything's a tool, tools modifying tools, genetic mutation) came to me. So, Nicole's ramblings became the key to understanding the Adriana-to-Adrianna story.

After I'd written *The Theory of Somethings* chapter, I'd realized it was prudent to do some research to be sure I wasn't recreating what already existed, labeling it as my own. Based on my verification research which included:

> *The Origin of Language Wikipedia page*
> *https://en.wikipedia.org/wiki/Origin_of_language*

my theory is unique. However, things got super-meta when it came down to naming it. That was hard work.

Ghostcloning

For many years since 1997 when I'd created a commercial computer graphics (CG) animation program called *FXtreme*, my interest in AI grew, specifically with regards to applying it to CG software. But in 2007 I began having serious thoughts about employing it. I'd initially started by looking into expert systems, fuzzy logic, artificial neural networks (NN), and such, but ultimately backed away from those and away from all external research. Why? I'd discovered the critical flaw in my approach: I was looking at the problem from the brain's physiology.

Sure, NNs are sexy in that you could model the function of synapse, but when the computing power and storage required to model a brain sunk in—not to mention that it would require an intimate understanding of all that the brain does... an understanding which science has yet to gain—I backed away from that. Fast. I realized that I needed to focus on the function of the brain, not the form.

I restarted, studying my own mind. Why I did the things I did. Thought the things I thought. Contemplating every little choice that I made. That sent me on an endeavor to understand human behavior. And *(gulp)* politics! Understanding the motivations of people, beyond the rhetoric, spin, and castigations. I studied more closely the concept of intelligence, what it was and what it wasn't. My conclusion? Knowledge doesn't beget intelligence, and massive accumulations of knowledge doesn't beget sentience. Emotions were key; the only way to achieve truly intelligent and sentient IAs is to synthesize/model emotion. This realization led me to create the concept of *ghostcloning*.

However, I needed the Lainey/Adrianna story to be present-day, not some far-flung future. I realized I could leverage today's society where people surrender so freely their anonymity and personal information.

(note: I've still yet to test my AI concepts. Time.)

Xendroid

On geek-based social media, I'd had heated debates with some about robotics and AI, where my stance was that there're more possibilities beyond robots, androids, and cyborgs. Adrianna is my response; she's what I've dubbed a *xendroid*.

Androids are robots with a human form. Because Adrianna's body also consists of biological structures, she's not an android. Technically, she could be considered a cyborg except that her organic parts are not DNA or RNA based, but something new, created through xenobiology. Why would anyone go through the trouble of developing this?

In the quest for more humanlike androids, designers use synthetics (e.g. rubber skin) that fail to fully mimic their real-world counterparts. It's possible to use living tissues, but keeping them alive and integrating them with technology would be mind-numbingly difficult (*note: I have no practical experience with this, it's just an educated guess based on my understanding of the problems*). The benefit of xenobiological structures is that they can be tailormade to fuse with non-biological components, allowing for the best of both worlds, clustered in an ad-hoc fashion throughout an entity. For example, Adrianna's eyes are a fusion of xenobiological (e.g. bioluminescent iris muscles for organic pupil dilation and emotional expression) and technological (e.g. hi-rez CCD-like devices instead of cones and rods). Also, her skin is xenobiological (segmented for manageability) while her joints and bones are tech.

High-Temp Hybrid Computing

I conjured the concept of a high-temp hybrid quantum and traditional computing based on my understanding of the problems associated with computer processing. I gained this understanding through my two-decades-plus of programming, years of building my own servers, and my interest in quantum computing. (*I'd naively thought I coined the term 'photonics' and the idea of photon-based transistors, but I learned that the term had already long been coined, and photonic transistor research had long been a thing.*)

Also, I developed a greed for speed from my work in CG image (CGI) rendering. Creating animation frames for movies, for example, requires a collection of servers called a render farm. All CGI centric companies, including PIXAR, ILM, Digital Domain, etc., have render farms and would love nothing better than to *not* need them in order to generate their images… in *real-time*.

The idea behind "hybrid" is a system that could allow for traditional computing at quantum speeds/unlimited parallelization. *Real-time rendering*. A man can dream, can't he?

Superpresence/Hyperreal Glass

The Superpresence/Hyperreal mesh idea was sparked by LED Christmas bulbs, the kind that don't disperse light at the ends (i.e. the ends are flat & clear). I noticed that at certain angles the light was bright and laser-like. Then I visualized what would happen if I were to miniaturize it (e.g. fiber optics), and create clusters of them arranged in inverted hemispheres, with some lensing that'd allow the viewer to see only one light in a cluster based on the viewing angle. Then I imagined the possibility of including tandem pressure emitters within each fiber, producing sound. In theory, the result would be absolutely indistinguishable from the real world… provided the mesh of hemispheres was dense enough… and there was a way to process a **massive** amount of audiovisual data in speeds upwards of 60Hz (*note: I'm guessing that would be a good baseline refresh rate*)… hence the hybrid computer.

Other concepts not mentioned were not so memorable in their birth, but I just made 'em up as needed.

Uh-oh… I'm Gonna Soapbox It!

After reading all that, you might think I'm very proud of myself. *I am.* After all, I took great pride in the process of creating this novel with the goal of producing the best work I could for my readers. So, why wouldn't I be proud of the finished work?

And, after reading all that, you might think I'm very down on institutionalized learning. *I'm not.* Quite the opposite.

First, I believe teachers are woefully undervalued and underpaid. If children are our future, why the hell are we leaving them in the hands of people we treat like crap?!

Second, it's relatively easy for me, coming up with ideas and presenting them as plausible. The *real* hard work is in bringing ideas to fruition. The biologists, mathematicians, computer scientists, archeologists, linguists, engineers, on and on and on, *they* are the ones who help us understand, define, and expand our world. Case in point, they made it possible for you to read these very words, and even to see them clearly.

Lastly, my great desire is that we do more to promote STEM, finding innovative ways to excite and entice students, especially Black students, into a lifelong pursuit of it, and for everyone to respect what science tells us about our world.

About the Author

Here's where you're supposed to learn little details that'd give some 'romantic' view of the author. Blurbs about my love of playing the saxophone. Living in some idyllic landscape with children, pets. Affinity with nature, lifelong love of writing. All written in 3rd person as if by someone at a publishing house, complete with a hero shot of my best side, conservatively Photoshopped. Well… I've none of that. And truth be told, I'm not all that interesting, and I'm camera shy, so…

I'm just a middle-aged African American man who grew up with a passion for drawing, and eventually became a professional illustrator, graphic artist, 3D animator for a major telecom. Dabbled in R&B/House music published on underground labels. Taught myself to program. Wrote some CG apps used on movies and such. Self-studied (and studying) artificial intelligence concepts. Currently developing a new creative software platform.

Where does writing fit in? *All of the above.* Every single bit of accumulated knowledge and experience allowed me to adapt to writing much later in life than the average author. And I love breaking down the craft of writing, and applying new principles that I learn and/or discover. By the time I'm done, I hope to have created many wonderful worlds in which readers lose and find themselves for decades to come.

Watch me. Read me.

www.ingramcontent.com/pod-product-compliance
Lightning Source LLC
Chambersburg PA
CBHW030323200626
46816CB00006BA/1900